Tears of Ink

Tears of Ink Series

ANNA BLOOM

CONTENTS

Chapter 1	1
Chapter 2	12
Chapter 3	20
Chapter 4	29
Chapter 5	40
Chapter 6	49
Chapter 7	57
Chapter 8	64
Chapter 9	73
Chapter 10	78
Chapter 11	90
Chapter 12	101
Chapter 13	111
Chapter 14	122
Chapter 15	130
Chapter 16	142
Chapter 17	153
Chapter 18	163
Chapter 19	171
Chapter 20	180
Chapter 21	189
Chapter 22	199
Chapter 23	209
Chapter 24	218
Chapter 25	225
Chapter 26	233
Chapter 27	241
Chapter 28	250
Chapter 29	259
Chapter 30	269

Chapter 31	277
Chapter 32	286
Chapter 33	295
Chapter 34	303
Chapter 35	310
Chapter 36	317
Chapter 37	328
Thank you	341
Acknowledgments	343

To love is to hope.
To hope is to dream.
To dream is to live.

One

A loud bang startles me and I almost slide off my stool. I wasn't asleep, though; far from it. My gaze is glued, with barely controlled fear, to a lump of untouched marble. The slab of rock is my Everest and I'm on a futile attempt to climb it wearing Birkenstocks. Between us has been a silent battle of wills. Me desperate to try to create a beautiful and exquisite creation from the gifts of the earth; the marble taunting me with its veined perfection until I've been almost frozen into not making a mark along its surface.

"What?" I holler. Everyone knows not to interrupt between the hours of nine and three. When the door shakes on its hinges, I consider it interrupting.

"Faith, open up."

I groan as I recognise the voice coming from the other side of the door and get off my stool. My back creaks with the unexpected movement and I wince. I walk like an eighty-year-old as I try to unknot the tight muscles along my spine. My fingers push my hair back under the bandana I have wrapped around my forehead. The stretch is good, and I point my fingers towards the high ceiling trying to unknot the stiffness in my spine. The few steps to the small hallway are like wading through thin wallpaper paste. Humidity is turning the air into a cloud of invisible glue. London is unbearable when hot. It's probably the only thing which makes me long for the sea air of home.

"Coming." My chisel is still in my hand and I have to remind myself it's not a weapon.

It's frowned upon to stab your lecturer, no matter how screwed up you are.

On my way to the door, I grab at a loose white cotton shirt and yank it over my shoulders, buttoning it up before I pull on the handle which I very rarely open during working hours.

I shouldn't be precious, I'm lucky I got the space to myself.

"Hi." I force a smile as Gerard darts through the door. Two years ago, my heart would have been in my mouth and I'd have been blushing like a teenager at him being close. Manly and broad with an impressive beard, he once made my heart pitter patter like raindrops on canvas. Then we fucked, and I got over it.

"Ger, I'm kinda busy." His eyes sweep along the cotton shirt and I know he knows what's underneath. Now he wants to know if he's on there, inked on my skin. Another regret in need of a permanent reminder. You'll never know.

"I know, babe, but I've got some news that can't wait."

I roll my eyes as he calls me babe, but I don't say a word. Instead, I point at the untouched Italian marble which is supposed to be my final second year piece—it should not be looking like it's straight out of the mine. Shit. This is bad.

I leave him to investigate the lump of rock while I grab my packet of cigarettes from the top of the small kitchenette counter. The lighter sparks as I light one and inhale deeply as I turn and lean a hip on the side. I watch him closely as he studies my unimpressive development. "Coffee?" I ask eventually, just to break the awkward silence.

He glances at me and frowns. "Are you mad? It's baking outside. No one wants a hot drink when it's like this." Giving up with my hopeless project—which isn't a project at all, just rock—he stands and steps closer. "Have you even been outside today?"

I shrug. "Not since I arrived." I can't even remember what time I got here this morning. It had been light; the streets were busy, but that's nothing new. Since then I'd been sitting on the stool, watching the rock; waiting for some form of divine intervention because, apparently, I'm all out of ideas.

Gerard shakes his head and steps closer. "Fresh air's good, even if it is sticky and humid. You need to take care of yourself; the best artists burn out because they won't stop." He puts his hand on my shoulder and pats gently, but I shrug it away and blow smoke in his face.

"I'll get some fresh air when this is getting somewhere." My eyes narrow at the rock. Bloody stuff. I should have chosen a different material to use. Glass would have been easier. I roll my head and try to release the tight muscles in my neck. Who am I trying to kid? My last effort at glass was a near on disaster, too. Every piece I've turned my hand to in the last five months has been a disaster.

Gerard shifts me towards the marble and I glare at it as his fingers knead my tight shoulder blades. "You're blocked, Faith. You've got to kick back a bit. Come out for a drink with me and we can chat, see if we can get to the root of everything."

His touch through the thin material sends waves of warmth along my tired limbs and I begin to soften a little.

My body's always been a traitorous bitch, her reactions can't be trusted.

I shrug away from his touch. The warm tingle in the pit of my belly berates me. *Spoilsport.* "I'm fine, this is the last hurdle before the summer and then I can relax."

His quick gaze slips over my face. "Have you thought about the summer, where you're going to go?" His unspoken question hangs between us and I shudder. *Are you going home?*

"I'm going to stay here. Get some bar work, something to get some cash, maybe look at some private jobs."

"I'm glad you said that." His face lights up and I know I've walked into a carefully contrived trap he's created.

"I'm not coming to your summer camp."

He grins. "Have I asked too many times?"

I can't help but chuckle. "Yes. I'm twenty-four, not an eighteen-year-old fresher."

Our eyes meet. He thinks he knows who I am, that I've shown him. There's a heavy pause, then he clears his throat. "So, how would you feel about a residential installation?"

I stare at him blankly. "Sorry?"

"A residential installation? I know someone who is creating one, and I thought of you."

I watch his face, my own is still blank. "But I've not graduated yet?"

He shrugs again. "So? It's the summer."

"But, you must have lots of post-graduate students who deserve that chance?"

Gerard's eyes fall on my untouched lump of marble. "Maybe, who's to say?" This is a ridiculous comment. What does he mean who's to say? I say. He says. People say. "It's a great opportunity, it will really get your name out there."

"I don't know if I want my name out there," I mumble.

Gerard catches my hand and squeezes my fingers with reassurance. I pull away and slide my hand back into the pockets of my shorts.

"You need your name out there, Faith." His face is serious. *Great*, I'm going to have a lecture. "Art isn't for fun. It isn't just for loaded people who can swan about and pretend to spend time doing things."

I grin teasingly. "Like you."

"Hey! I work." He smiles, and it sparkles. His face warms as his freckles crinkle around his eyes. I remember all too well how he convinced me into his bed and it had nothing to do with vodka. "I teach you, and some other truly awful students who I can't possibly name." He shifts away, and I finish my cigarette, watching as he starts picking things up and tidying. He peers into one coffee mug with a disgusted look and I chuckle. Housekeeping has never been a passion of mine. I'm more a 'wreck it and trash it' kind of girl, than tidy it up and put it away.

Gerard Steers is easy to like, and he's been kind to me. When I arrived nearly two years before, I'd expected all the tutors to be stuffy and old. Gerard wasn't either of those things. With red hair and fiery freckles, he'd captured my attention, and his lessons had always been my favourite.

Then for a short while, he'd been my favourite everything. Smell, taste, touch. It had been impulsive, torturous, and *very* short-lived.

Now we are something in between university lecturer and student. Not friends, either, and definitely not lovers.

Ignoring his indiscreet tidying, I step back up to my own personal Everest, running my hand along the pitted and cool surface. "So, the installation?" I prompt, using any excuse I can not to mark the marble with my chisel.

Although I'd be crazy to ignore the possibility of my

own exhibit. They are rare and hard to come by. Especially for unheard of students.

"An old friend of mine is drawing attention to his, er, family home." Gerard fiddles with the cuff of his pale-blue sleeve.

"What, is it some ironic installation in a council house?" I ask. Not that I'm opposed to irony. My life is one long ironic moment.

"No," he hesitates, "it's a place called Bowsley Hall in Hampshire."

"What?" I stare at him waiting for a smile to crack. "Are you kidding? Your *old* friend lives in a place called Bowsley Hall?" I snort and chuckle as I move around my lump of marble, looking at it this way and that, trying to visualise what it could be—other than a lump of rock.

"It's not as posh as it sounds. It's skint. The ceiling is like dry cheese, there are cracks in the plasterwork a refugee family could live in, that type of thing; so he's opening it up to the public. Well his mother is, and he asked if I had any ideas."

"And you thought of me." I narrow my gaze. I could do with another cigarette right about now.

Bowsley Hall?

"Well, I figured you wouldn't be going anywhere, and you could use the money and the exposure, right?"

I nod, meeting his pale gaze. "Money is good." With a wry smile, I shrug. My art degree is full of different people —lots of them rich, their voices dripping with education and money. Then there are the likes of me. Not rich, covered in tattoos, and so anti-establishment I could be put on display myself. "Any particular themes?" I dab at a bead of sweat as it rolls down my chest under the shirt. His eyes trail across my skin. Not going there again, Gerard.

"Come on, Faith, take a break. We can go and grab a coffee, wine, whatever, and discuss it more." He fans himself dramatically. "It's too hot to breathe in here, let alone talk."

"I've got to come back, though." I'm not so worried about the sculpture still sitting undone, but rather making a statement that I won't be ending the night in his bed.

I never go back for seconds. Not ever. It's the only unbreakable rule I have.

He grins. "Of course, I wouldn't presume otherwise. This is just a lecturer offering his student a coffee to discuss summer work."

I shake my head. "You make that sound all levels of dirty."

"You hear all levels of dirty."

I exhale a deep breath and step away from the gleaming rock. "Come on, I could do with a coffee."

"I mean you've got so much you could use."

I frown over the top of my wine glass. It had taken no persuading to veer me off the proposed coffee. "Yeah, but there is nothing tying them together... they aren't cohesive. There is no theme there that can be used."

Gerard shrugs. "That can all be worked out, though." He looks thoughtful, his hands linked together as he ponders the erratic collection of pieces I've managed to grow. "There's got to be a theme running there; you're just too close to it to see."

An installation? Could I do that? In a stately home?

I shake my head. "Suggest Meg. She's far more sensible." I pause before adding, "And reliable."

Gerard's gaze is scorching. "Meg's not as good."

I mock gasp and pretend to fan myself down. "I'm better than Meg?"

He rolls his eyes. "You know you are, don't make me tell you again."

I grin. I fucking hate Meg. With her long legs, blonde hair, and gallery friendly demeanour.

"So, can I tell them you'll meet?"

"Meet who exactly? Your friend?" I sound about twelve and take another deep sip of wine to counterbalance the child in me.

Gerard grimaces, much like he did earlier looking at my mouldy coffee mug. "No, his mother probably."

"And it's just for the summer?"

"Yeah, just the summer, for four weeks only. I wouldn't suggest it if I didn't think it would be great exposure for you."

"And they're really paying me five thousand pounds? Just for the summer?"

"Yep." He nods and drains his glass of beer.

"Why don't they just invest the money in the property if that's what it all comes down to?"

"I guess they want to do something a bit better than investing money in a leaky roof." He glances at my glass. "Fancy another? I'll walk you home after."

"Sure," I pass him my glass, "but I'll get a taxi, no need for you to walk me."

He wanders off to the bar which is packed with a Friday night crowd. Conversation is humming loudly, girls laugh, and glasses clink. I love this pub although not so much on a Friday night. Normally it's filled with regulars and their dogs. But, there is always the after-work crowd drinking pints and drowning the week in Prosecco. I glance up and find a pair of dark eyes watching me. I stare and take in the package containing the dark eyes: tanned skin; light brown hair; plump lips—perfect for kissing. I smile and drop my gaze, concentrating on the bangles on my wrist. When I glance up again from under my lashes, the guy's moved closer around his edge of the table, ignoring the conversation around him as he focuses his attention on me. Game on.

By the time Gerard comes back, I'm stuck into some serious eye flirting.

I'm not interested in conversation, never have been. The opposite sex are an itch that needs to be scratched.

"What are you staring at?" Gerard slides my glass of wine in front of me, and I watch the flicker of disappointment flash in the dark eyes of the man on the opposite table.

"Nothing." I grin and shake my head. Last thing I need is a pissing competition between my friend/lecturer and a random in a bar.

Gerard pulls my hand closer and turns it palm up, cradling it in his hand. His thumb traces the lightning strike I have inked on the delicate skin of my wrist. "Tell me about this one?"

I glance at the zigzag with its blurred edges. It's old now, one of my earliest lessons I marked myself with. Lightning doesn't strike twice, apart from where you let it.

I smile wryly. "Lightning doesn't strike twice." I hold his gaze, making my message clear.

His lips turn down, and a light frown mark wrinkles his brow. "Why do you pull away? We had a fun thing going, Faith. I would never have compromised your position with the faculty or the art board."

"It's crazy to stay still too long. Don't you feel it?" I lean forward and his eyes graze along the opening of my shirt. "It makes you age, the longer you stand still; the more you cling onto things that have already happened. How can we innovate and inspire if we can only see the past?"

The frown on Gerard's face deepens. "So, you're never going to have a full relationship because you're worried about becoming stagnant?"

I shrug. "Maybe."

His thumb runs along the skin of my palm, and in my peripheral vision, I sense the guy with the dark eyes shifting away, his quarry stolen from under his nose. I don't want that. I want to scratch the itch burning in the pit of my belly.

"You are an enigma." Gerard relaxes. He knows I won't change my mind.

"It's the best way, baby." I laugh and tilt my head back, a spurt of euphoria rushing in my veins. Half my wine slips down with ease and then I gulp the rest. Sliding off my seat, I pat Gerard on the shoulder and lean down to kiss his cheek. "Thanks for the heads up for the installation. I'll apply if you think it's best." A flap of unsettled butterfly wings causes my stomach to clench.

He sighs. "I've already applied on your behalf."

My hand pauses on his shoulder. "You did?"

His eyes settle on my face. I can't read his expression. "I won't let you mess up, Faith. You are too special."

I don't know whether he's talking about my art, my untouched marble, or my life. So I don't say anything, I don't know what I'm thanking him for.

I weave through the tables. As I pass by the man with dark eyes, I run my finger across the sweep of his T-shirt covered shoulders. He straightens his back and I sense his gaze burning as I head through the exit. I wait around the corner of the bar, watching a long shadow walk towards me.

"I thought you weren't going to come."

The stranger appraises me, eyes drinking in the loose fit of my shirt, the cotton trousers that cover my skin.

Lips meet mine, and hungrily I eat them up, burning with a fire of need, a dart of danger. "You seem like an opportunity not to be missed." His words come in breathy gasps as he nibbles and nips my throat.

"I live around the corner." My legs weaken, the pit of my stomach hot and tender. Girls are told not to take strangers home—I'm not most girls.

"Good."

Two

The leering grin taunts me from across the cafeteria. It's as though I can read from his face everything he knows about me. And he knows everything. The tray of food I don't intend to eat trembles in my hands. Who can eat when their stomach is tied into knots? It's impossible. If I shut my eyes, I remember his hands on my skin. The taste of his tongue. The sharp sting as he pushed inside me.

I wave, wondering if I should go across and say hi. I think we are past hi, but I'm not sure. Hesitation roots my feet to the floor. He doesn't wave back; his eyes slide to the side and my stomach rolls. Maybe he didn't see? I try again, "Hi," I say it this time.

Slowly, his eyes meet mine. Everyone at the table he's sat on all turn to look my way. Then he laughs, and with a shuddering shock I know what it's like to burn under the scorch of the lightning bolt. It crashes into my chest, stealing my breath.

His laughter draws attention and then everyone's eyes are on me, their gaze burning.

I turn, place my tray on the table and run. As I reach the gate, I understand the futility of running. I don't have anywhere to run to. With no clear direction in mind, I turn *towards the town filled with its salty air. There, down a side road, I will find a hiding place. I jangle through the door.*

"Faith, what's wrong?"

I hold my wrist. "Make me remember."

Grey brows scrunch together. "You aren't eighteen."

"I don't care. Make me remember."

So he does. With a tender touch and painful needles, my skin reminds me to never give myself to anyone more than once.

A heavy arm rests across my waist, and I stare at the ceiling. I managed to doze a bit, ignoring the strange form next to me in the bed. I don't know where that dream came from. What was that, eight years ago? Sliding out from under the stifled snores of the man from the bar, I tiptoe across the wood floor and grab my phone.

Me: I was thinking of my lightning bolt. How are you?

I don't expect an answer, so I shove my phone back in the recess of my leather tote and head to the kitchen. I need coffee. The wine from last night is making me blurry-eyed. I hate it when the buzz of the short-term fix eases and leaves me exposed. In the bedroom, there's a stir from the bed. This is always the awkward part.

"Hey." I spoon coffee into one mug.

"I'd love one, thanks." The guy, Mike... Matt, maybe... comes up behind me and wraps his arms around my waist, his chin resting on my shoulder. Yeah, that's not comfortable. I squirm out of his grasp.

"Look, I've got to get on, I've got a project due." I carry on making one coffee.

"Hey." His fingers catch mine and he turns me around. Honestly, he looked so much better after three large wines. This morning, what was an olive-skinned charm is more swarthy and blotchy. Got to turn those beer goggles off, Faith. "We had fun, didn't we?" he asks, oblivious to my critical observations.

"Sure. I'm just busy, you know? It's nearly the end of term. I've got lots of finals to complete."

"And you're doing an art degree?"

"Fine Art," I clarify. I must have told him that on the way home. I don't remember much conversation taking place once we walked through the apartment door.

His eyes drop to my skin. "And you don't want to be a tattoo artist?"

I level him with a stern gaze. Whatever happened to not judging a book by its cover. "No."

"What are all these? Why so many?"

I hold my breath as his fingers graze along the coloured ink across my skin. "Just thoughts and observations." And lessons, but I don't tell him that.

"That's some observation." He smiles, but I see right through it. In his eyes is half panic that he's woken up with a crazed tattooed lunatic, and part desire that I might be willing to submit myself to him like I did last time.

I won't.

"This has been great, but you need to leave now." My lips stretch into a tight smile. No messing with the shit I'm telling him. My message is clear. It doesn't stop him trying though, his hand snakes around my upper arm.

"Come on, babe. I showed you a good time."

I step back, my hand reaching for the catch of the front door. The apartment is cramped and small. Nothing is further than one reach, or one step away. "Real good, but now it's over."

He stares in shock before shrugging. "You've got problems."

I open the door and swing it open, waving my hand toward the dingy corridor. "Yep, and you leaving makes one less."

I shut the door, listening to his mumble about the "crazy bitch" as he walks away. I chuckle. He wasn't complaining about it last night when we were going for it, two strangers tangled in the dark.

It's just a physical release.

I go back to the kitchenette and think about my encounter. Unremarkable, our enjoyment had been one-sided as are so many of my moments of intimacy.

It's a craving which lives deep under my skin. A need for touch, warmth, delicacy. But when I get it, it's never quite what I hope for.

And, as always, I'm left washing away a flavour of bitterness with my morning coffee.

I drain my mug, scorching my tongue, then walk to the small bathroom. Compact but relatively clean—for me. I switch on the shower, yanking the old-fashioned curtain back before stepping into the tub. The hot water works on my muscles and I finally wake up. My skin bears no marks from the night, though even if it did they wouldn't show. The suds from my shampoo run down my arms and I find myself glancing at the lightning bolt on my wrist. I touch it as if it's still going to burn hot and tender. It's old, its edges faded. My eyes close and I breathe in the steam. It was a long time ago, and I don't have to remember those times anymore. I shut off the dream that chased me awake. All those days are in the past, and I don't need to worry about them anymore.

I'm untouchable here.

Towelling off and scrunching my hair with the rough cotton, I think of Gerard's suggestion for the summer.

Could I do something like that? He's right about one thing: I don't plan to go home.

I'm pulling a pair of black skinny jeans up my hips, noticing the waistband seems looser again, when my phone rings. I glance in the mirror. Dressed just in jeans and my bra I'm a sight to be held. I grab at the black baggy shirt and pull it on before grabbing the phone. My heart pounds at the flashing screen.

"Hey."

"What are you thinking of that old lightning bolt for?" A deep voice rumbles down the other end of the line and a squeeze constricts my chest.

"You okay? You sound out of breath."

"Hey, don't be rude." A hearty chuckle turns into a phlegmy cough. "You got to be kind to your old Uncle Al."

"I'm always kind." I slip my feet into some ballet pumps and check my keys are in my bag. I'll have to walk and talk. I haven't got time to be anywhere apart from at the studio and staring at that lump of nemesis. "Tell me the truth," I insist.

"I'm fine. Tell me why you were thinking of your bolt."

I sigh but carry walking silently on.

"Are you dreaming again?"

There isn't any point lying. "Yeah, a little, just occasionally."

"And you haven't heard from your old man?"

I snort. "No, though I'm not surprised."

"He'll come around."

"I don't want him to. It's better this way."

There's a pause, and I can't help but focus on the rasp in his breath. It's getting worse. I need to try to visit him over this holiday. An unsettled ache shifts my stomach when I think I might not get that many chances to see him again.

Although I guess my skin will always remind me of my favourite "uncle".

"Don't talk nonsense, Faith. Anyway." His voice picks up. "Talking about lightning bolts, guess who came into the shop yesterday?"

I roll my eyes. It could be anyone, Brighton is a big place. "Surprise me."

"That guy, the one who messed you around."

Another eye roll. Narrow it down. I snigger at my own dramatics. No one's really broken my heart. Truthfully, I don't have one for them to break. If you lock something up so tight that no one can touch it, it keeps you safe. Keeps you whole.

It leaves me to roam with my body and mind, mapping the journey of my life on my skin. All the while the space above my heart remains untainted, untouched, uninked. Mine.

"Yeah, what did he want?"

"A tatt. What a loser." A spark crackles down the line.

"Al, are you smoking?" I'm genuinely shocked.

"Faithy, babe, I'm on my way out anyway. Fuck if I'm not going to enjoy myself while I go."

Tears sting my eyes, but I don't let them fall. Al would hate my tears, hate my sadness. "They still might find a cure."

"It's lung cancer, Faith, I think I'm fucked."

"Bout time you got laid."

He roars with laughter, and I grin. "So, tell me about Stuart's tattoo." I'm outside the door to the upstairs studio on campus. It's only a couple of roads from the small apartment I call home.

"I got Dan to do it."

"Dan?" I frown as I slide my key in and out of the lock.

Al snorts some more but I can hear him trying to control his devilish cough. "I told him to do his shittiest job ever."

"Did he?"

"I got him to take pictures, I'll send them over."

"Al, that's not professional."

He chuckles again, this time breaking into a cough. "Have you thought of coming back to the shop for the summer? We could use you. It's going to be hot and you know that means lots of drunks who lose all common sense."

"Your best customers then?" I chuckle a little clutching the phone. I don't want this call to end.

The echo of the hum of machines, the tang of disinfectant and cleaner barrages my memory. I can't go back though.

I straighten myself up. "Hey, I've been offered the chance to apply for an installation." I pause to allow my words to sink in. "It would insane to not take up the chance."

"True thing, babe."

"I've got to go, Al." I don't want to add that my chest aches a little and I want to crumple into a ball because one of my favourite people in the whole world is being eaten alive by cancer. "Hang in there, I'm coming to see you real soon."

"I'll tell Dan."

"Don't. I could do without the puppy dog eyes and general moping."

"You two will end up married one of these days. I know you pretend to hate him."

I laugh. "You're losing your mind, old man. Dan and I will marry when hell freezes over."

"That's good, we'll all be together down in hell anyway."

"Love you, Al."

"You too, bright spark."

I smile as I hit the red button at his familiar use of my childhood nickname. Seems silly to be called a bright spark at the age of twenty-four, when there is nothing bright about me at all anymore. But I still like it, just like the six-year-old version of me did before my shine was eroded by darkness.

I pace up the stairs and launch into the studio, pulling the cloth I'd thrown over the marble the night before onto the floor. Sadly, nothing has changed. It still remains untouched, just like it has been pulled from the earth.

What am I going to do if I can't finish it? What will I hand in instead?

Why the hell can't I get to grips with this bloody lump of rock? I've never struggled before. That's why I'm studying Fine Art and sculpture... because I'm good at it. Well, I used to be. Now I'm not sure if it wasn't all a bit of a fluke.

Yet, Gerard had put me forward for that installation with no hesitation. It could open so many doors. When I get home and haven't been waylaid by wine and stranger sex, I'll look up Bowsley Hall and see what it's about, what they are trying to achieve. That's what the internet is for right? Some light stalking and research.

Unbuttoning my shirt, I fling it on the back of a chair and place my apron over the sports bra, tying it around my back. Then I grab my chisel and step up towards the marble like I'm going to war. Which I am. I'm fighting for my degree, the First class honours I'm so desperate for, and the future that will never take me back to that tattoo shop in Brighton.

Three

The chilled wine slips down wonderfully and with a deep sigh I shut my eyes for a moment and rest my head back on the sofa. My muscles ache from hunching and sitting in a scrunched position for hours. I give my shoulders a stretch, lifting them to my ears and dropping them back down. They are stiff and reluctant, and I straighten up having another sip of wine that I'm pretty sure will help ease them. Before I can drift off and lose focus, I pull my laptop onto my lap, opening the lid and quickly adding my password one-handed so I don't have to put my glass down. My hands are sore—light cuts and nicks scratch the surface of my skin. They're all chisel inflicted, although I'm aware of how they look to the untrained eye. It's why I came home and declined Gerard's call of a drink.

I type in "Bowsley Hall" waiting for Google to provide me some insight into my possible summer accommodation. Could I live in a strange house for the summer? I don't play well with others. It's why I've lived by myself the previous two years of my degree. That and the fact I started older than the other students. And I look different. Not that I give a flying fuck about looking different, being different. But girls stare at me in alarm, and guys want to see how far the tatts go. They see a girl who's free with ink and think she will be free with her morals. Sometimes I am. Sometimes I'm not. It all depends.

Bowsley Hall... I blink when images fill the top couple of results. There is no way! I can't stay in that; it's nothing short of a huge castle. Spiralling chimney stacks—more than surely any building could hold—and turreted corner wings, focus the sprawling mass of red brick. Architecture and buildings aren't my speciality, what with me being more concerned about what goes inside buildings than outside them, but I'd hazard a guess and bet my favourite potter's wheel on it being Elizabethan in origin; at least the main part of the house with the chimneys. I remember being in a lecture once on style and the lecturer had pointed out that the more chimneys, the greater the wealth in the Elizabethan period. Rather like when a hundred or so years later there had been the glass tax and all the many windows of splendour had been covered with brick. This house had all its windows and all its chimneys—honest, I felt sorry for the cleaners.

I scroll down, ignoring the looming presence of red brick and try to discover more about its owners. Gerard had said it was his friend, but that couldn't be right, surely? Some images flash up of a couple and their children. They look wealthy, their clothes simple yet expensive. Smooth and manicured, tailored and sharp, without trying too hard. Lucky for them.

I open Facebook and click on a Messenger chat. Gerard's online as I knew he would be. He's a social media addict, although he'd deny it to anyone. I thought it was strange at first when my lecturer friend-requested me, but then when I looked at his friends list I realised I wasn't that special at all. He's friends with as many members of the world's population as Facebook allows. I type a quick message.

Faith Hitchin: I can't stay in that house. Offer it to Meg. She will fit in so much better.

Gerard Steers: Too late. Mrs Fairclough wants to see you next time she's in London.

Next time she's in London? Is she swanning in to check the sights?

Faith Hitchin: It's a bad idea. Please give it to Meg. Leave me to serve warm beer all summer. I'll enjoy that far more.

Gerard Steers: This is a big opportunity. It could lead to galleries wanting you. If I know the Fairclough's, then there will be press all over this.

I cringe and shut the laptop with a bang. For a moment, I lean my head back and close my eyes. The press. I don't want them anywhere near me, or anywhere near my work. But then if I want to be an artist—a world class artist, no less, the kind who has galleries in London begging for their work—won't I need them?

Shaking my head, I stare at the crack in the ceiling.

I could go back to Brighton, pick up a tattoo machine and do that for a living. It's good money. *Very* good money. But then who would I be? The girl from the fucked-up family. At least here in London no one knows me. They might look, but I'm hidden behind the ink they see first.

Uncertain I open the laptop back up and swallow down more wine.

Faith Hitchin: I'll meet Mrs Fairclough and see what she says.

Gerard Steers: So I should let you know it's actually Baroness Fairclough…

I splutter on my wine. *Baroness*. Is he having a laugh?

Faith Hitchin: You're kidding, right?

Gerard Steers: I'm not a joker.

My heart palpitates. I can't meet a Baroness… look at me for fuck's sake. I've never cared about my choices, never once questioned why I've done what I've done. Each touch of ink a cathartic release from a memory I've wanted to forget.

But right now, I wish I'd left it at a sleeve, maybe half a sleeve.

There is no way a Baroness will allow someone who looks like me into her house. I'd be wasting her time and my own. Artists are loose with rules and regulations. But I've taken those rules and destroyed them with my hammer of pain.

Gerard Steers: have you slumped into a coma of shock?

Faith Hitchin: Maybe.

Gerard Steers: Get some sleep. It's the end of term in a couple of days, but you've still got to look interested during my science of materials lecture tomorrow.

Faith Hitchin: I'm an artist, not an actress.

Gerard Steers: You wound me with your sharp words.

Faith Hitchin: Insert *smiley face* here.

I giggle. It's easy to roam into flirting behind the safety of a screen. I could close my eyes right now and think of the night we'd spent together last summer. Hot and sticky, he'd taken the time to explore every inch of my skin, and every tale marked on its surface. It had been intimate, revealing, and I'd surrendered to his touch as a friend, lover, and student. I couldn't allow the night to roll into more, but it had been sweet while it lasted.

He was probably the last decent lay I had.

Thinking about it makes me ache for a physical release. The wine is swilling around my head, those beer goggles slipping back into place.

I don't want anything other than a nameless face on me, inside me, smothering me with every sensation under the sun.

My eyes drop to my lightning bolt. Curse that dream for making me remember the scorch of the burn. I've always managed to keep things locked and in place. Now the memory is running free, careering like an out of control freight train.

I must remember to get Al, or Dan, to send me the picture of the tattoo. I hope it's bad, real bad. Silly, to hold on to the past from eight years ago, but my history is a dark demon that lives in my soul.

I fought to free myself from its sharpened claws, but it's never far behind, chasing me, tempting me, whispering in my ear. Goading me to step back and reclaim the misery I ran from.

Ignoring the unsettled sensation building from my tummy and shifting through my body until my limbs ache, I swipe my thumb over the surface of my phone, scrolling through my contacts before hitting FaceTime.

"Hey." I light another cigarette with my greeting and watch smoke curl into the air.

"Faith fucking Hitchin. I thought you'd flown to the moon, Sista."

I laugh and stick my tongue out. Abi laughs and sticks

her own tongue out. What did two best friends do before video-calling?

Brighton isn't far away, just a train ride, but sometimes, since I left, it seems like the other side of the earth.

"How are the kids?" There are shouts in the background, a clamour of screeching despite the late hour.

Abi and I have been friends for fourteen years. While I fell apart and faced my demons, allowing the truth of the past to tear me into a million tiny shreds of regret, Abi had two children. I don't know how it happened. One day I woke up, coming out of the fog of destruction, to find my oldest friend had grown up.

"Fucking awful. I kid you not, Faith, don't ever have kids. They are a curse on all existence."

I laugh and inhale more nicotine until my lungs burn. "You don't mean it. How's Adam? Still working hard?"

"Of course. He'd rather be at work than home with me nagging him."

I wonder what it would be like to have someone to nag. Am I even the kind of woman to nag? I shut the thought out, it's irrelevant. Anyway, Abi nags enough for the both of us. "So... question." I take another drag. She's going to be all over this summer idea. I'm not asking the right person for advice, but hey, my options are severely limited.

"Ooh, I love grown up questions." She stares at me intently through the phone, opening her eyes. "Better than constantly hearing 'What's that? What's that? What's that?'"

I snort, choking on my smoke. "Charlotte is adorable. Don't be mean to my goddaughter."

"Hold on, I haven't finished yet." Abi wags her finger at me like I'm her two-year-old. "What's that do? What's that do? What's that do?"

"She's a highly intelligent human being."

"Yep, that girl, she's got us all running around at her beck and call."

Abi and I stare at one another for a moment, and an odd, unwelcome yearning for home washes over me.

I'd do anything to go back… back to a time before destruction and violence.

"You okay, Faith?" Abi drops all humour. She knows me well. Has seen me at my high and at my rock bottom, with varying stages in between. "Are you dreaming again? You look tired?"

I shake my head, but to my horror tears prickle. "No, no, it's stupid really. I just dreamed about my lightning bolt."

"Babe, I told you at the time and I say it again now. Boys are fucking shits. Some of them are just about good enough to marry and make decent, but the rest are bastards."

"Hey," a voice calls off-camera. My view swings like I'm on a Waltzer, and the next moment I'm staring up Adam's nostrils. I hadn't even known he was there. I'd presumed he was at work. Abi's so bloody nuts.

"Hi, Adam." I wave weakly, grimacing an apology. "You know you're one of the good guys, right?"

"Too damn right, Faith. I'm one of the best fucking bastards around." He waves and gets up from the sofa, but not before pecking a kiss onto Abi's forehead.

"So, anyway. What did you want to tell me?"

I have to think for a second. Oh, Bowsley Hall.

"Oh yeah, I might get the chance to do an installation this summer."

"What are you installing? A toilet? Plumbing? Windows?"

I chuckle and stub my cigarette out. "Don't be funny, you know what I mean."

"Oh... you mean that glamorous life you are going to lead, selling super-expensive bits of odd art to super-rich twats who don't know what they're buying."

I blink at her before rolling my eyes. "Yes, that exactly."

"Well, that's good then isn't it?"

"I don't know, Abs. It's at some crazy posh stately home. I can't fit in there."

"What because you're covered in tats?"

I glance down at my exposed skin, at the multitude of colours. "No, because I'm me. I come from the scummy end of Brighton and grew up in a tattoo parlour." I frown and rub at my face. My eyes sting; the lack of sleep I've been culminating is starting to catch up. "I'm hardly the manicured lawns and afternoon tea type."

"Hey, we can have PG Tips any afternoon you like." She pauses as a crash filters from her kitchen. "Will you lot keep it down, I'm on the phone!" she hollers before turning back to me. "Fuckers. I tell you, Faith, they don't stop." Her face drops to her serious expression and I know my pep talk is coming. "Listen, you can fit in anywhere you want. You are crazy talented. People would pay thousands to have you ink their skin, and I'm not talking about all the poor bastards lining up because they want to bang you senseless."

My cheeks flame. "Abi!"

"Do it. Get your art out there. Do whatever it takes to make your dreams come true, and then one day come back to the scummy part of Brighton and show every fucker who ever doubted you just what you can do."

I grasp at a lungful of air. "I'll have the meeting with Baroness Fairclough and then decide."

Abi peals with laughter. "Baroness? Hahahaha, you didn't tell me that. Good luck, Faith, you'll fit in a storm."

I squint my eyes giving her a well-practiced side eye. "Thanks."

"Always a pleasure. Some of us will have to see your feet firmly in the shit when you are being touted all over the world."

Blowing her a kiss, I cut the video call, slumping back in the chair. I suppose I should get some food.

I reach for my packet of cigarettes instead. That will do.

I fiddle with the neckline of my silk blouse. A pale-blue, the material is just thick enough to keep my secrets hidden underneath. I stare at myself in the reflection of The Ritz's glass window. I'd laughed until I'd cried when Gerard had told me the meeting with Baroness Fairclough was going to be at The Ritz. Who goes to The Ritz apart from tourists? Apparently, she does.

I've had three showers this morning, but I'm still uncomfortably hot and sweaty. I wish the rain would come and clear the air, but there hasn't been a drop for weeks. I hike my leather tote containing my portfolio up onto my shoulder and push through the revolving door. Cool air from the air conditioning greets me as I step inside, for which I'm very grateful.

I wished Gerard had accompanied me, but he'd told me it would look better if I came alone. Bloody arse. Who sends a young woman by themselves to meet a baroness for a job interview? Gerard Steers does that's who.

He prepped me last night though over a glass of wine and some crackers. I couldn't eat, my stomach too twisted with knots. I approach the lounge, walking with my head held high in front of the reception desk. Once there, I'm stopped by a neat sign telling me to wait to be seated.

I glance around. The room is hushed with whispered conversations; groomed and coiffed heads tilted towards one another. Some of the tables have papers on them. People working in luxury.

It is luxury. Even the air smells rich and clean. Crisp. There aren't that many obvious tourists. I was expecting a few overweight sightseers with their cameras flung around their necks on straps.

A waiter sees me and inclines his head in my direction while he continues helping another elderly couple. I smile and fiddle with the neck of my blouse. *Calm down, Faith.*

It's hard to calm down. I've never been anywhere like this. The nearest I've got is a wine bar.

"Good afternoon," the young man greets me warmly, his face open and friendly. Nothing forced, no sign that he hates his job or the rich people he must serve. "Are you joining us for coffee, or lunch perhaps?"

My tongue nearly falls out of my mouth, but if he notices my discomfort he calmly ignores it. How can he be calm in this place? I want to puke. Coughing and clearing my throat, I attempt to pull myself together. "I'm here to meet Baroness Fairclough." I'm surprised by my voice coming out so calm and level. Inside I'm flapping about like a fish out of water. He hesitates before smoothing his expression. "Could you wait just one moment?"

My palms slick with sweat and I clutch my bag tighter, so I don't wipe them down my silk blouse. "Sure." I smile.

He walks off and ducks his head into a booth in the corner. A moment later he returns and asks me to follow, guiding me with his outstretched hand, careful not to touch me in any way. "Can I take your bag?"

I clutch it closer. "No, thank you, I'll keep it with m—" my words die on my lips as I glance inside the booth.

This is no baroness. Not unless I've spent my life misunderstanding the title.

Instead of the middle-aged lady I'm expecting, there sits a man in the sharpest, neatest suit I've ever seen. You could cut bread with the edges of navy material.

Google has failed me. *I'll never trust you again Google.* The man stands and towers over me, a clear head and shoulders higher than me, and his broad shoulders block the light in the room. His hair is close cropped, a dark fuzz; but it's his eyes that render me totally mute. I've never seen anything like them, as deep as lapis lazuli, they are more vibrant than any gem I've ever seen—and I've seen a few. I'm an artist for God's sake.

"My apologies for the confusion; Miss Hitchin, I believe?" Oh God, his voice is soft, low, devilish. It licks warmth along my reeling insides.

"Faith. Your Faith." *What?* "Sorry. I mean, I'm Faith, yes." I brush at the ends of my ponytail, but there is no hiding the scorching burn travelling up my cheeks.

"You were expecting my mother, but she's been held up." His stunning gaze sweeps over my face. His own is open, his lips turned slightly at the edges as if something is amusing. What could possibly be amusing about this I don't know. He's tanned, his skin a dark gold, and a faint stubble darkens his jaw. I don't think I've ever met a single human being in the flesh who is quite so beautiful.

"Oh, I'm sorry. Is she running late?" I don't know whether or not to take a seat. I'm experiencing total loser syndrome.

He takes control of the situation, smoothly moving around the booth and motioning for the velvet seat opposite his own. "She's in New York. She got muddled with her dates," he says as I slide into the seat.

"Oh," I stutter. "Oh. Has she changed her mind?" I'm officially going to kill Gerard for making me deal with this. This is hell.

"Well, no, she wanted me to do this on her behalf."

"Do you know a lot about art?" I snap. This was a waste of my time and anxiety, not to mention the packet of smokes I consumed as I paced outside the back of the hotel while I summoned the nerve to come in.

He lifts his shoulders, but his eyes never leave my face. It's unsettling. "I know some, I guess."

I raise an eyebrow. I bet he knows jack about art. "And you're familiar with installations, and how they run? You know your mother's plans and how she intends to use my time invested pieces to create her exhibition?"

He doesn't answer but his lips twitch at the edge. I slide back out from my seat, and as I straighten my legs, I drop my bag on the floor. Curse it.

"You'll forgive me if I cut this meeting short." I bend to pick up my sprawled belongings but he's already there, a long arm sweeping down to the floor, his slender fingers picking up my glasses case, and portfolio. I stand and hold out my hand to the outrageously handsome man in the expensive suit. "Please," I say gesturing at my belongings.

He flicks through the pages, his focus settled on the sheets of my dreams and aspirations. "Sit." He motions for the chair.

I glare. I am not a golden retriever. "I think I'll stand."

My rebuke is met with a casual lift of his shoulders. Digging somewhere deep inside me, I find the will to stand tall and nonchalant as he carelessly flicks through images of my soul's work.

It's like being exposed naked and gawped at. I've shown the portfolio to other people—of course I have—but I've never shown it to someone who looks quite like that in a suit before.

My nonchalant stance is undermined by the fact my damn eyes won't behave themselves and sweep over his broad shoulders every twenty seconds. His hair is so short; really, it's nothing more than a buzz cut. I don't know why I thought rich people in suits like that would have artfully styled hair, straight out of an expensive salon or barbers.

I'm so busy on my internal discussion about his military buzz, I don't notice his eyes lifting from the pages of my bound book to my face. I'm just staring at him. Maybe with drool. I lift fingers to my lips just to check. If he sees my indiscreet drool wipe he doesn't acknowledge it. And, why would he? He looks like that... he probably has women launching themselves at his feet and hiking their skirts while he walks down the street.

Jesus, calm down, Faith.

In the three minutes he's been staring at my work I've become ever so slightly psychotic.

"So, how do these pieces tie together? What's your underlying theme?"

Gah, that level deep voice rumbles under my skin.

Does he realise how incredibly attractive he is? Probably.

I can't think straight.

"I'd rather discuss this with your mother. I can't help but think she'd be my beneficial audience."

His stare is flat. Direct on my face. It doesn't once drop to the neckline of my shirt where I know ink teases and waves from under the silk. "Gerard mentioned you were incredibly difficult," he mutters.

Did he indeed? Gerard clearly wants a black eye.

I hold my hand out. I don't have time for this. I have bar work I need to search for. Or... I need to think of going home...

He sighs and smooths his hands across the white tablecloth. Those fingers... my eyes stalk out on sticks.

He stands, and I assume he's going to give me back my book and let me scurry away. Instead, with another small, half repressed sigh, he holds out his hand again to me in greeting. "Let's start again." His smile when it hits my face is like the beam of a lighthouse. It's just... just... I don't have anything to describe it with. It shines, it dimples, it glows with the light of a thousand suns. Okay, maybe I do have words, but they are the crap ramblings of a twelve- year-old.

"Elijah Fairclough." The smile is still focused on my face. I don't know what expression I'm pulling but I'm guessing it's amusing because his smile morphs into a smirk.

I should leave, grab my bag and go. The wild beating of my heart I have going on is pathetic. If there is one thing I don't do, it's pathetic.

I shake his hand. "Faith Hitchin."

He gestures for the seat and my legs instantly fold.

"I'm sorry she's not here. What can I say? She's easily waylaid at Barneys."

I don't smile. "Is this even a serious project? I don't want to waste my time. This is my last summer before my final year."

The lapis gaze locks onto my stare. "I can assure you this is a very serious project. Bowsley Hall is in need of a cash injection. We want to turn it into something useful to the community, to create a lasting initiative that will improve the fortunes of the building."

"And an installation will do that how?"

"It will give an old tired house a new purpose."

"Old and tired? That's not much to say about your home."

He chuckles wryly. "Oh, I don't live there. Hell no."

I raise both my eyebrows. "You aren't selling it?"

He leans forward; his gaze hasn't once broken from my face. "It's got prospects I think you will like."

"How do you know?"

He pushes my black bound book towards me, but I allow it to sit between us on the table. "I can tell."

I narrow my gaze and his lips curve at the edges again.

"Can I offer you a drink? Or would you like lunch? We can discuss more."

The thought of eating in front of this man makes me want to stab my eyes out with the silver fork on the table. "A drink would be okay." *Faith...*

He waves for the hovering waiter. "What would you like?" Jeez, that gaze is unlike anything I've ever seen. It makes me want to go home and grab out my paints and churn through them until I've found the perfect shade.

I haven't touched my paints for four years.

"Whisky on ice."

He raises two fingers to the waiter without saying a word. His other hand rests on my book and I want to snatch it away and run for the door. "I'm sorry about the setting. I don't know why my mother insists on coming here."

I sit on my hands because for some inexplicable reason they are shaking. "It's an interesting choice."

"Have you sold many pieces, Faith?" His change of direction takes me by surprise.

"Some. Gerard hooked me up with a couple of galleries who've sold pieces of my pottery."

His eyes flick across my face at Gerard's name and I

can't help but wonder what he knows. Does he know I slept with my lecturer? Did Gerard kiss and tell? I stare back, swallowing painfully.

"What do you prefer, sculpture or ceramics?"

I hesitate as he says ceramics. Most people with no knowledge say pottery.

My shoulders lift and fall. "Either."

That unsettling blue lands directly on my face, dropping to my lips. "Sure."

A frown scrunches my face. "Are you saying I'm lying."

"No."

Surely this doesn't need to be so uncomfortable? What's going on? I want to slap myself. This is the opportunity of a lifetime and I'm screwing it up, and all because his suit fits like it was cut onto his skin and his eyes are sharp enough to slice the surface of my skin. Who cares? It should be his mother I'm meeting.

The waiter brings our drinks, the ice clinking in the glass. I pick mine up as it barely touches the table and take a sip. The whisky is peaty and heady with malt depths. I lick my lips, enjoying the sour tingle on my tongue.

Maybe the alcohol will help me behave like a normal human being. Maybe.

He doesn't touch his glass. If he's not too careful, I might shoot it back.

"So can you tell me more? Why a residential? Why my sort of art? Wouldn't a painter and a painting exhibition have a wider appeal?"

His fingers fan across the table, his right index finger still touching my book. "We don't want to do something normal, that's not the point."

"Is this a royal we?" I smirk and take another sip of my drink. It burns in my veins and I welcome its warmth.

He frowns, his dark brows pulling together. "No, Peter is 18th in line to the throne. I think the chances of him making it onto the throne are slim."

I watch his handsome face for a crack of humour, but no cute dimple appears. "Sorry, what?"

"Oh, I thought you were digging at the royal succession."

My eyes widen. "No, I was taking the piss, oh, I mean the mick, uh." I decide to stop talking, but then another question pops into my head. "Who's Peter?"

There's a pause and Elijah Fairclough's face grows pensive. My hand itches for my paints. "He's my elder brother."

"Two of you?" Oh my god, I sound like a wanton lunatic.

"Three of us. Me, one older brother, and one baby sister." His face hardens into an unreadable mask.

"And your mother is a baroness?"

He nods, but his gaze lingers on the pristine tablecloth.

I lean forward. I've never met a member of the aristocracy before. "And Peter is going to be the baron as well as in line for the throne?"

When Elijah meets my gaze, I'm sure I catch a flicker across his lips. "It's an unusual succession, quite old and embroiled in tradition."

"And you're the sibling who got lumbered meeting me today?" I take another sip. "Shame for you."

Finally, he picks up his own glass, and I watch mesmerised as he allows the iced liquid to slip between his sumptuous lips. *Sumptuous lips? Someone shoot me now.* "Something like that."

I glower. "Maybe I should meet your mother when she's back from her trip?"

"Maybe."

"Okay." I go to get my stuff. Honestly, I can cope without sitting at a table in a poncy over-priced bar with an egotistical prick who doesn't want to be there.

"What gallery sells your work?"

"What?" I turn back to face him. He doesn't seem to realise I'm leaving.

"What gallery sells your stuff?"

"Uh, Whitlocks in Whitechapel; they are only small."

He nods.

"You know them?"

"Yes, I've bought a few bits from there."

"You have, or your mother?"

He smiles, enigmatic. "I like you. You're sharp, different."

He doesn't know how different; he doesn't know that under my silk oversized blouse I have a multitude of secrets written on my skin.

"How's your final piece for the year?"

"Sorry?" I'm going to get a migraine if this conversation carries on this way.

"You must be working on a final project? Next year will be the big pieces, right?"

"How do you know so much about it?"

Another shrug. "So how's it going?"

"Terrible." There's no point in lying.

"Maybe you'll let me see?"

I shake my head. "Not a chance." Finding the will to move my stubborn legs, I step up from the table. "This has been different."

He stands and holds his hand out again. His mummy must have trained him well. "We don't seem to have got along."

I chuckle a small laugh. "No, I'd say not. Maybe your mother can call when she gets back and then we can see how this might work. I'm guessing you have other people to see, maybe your meetings will go more smoothly with them."

He inclines his head. "Maybe."

"Good bye, Elijah," I straighten my shoulders and swing my hips for the door, keeping my head held high.

That was fucking weird.

It's only when I'm on the sweaty bus home, I realise I've forgotten my portfolio.

Shit.

Five

"I can't believe you sent me out to the lion's den like that."

Gerard has his hand on the front door of the studio, but I've got my foot against the door. I'm too cross to be making small talk with him at the moment.

Bloody Elijah Fairclough. Gah, the gall of the man. 'We don't seem to have got along'.

I don't know why it's burned under my skin so bad. Let's be real, he's not the first guy to say those words to me. Normally, though, I like to say them first.

"It was The Ritz, not London Zoo, Faith." Gerard tries to peer around the door. I know he wants to see my project, but right now he can kiss my arse.

"Tell that to Elijah Fairclough, the guy is seriously lacking in social skills."

Gerard snorts loudly despite the fact he's standing in the hallway. "Says you."

I narrow my gaze and then swing the door in his face. I can hear him sigh through the wood. "Get my portfolio back," I shout after him, before walking back into the studio and staring at the tragic mess I've made.

It's unsalvageable. I'm going to have to order new materials. Turning slightly, I stare at the canvas covered in blue.

Fuck. It's been an obsession the last two days.

Blues everywhere in everything. I even bought a blue orchid today. Not that I can afford fancy flowers or have the ability to keep them alive.

It's all shit.

I can't stop thinking about the pensive expression on his face as he watched me across the table. I can't stop remembering that low rumble of his voice, or the way his body packed out that expensive suit.

So, in fact, I can't stop thinking about him.

Player, he's a player, Faith. A rich one.

But he seemed so serious. There was this quiet *something* about him. I can't work it out.

Like, if I didn't want to be there in The Ritz talking to him, then he really and truly didn't want to be there either.

Maybe he didn't like my outfit. Maybe he just didn't like me. Maybe he wanted to be off shagging someone and I was an inconvenience.

Maybe.

I thought I might have heard from the baroness herself. Perhaps an apology for standing me up and leaving her arsehole son in charge. But I haven't.

So, tonight I'm going to look for a bar job. I can't leave it any longer, and obviously the summer installation has fallen through.

My phone beeps and I can see Abi's face, but my mood is black—dangerous.

The phone rings off and I crank on the shower to clean up. Before I climb in, I flick through the small wardrobe I keep at the studio as the water runs through warm.

With a decision of black harem trousers, a black skinny vest, and a leather jacket, I choose my outfit for my mood. With no blue in sight.

The shower does little to settle me down, so after I've dried off, I fling on my clothes and tip my head upside down and scrape my fingers along the damp strands of hair, dragging them into a high ponytail which I twist and secure with pins.

My phone rings again but I ignore it. People should know by now if I don't answer the first time, the chances of me picking up from that point on dramatically decrease.

I grab my purse and keys and open the door. It's time to get drunk, find a job and hopefully find some indiscriminate screw who can help me forget the colour blue.

"What the actual fuck?" I curse as I swing into a hard chest the other side of the studio door.

"Miss Hitchin?"

God, no! It's the gem deep eyes of loserville.

"Fairclough." I snap. "What are you doing here? My eyes, they won't stop or behave themselves and they rove all over his chest, over the muscles straining against the tight stretch of his T-shirt. He's wearing dark jeans and sliders. The short hair and casual combo give him a rugged edge that's kind of hard to stop staring at. Two days ago, he was suave and icy. Today, he's beach bum, rough and ready chic.

"I thought you might need this." He lifts the black book containing every documented precious item I've ever produced and holds it out. I grasp its edges. That baby is mine, and it needs to come home. He holds onto the spine though, and I stare up into his face. When I meet his gaze, my tummy tightens. *No, Faith, that is not an indiscriminate screw.* "Also, we got off to a truly awful start, and I was hoping we could try again," he says.

I glare at him, but he spreads the most charming smile across his handsome face. And crap if it isn't the most handsome face I've ever seen. Sharp cheekbones and soft lips—

and those eyes. "Totally my bad." He steps back from the door and lets go of my book. "I can leave if you think my failed attempts at interviewing are past redemption."

My lips twitch with an annoying urge to smile. "The single worst interviewing skills I've ever come across," I reply.

He nods sagely, the little dimple on his right cheek growing. "It's as I thought. I suck."

"So much so I'm about to go searching for bar work." My eyes narrow as I scrutinise him. He could not be more different than the man I met in The Ritz. I'm wondering if he's a twin, and this is some weird sibling game called "let's fuck with the girl's head".

He holds his hands to his heart, knitting his fingers together like a child begging. "Don't let me be the one to set you on the path to inhospitable working hours and drunken leering old men."

"Maybe I like drunken, leering old men." I smile, just a little.

"Oh, well, in that case we have many of them at Bowsley Hall, you will be inundated."

"Inundated? Now you're talking."

For a moment we stop and stare.

Then he spreads his hands to his side and raises them up. His arm muscles flex—not that I'm noticing. "What do you say, Faith? How about we go for a drink and attempt a half normal conversation?"

"Half normal, are you sure you can manage?"

The left side of his lips quirk into a smirk and he runs a hand through his cropped dark hair. I wonder what that feels like? "I can try."

An unsure hesitation roots me to my doormat. He is extremely attractive. Staring at his face for a couple of hours wouldn't be a hardship. But then he does seem to be a complete arse... and there's the fact I'm desperate for a screw. That wouldn't be a good idea. Not at all. Terrible. Also, did I mention the fact he is extremely attractive, in a panty-melting, I'm-going-to-smile- that-underwear-straight-off-your-body kind of way?

His eyes sweep behind me into the studio. I could invite him in, show him some of my more successful work. Obviously not the pile of marble dust I've created. This way I might still stand a chance at the Bowsley summer job. I don't though. I don't even know if I want him seeing inside my studio; it's strangely intimate.

Then I notice his gaze has settled on the exposed row of roses I have displayed across my collarbone. He doesn't say a word, and I refuse to shift my jacket to cover them up. He's the one who turned up unexpectedly, ruining my chances of getting laid.

"Okay let's go." The words escape before I have any chance to think on them further. Which is probably a good thing. I could have stood there analysing all night.

He flashes me that dimple and cute smile.

"Not The Ritz, though. You could come out of that place in a wooden box." I slide my portfolio across the floor of the studio. There's a low snigger, and he shoves his hands in his jean's pockets, the epitome of casual cool. He could have fallen off the front page of GQ. I wonder how many people have tried to take his photograph.

"I think I can manage something better than where my mother goes for a glass of sherry."

"Nothing fancy, though. You don't want to make me uncomfortable."

His eyes settle on my face, and I melt under their weight. "No." He pauses. "No one would want that."

There's a flicker across his lips, but I don't know what it means so I start to walk down the hallway to the stairwell with him trailing behind. It's all I can do not to fall over my own feet.

Out in the narrow street, the day is winding down. The streets are noticeably emptier of people, no doubt home now their day is done. I hadn't realised how late I'd been murdering that piece of rock. "Walking?" I stop and wait for him; the pavement could lead me in two different ways.

He slides his hand out of his pocket. "I drove," he shrugs sheepishly. "I didn't know if you were going to repel me."

"Repel you? Are we in an Austen novel?"

"Repel me with your cantankerous bad attitude."

His eyes challenge me, so I switch things and grin. I can't help it. I know he could mean a job for the summer. I know being on the right side of his family could mean more exposure than I could spend the next ten years trying to build. But I can sense a game building, a challenge.

I also know he's damn annoying. "Lucky for you, I'm feeling friendly today."

I could be very friendly towards him. I could tug him back into the alleyway behind and show him just how friendly I could be.

He laughs. I'm sure he knows what I'm thinking.

"Your carriage, my lady." He steps up to a navy car. Smart and sleek, its trim is a gleaming silver.

My mouth falls open. "You have an MG Roadster?" I step up, completely forgetting myself, and run a hand along the immaculate paintwork. Oh my god, this car looks like it's just out of the factory.

"Yeah?" He can't disguise his surprise.

"What is this, a nineteen sixty-six, mark one?"

His mouth falls open, which is all levels of funny, but

I'm too taken with the car to use it to my advantage. "Yeah, how do you know?"

"My dad used to have one." The words slip out before I can contain them. A sharp slice cuts me some place around my chest.

"Nice."

I can't breathe, though. For a long moment, standing here in this shady Islington street I'm lost in forgotten memories. *Faith, don't put sand all over the leather.* A squeal of laughter echoes from the past.

"Would you rather walk?"

I glance up into Elijah's face. There's a frown between his eyebrows.

"No." My answer wobbles. "No, it's okay."

He opens the door and I slip onto the leather, sinking deep.

"Where are we going?" I try to switch it back on. Switch the me of now back on.

"I know a good pub, if you fancy a pint somewhere?"

"It's London, there are thousands of good pubs."

He doesn't answer but fires the ignition and coaxes the car out into the weave of black cabs and post rush hour traffic.

As we sit in the car, silence laps between us. "Did you have nothing better to do than come and give me back my portfolio? You know you could have given it to Gerard."

His head flicks in my direction. He drives sexy. Confidently weaving in and out. Strong fingers flick the indicator and shift the gears.

Stop it, Faith.

"That wouldn't be very gentlemanly."

"Are you always a gentleman?"

He flicks those blues onto me again. "Sometimes."

Yikes.

"So where are we going?"

"The Green Man."

"Could you narrow it down? There are at least a hundred and fifty Green Man pubs in London."

"Have you counted them all?"

I've got to laugh. "Not personally, but I have it under good authority."

He laughs too and the car fills with the sound of our mingled mirth. "How do you enjoy London?"

"It's okay."

"And you were in Brighton before?"

I cast him a side eye. "Have you been stalking me?"

"No. My mother found out when she was talking to Gerard about you."

I blush a little. That makes so much more sense than him stalking me.

"And I've been Facebooking."

"Facebooking? The baroness' son is on Facebook?" I chuckle under my breath. "What is your title? If your mum is a baroness, what does that make you?"

He turns, his smile enigmatic. "Elijah, it makes me Elijah."

He flicks the indicator and turns into a small car park lined with rose bushes. I lean closer, peering through the windscreen. The roses are a similar colour to the ink on my chest: dusky pink and cream.

"I saw your tattoos and thought of this place."

"You didn't plan to come here?"

He shrugs but neither of us move to get out of the parked car. "I change my mind frequently."

That sounds dangerous. I swallow hard and reach my hand for the chrome handle.

"Why?" I ask.

"It's just who I am."

The lapis blues meet mine. Message received perfectly clear.

Like a scolded child, I want to take back every giggle I've bestowed on him.

Six

"Why London? You could have gone to so many other places to study Art? Couldn't you have stayed in Brighton, even?"

"What have you been looking at on Facebook?"

He smiles over the rim of his coke. The barmaid had known him by name when we came in. I tried not to let the fact irk me as I'd stood and ordered my wine. It wasn't any of my business anyway. "Nothing, really. It's clear you only have contacts in Brighton, and a few from London. Gerard Steers being one of them."

His gaze makes me squirm on the hard, wooden chair.

"You know, you could have friend requested me instead of just lurking and judging my friends and contacts."

"We aren't friends, though."

I take a sip of wine. "No, we aren't."

"I could, though."

I shrug. "You could."

"Would you accept?" There's teasing in his smile.

Another shrug. "Maybe. It depends how busy I am."

"I looked through your portfolio." His change in conversation blindsides me. "You are exceptionally talented."

I flush, but my instant reaction to protect myself flares into action. "Thanks. Are you an expert?"

He shrugs and makes it look far cooler than I do. "So, what do you do with your time?"

"Stuff."

"Stuff? That sounds vastly entertaining."

"I manage to keep myself amused."

Sure you do. God, this man is making me regress to teenagehood. Is there such a thing as teenagehood? If there is, I'm hurtling towards it at a great rate.

"So... you and Gerard. How long have you been friends?"

He shakes his head, cutting me off. "Peter is Gerard's friend."

The pointed way he says it makes me frown.

"Well, he's been good to me. He's made me stay the course when I could have left so many times."

"Course he has." Elijah's face hardens.

"What does that mean?"

He spreads his hands and shrugs again. "Don't mind me, it's schoolboy history. Oh, and call me Eli, please." He smiles broadly, and I stare, my eyes open wide. That smile... have I ever seen anything like it? "Elijah makes me feel like I've stepped right out of the bible."

"Highly religious, are we?"

He gives a small shake of his head. "You're like a razor."

"Don't get too close then," I retort.

His face falls flat, all signs of joking evaporating. "I won't."

"Good," I say. Whether I mean it or not I don't know.

"Tell me about the roses."

My hand flutters to the skin under my collarbone.

"There isn't much to tell. Before I came to London I fancied something pretty."

"Who did them?"

"My uncle."

"Wow, that's a delicate hand for a man."

"I drew them." I blush. I don't know why. He's had my portfolio for two days, it's not like he doesn't know what my drawings look like. These are different though; they are mine and on my skin.

His gaze burns hotter than the pen used to draw and colour them. "How did he get the blending like that?"

"A nine pin needle." I'm exposed under his scrutiny and I pull my jacket together, cutting off his view. It doesn't help. That unsettling blue drifts to my face like he can read everything there.

"Will you come to see Bowsley? See if you think it could work for you."

My shoulders sag. This could be the opportunity of a lifetime, so why does it seem so dangerous? "And you don't live there?" My face scorches.

He grins. "Am I so awful that's the deciding factor?"

"Yes, that exactly." I giggle again—someone get me a training bra please.

"I don't live there; can't think of anything worse."

"You don't need to make my decision not to come any easier."

"My mother lives there—"

"When she's not sipping sherry at The Ritz," I interrupt.

That gaze brightens on my face again. "Well remembered. She's um, determined."

"In what way?"

"In the way that we should all be doing the right thing. Marriage, children, heirs to the family name."

I blanch. "Married? How old are you?"

"Twenty-eight."

Four years older than me. *Why am I even working that out?*

"Tell her to worry when you're forty-eight and still driving around town in that chick catcher car."

He laughs so loudly the rest of the pub garden turn to look. "Chick catcher?"

I wiggle my eyebrows. "You know what I mean."

He holds his hands. "Guilty as charged, apparently."

"I'll come." The decision is made.

"Thank you." We watch one another, and I study the profile of his face.

"You know, if you turn to the side." Leaning across the table, I tilt his face so the soft rays of the setting sun land along his nose and the tip of his chin. "You look like one of those beautiful cameo brooches the Victorians used to wear."

He turns, my fingers still on his chin. Is it me or is his skin alarmingly hot?

"Aren't they usually female profiles?"

I shrug, my hand still on his face. "Let's not be sexist about it."

His lips turn at the edges. "You just called me beautiful."

I drop my hand. "I did not."

He laughs, his shoulders rising and falling. "You did. You called me beautiful."

Glaring, I narrow my gaze into a steely look. "I'd better go home before I change my mind about Bowsley." I drain my glass.

I can't sit here on this bench any longer.

In an hour with Elijah Fairclough, I've spoken more words to someone of the opposite sex than I have for five years —excluding Gerard. Normally there aren't any words at all.

It's been three days since my unexpected but short drink with Elijah Fairclough. I thought maybe I'd hear from him about visiting Bowsley.

Gerard's been forgiven. Not because everything is all hunky dory, but mainly because I need him to help look at my pieces and decide which ones might be good enough for Bowsley. I've nearly finished with the marble, but it's not what I intended to do with it—nowhere even close.

My phone rings and I see Abi's face on the screen. "Hey, you."

I give her an enthusiastic smile and shuffle myself around to hide the three sheets of blue silk I've hung from the ceiling.

I'm obsessed with the colour. And I can't stop thinking about Elijah—no matter how hard I try.

"Why are you smiling? What man was it, and what did you do to him?" she quizzes.

"Why do you always think there's a man involved?" I plop down on the small sofa and grab my packet of cigarettes. Sliding one out, I light it quick.

"Normally you only smile when you are on a sex come down. You're basically like a praying mantis who needs to eat males."

"I am not a stick insect." I chuckle and suck in a lungful of smoke.

"You know what I mean. You've always been like this. You're a predator: no feelings, no attachments, just sheer pleasure."

I screw my face up and remember the guy from the bar the previous week. I'm not going to tell her there wasn't much I found pleasurable about that. Why ruin her high expectations?

"What you up to this evening?" I change the subject away from my sex life.

"Oooh, it's Friday. So, uh, I think I will stay at home and watch the telly."

"Can't you get a babysitter and go out somewhere? You are allowed to have fun."

"We can't all be single and shagging our way around London, in some free-wheeling display of independence."

I frown and drag on my smoke. Seriously is that what she thinks I do all the time?

"Listen, I saw Al yesterday."

My chest tightens. Abi has her serious face on. The one I don't like. "Yes?"

"He's not looking good, Faith."

"What do you mean by good exactly? I talked to him the other day and he seemed fine." I run my finger over my lightning bolt, my heart pinching a little into a sharp ache.

"He's weak. You can just see his body is giving up."

"So why isn't he in hospital? Getting treatment… help?"

Abi's eye is steady on the camera. "It's too late for that. Dan says he just wants to live while he can."

The blood in my veins runs cold. I can't imagine making that decision. Can't imagine saying the words "That's it, it's my time."

"How is Dan?" I light another cigarette, knowing I'm

being ridiculous doing so when I'm talking about one of my favourite people of all time succumbing to cancer.

"He's okay. Says the shop's keeping him from worrying too much. But I think he's struggling." Underneath her innocent statement are unspoken words. I should come back and help... I shouldn't leave them all like this.

How can I not? I can't be there. Not now.

"What they going to do when he gets worse?"

"Dan says Al has chosen a hospice."

God, I want to be sick. I want to wash away in a sea of tears, never to surface again. What's the point of living if it all comes down to this?

"Have you really not got any plans for the weekend?"

Abi offers me a little smile. "Wine, television, family time, and maybe some sex with my husband. I'm content with that."

A little stab digs deep in my stomach. I can't imagine what it must be like to have sex with the same person time and time again. It's the one rule I will never break.

"You should try monogamy some time, it's not all bad." Abi cracks a grin.

"Who, me?" I laugh. "One guy, forever? Please just shoot me and put me out of my misery."

She chats about her children for a while. "Anyway, what's the latest with you?"

"Well, I'm going to see Bowsley Hall tomorrow."

Abi chuckles. "Wow, I still can't believe you are considering living in a stately home for weeks."

I grin back, my smile for my friend growing from the inside out, genuine and honest. "I can be a lady."

Abi howls laughing. "Okay, Lady Hitchin."

I giggle. We say our goodbyes and end the call. Standing, I turn and find the angled free-standing mirror. In my denim cut offs and scrappy vest, with my stories on my skin I am very, very far from being a lady. And that's a good thing. I'll go surprise Abi on Sunday. It's only a train ride, and I want to see Al. It's as though time is ticking too fast and it won't slow down. But he's my champion, the one who's always had my back, and I can't allow my time with him to pass. I can ignore those I don't want to see, those with distrust in their eyes, just so I can spend time with those I care about.

I still haven't decided how I feel about Bowsley. Whether it's a ridiculous mistake, or is an opportunity not to be missed.

I slip on some espadrilles and grab my bag and keys. I need to go shopping for something to wear tomorrow. And I need to get laid. Maybe then I'll stop thinking about Elijah Fairclough.

I check all my appliances are off, and glance at the remaining marble. A fine sliver of marble, sanded until it's nothing more than shell thick, holds an etched profile of a delicate sloped nose and a high brow. It's the most fragile thing I've ever made. I won't be able to hand it in, though—it's too far from my style, from the coursework I've created to go with it. It was supposed to be a solid piece, not a glorified item of jewellery. On a whim, I pick it up and place it on my bookshelf. Then I turn and go to find the smog of London, some new clothes, and hopefully a release from the unsettled sensation in my chest.

Seven

It only takes me an hour to find a pleated, black, ankle-length chiffon skirt. The material is see-through, but underneath is a shorter underskirt. The material is just dark enough that the pictures on my thighs won't show. Not that I particularly care.

I found a matching blouse with a cute collar I'll be able to tuck in. Pleased, I head back to the apartment. There isn't anything at the studio left for me to work on. Only the mess I've created with that damn marble. What was I thinking?

I wonder if the guy with the surfer blonde hair found his friends again? It had been easy to walk into one of the packed bars of Covent Garden and find a random and take advantage.

Maybe I am a praying mantis?

My phone vibrates, so stopping in a doorway I check out the message. I know I only spoke to Abi this morning, but every time my phone makes a noise, my heart leaps into my mouth thinking it could be the call I never want to arrive.

It's a Facebook notification. Pressing it and opening the app, I hold the phone closer to see who it's from.

Eli Jones.

I don't know an Eli Jones. There isn't a profile picture, so I click on his 'friends'. There are only five and none of them are anyone I know. But I do know an Elijah. His words come into my mind. *Call me Eli.* Then there was our conversation about Facebook friends. *Would you accept?*

Is that why he's Facebooking me? To find out the answer? But then maybe it's about tomorrow. I accept the request and shove my phone back into my bag. It's hot and sticky, and I want to go home for a shower.

The water does its trick, washing away my London encounter and the grime of the city. When I come out, I wrap myself in my giant bath towel and open the lounge windows. I love this building, it's perfect. Art deco and with wonderful windows, it might be tiny but it's a little slice of architectural perfection. Overlooking the Thames from the south, I'd fallen in love on the spot. What the rooms lack on cubic square feet, the ceiling makes up for in height and vaulting. I could never have afforded this in my wildest dreams, but when Al gave me the chance to work in his shop to save money for my escape to London, I saved every penny. Men pay a lot to be tattooed by someone like me. I sometimes wonder if they get an erotic kick out of my inflicting pain on them. Oh well, I don't care if they pay well.

I light a cigarette and grab my phone. A Facebook message is on the home screen.

Eli Jones: I decided to stop stalking.

I roll my eyes and drag on my smoke.

Faith Hitchin: Thanks. I feel so much safer now.

I go to throw my phone onto the sofa, but it beeps before I have a chance.

Eli Jones: I've increased your London friends by 50%

Well that's damn rude.

Faith Hitchin: Don't do me any favours.

Eli Jones: Actually, can you do me a favour? Can you send me a screen shot of your roses?

I stare at the screen. Can I do what exactly?

Faith Hitchin: I am not sending you a picture of my chest.

Eli Jones: I'm not a pervert. I just need to see the colour.

Faith Hitchin: Why?

I'm going to send him a get-the-hell-lost-you-weirdo response, or maybe I'm going to just shut off my phone and ignore his random request. Or perhaps I will take a picture of the roses along my collarbone and send it.

Yes. I'll do that.

I don't hear back. Nothing.

Well, that was weird, and don't I feel like a dick for sending him a picture of my skin.

I grab my laptop and Google *Elijah Fairclough*. If he was being serious the other day and his older brother Peter is something in line to the throne—how completely ridiculous—then surely there's got to be something about the younger brother on the net. Everything's on there isn't it? If Elijah had had the foresight, he could have Googled rose tattoos with Brighton and it probably would have bought up some image floating around of my roses. Al's a bugger at spreading his work, especially when he's proud of something.

I light another cigarette and squint at the screen. My glasses are over the other side of the room, and even when dressed in only a towel and completely by myself, I like to maintain my vanity.

Some younger images of Elijah flash up. His hair's longer, less severe, but those eyes are the same. I zoom in. What colour are they? Now I look closer I'm not sure if they are Lapis... What do they remind me of? I open another tab in Google and type in porcelain. Images flash up of blue on cream. The blue is vibrant, but it's not quite right. Another tab and I type in Wedgewood. That's too pale, too wishy-washy. Not piercing enough.

In the end, and cringing as I realise I'm the worst artist in the world I type *vivid blue flowers*.

I scroll the results knowing I will see what I want when I see it. I can get like this, I hate not knowing something, especially when it's right there on the tip of my tongue.

Then I see them. Tall and brilliant, a bunch of delphiniums. That's the blue. Delphinium blue.

I flick back to the tab with the images of Elijah and then to the one with the flower. Yes, that's definitely it.

I read some of the words on the screen, but my eyes constantly wander back to the pictures. There are numerous photos of him at racecourses, normally with a blonde on his arm. Not always the same blonde.

Player.

Then I see the words that finally snap my attention from the images.

Younger son of Baroness Fairclough announces engagement to socialite Sienna Richards.

I drag on my cigarette and read the words again.

What is a socialite? Is that actually a job?

So he's engaged. That's good, because it means next

time I think about those *delphinium* blue eyes, I can tell myself to get a grip on reality and concentrate on the work I need to do.

This is what I need. A stiff slap of realism. I can get *carried away*. I want something, and I pursue it despite the cost. Look at what I did with Gerard. I wasn't going to let him go until I had him and then when I had it was enough. I lost interest. And even though he didn't understand, apart from maybe on some level realising I'm totally fucked up, I knew I couldn't break my one-time rule.

I'm guessing Elijah Fairclough and Sienna Richards don't have a one shag only rule.

Of course, they don't. I'm the only one with that rule.

I shut my laptop, my snooping complete. It hasn't made me any happier, but it has wasted what was left of the evening. I slip into bed knowing that tomorrow I'm going to Bowsley Hall and that it could be the start of an opportunity of a lifetime.

I don't sleep, my dreams are twisted. Sharp pens and ink chasing me. And I dream of Dad and his face when I tried to tell him the truth.

Unrested and jittery, I get myself together. Elijah is going to be here soon; he said ten. I check my phone to see if I have any messages but there is nothing. God, I wish Gerard was coming with me. I call him, to beg, but he doesn't answer. It is Saturday and almost the end of term. I'd say he has better things to do than listen to my ramblings and worries.

I shower again and tell myself it's the sticky air making me sweat despite standing under water. My outfit is all wrong as I pull it on. Maybe I shouldn't cover my tattoos? Maybe the outfit is too formal? But then isn't this a job interview?

Why is this so damn hard?

I'm hating Gerard for telling me about this. He should have given it to Meg and been done with it. Meg would have known how to cope. She would have sailed in there, crafted them some pots, made everything all pretty, and it would have been hunky dory. Instead, here I am sweating in chiffon.

My phone beeps dead on ten a.m.

Eli Jones: Where are you?

Faith Hitchin: Waiting for you.

Eli Jones: But I'm at the studio.

I realise my error. I need a serious bitch slap.

Faith Hitchin: I'm sorry. I'm at my apartment. I thought we were meeting here.

Eli Jones: even though I don't know where it is…

I don't know what to say. This is not a great start to a second interview.

Before I have a chance to respond, my phone beeps again.

Eli Jones: Send me your postcode.

I do, along with my road address and door number. I've gone overboard on the details, but I'm not chancing anything again. Then I sit on my sofa and chastise myself for being the world's biggest idiot. I should have just made my own way to Bowsley. Why did I agree to the lift? Why did I even agree to go?

Twenty minutes later, there's a buzz on the intercom. "I'm coming down," I shout. Grabbing my bag and my portfolio, I launch myself out the door. I'm too slow. He's stood at the other side in a black suit with a grey striped tie. My mouth pops open a little.

"You're very dressed up," I say.

One side of his mouth lifts. "It's business?"

"And the sliders the other night?" I find myself standing still, just watching his face.

"An apology." His steady gaze is on my face. "Are you ready?"

I nod, my cheeks flaming. "Yes, I'm sorry about the confusion."

"Don't worry, I called ahead and told them lunch was going to be a bit late."

"Lunch?" My heart starts knocking in my chest.

"Of course. You are going to need to meet everyone and talk through plans. Surely that would be better over lunch?"

I hadn't even thought...? Suddenly I realise I haven't been sensible about this at all. This is just another classic example of me being hasty. What was it my dad always used to call me? *Flighty*.

I lock away thoughts of my dad and straighten my shoulders. "Okay, let's go. I wouldn't want to make lunch later than it is."

He grins, and it does something funny to my stomach. *He's engaged, Faith.*

I follow him down the landing to the stairwell, breathing in deep. I can do this. I can do anything that stops me going back to Brighton and living my life in the shadow of the past.

Eight

The car ride is awkward. Two strangers stuck in a small sports car for two hours. He tries to open up conversation, but my stomach is twisted into knots and I keep focusing on the movement of his wrists as he drives. So strong and controlled, his watch every so often flashes a ray of sunlight.

I'm paying so much attention to his wrists smattered in fair hair, I don't hear him speak. "So why don't you have many London friends on Facebook?"

I swivel in my seat to stare at him. "What's the obsession with Facebook friends?"

He shrugs, his fingers flicking the indicator for a left turn. *His fingers... Oh my god, stop it, Faith.*

"I just figured that's what people gauged their lives by?"

"Do you? I checked your profile; you don't have many friends on there, either." I'm not worried about my lack of online friends. I've never been a people person. That it should extend to my digital life is no skin off my nose. What am I going to do? Tell people on a daily basis that I forgot to have dinner and instead had a cigarette and a handful of crackers? Or that yesterday I shagged a stranger in the changing rooms of Topshop because I had nothing better to do. Those aren't the sort of things people want to know.

"You checked my profile? Are you stalking *me* now?"

I roll my eyes and stare out of the window. I wonder if he'd let me smoke in his vintage car. I'm thinking not. He doesn't look like a smoker. He looks like someone who works out, and eats salmon and broccoli for breakfast, probably brought to him on a silver platter by his skinny socialite fiancée.

"It would be foolish not to see who my boss is."

I glance back at him just as he looks at me. Our eyes meet.

"Technically my mother is your boss."

"Is she going to be there today?" I don't know why but the delayed meeting with the baroness is starting to freak me out. "Or are you our permanent go-between?"

"That's one of my favourite books?" His words make me sit up straighter.

"Pardon?" My palms slick a little—crazy overreaction. "L. P. Hartley is one of your favourite books?"

He nods, and those insane bright eyes glance over me. "Have you read it?"

I cough a little. "Uh, yes."

"And?"

"I was obsessed with it as a child. That tension, the build up, and the final tragedy." I studied The Go Between for my English exam before my life went to shit. It's one of my last stable memories: sitting in my room, flicking the pages; trying to get to the ending, but then realising that the exciting bit was shocking, and it hurt to read. A bit like life. "It's hard to forget." I add, and my voice wavers a little.

"The past is a foreign country," his words hang in the air.

"They do things differently there." I finish the famous quote.

"You surprise me, Miss Hitchin."

I glare at him but find him grinning at me.

"You don't surprise me if you only see as far as the surface," I snap.

He chuckles to himself like he's so damn amusing and I seethe in my seat. Bloody ignoramus.

When he flicks the indicator towards a small entrance in the centre of a huge brick wall—a wall we've been driving past for a long while without me realising—his relaxed demeanour hardens. It snaps in the air like brittle glass.

I watch through the window, his change in body language causing a shiver of apprehension to tingle down my spine. We draw up in front of what can only be described as a palatial building. It's bigger than a mansion. In fact, it would make a mansion look like a cottage.

"Jesus," I mutter. He snorts, but it lacks the warmth of a few minutes before.

"Welcome to the crazy house." He announces.

By the time we've made it up broad, pale stone steps, I'm glad of my outfit choice. If I've got to sell myself—convince these people that my work belongs in their frankly giant house—then, hell, I'm going to dress right for it.

The door opens as we arrive and a man in a suit bows as we walk through. Please tell me that's not a butler.

"Jennings." Elijah greets the older man, clapping him warmly on his arm and handing him his keys.

"Elijah, it's good to have you home." The man's deep brown eyes sweep over me. "And not alone. Miss Hitchin, we are pleased you could come."

"Thanks," I stutter.

The fall of footsteps draws my attention, and as I turn towards them, I catch Elijah stiffening out of the corner of my eye.

"Darling, you are home." A woman of middling years walks towards us, a waft of pungent perfume which I believe may have been made in hell by Chanel precedes before her. She's an apparition of immaculate perfection. Hair carefully coiffed, face smoother than my own which is impressive considering she must have at least twenty years, if not more, on me. Her suit is Chanel. She air-kisses Elijah and he shoots me a small smile over her lilac-suited shoulder.

She pats his shoulders, taking in the full view of his face before turning to me.

"Faith, I am so pleased Elijah was able to convince you to come." Her smile is bright. But, Elijah doesn't get his blues from her. "My apologies about our meeting at The Ritz. I am just so unorganised. Hopefully, Elijah acted like a gentleman and explained the situation."

I flick my gaze towards him. His face is cautious, perplexed, although I have no idea why. She grabs my arm and wheels me around, not giving me time to answer. "Now, come, let's start a tour, or do you need a drink after a drive in that awful rust bucket Elijah insists on keeping. Sentimental fool."

"Why's he a sentimental fool?" I want to turn to see him, but she's marching me away down a marble floored hallway at a great pace.

"Oh, it's silly. It is the car his grandfather used to drive. When Elijah passed his test, he found someone selling it. Somehow, he managed to match it up with old photographs and bought it. He has spent far too much energy on fixing it up, I can assure you." She clucks her tongue against the roof of her mouth.

Elijah fixed that car? I don't know why this surprises me, but it does.

We are speed walking through an airy hallway. Arched windows stud the wall at regular intervals. How many windows are there? I can't stop to count, she's towing me so fast by the elbow. I glance up and see a beautiful domed ceiling, decorated with gold stars on white. It's quite beautiful.

"Wait." I pull on her hand, holding her back.

"What is it?" She looks genuinely perplexed that I might want to do this walk slowly.

"Can I take a moment to see this room? It's amazing." I slide my chiffon-covered sleeve out of her grasp and step away. I need to breathe air not tainted by Chanel. I turn on my heel and take in the impressive length of the room.

It reminds me of the type of room Jane Austen would have had her characters "taking a turn of the room" in. Blimey, if they'd had Fitbits in those days no one would have had problems getting their steps in.

"Faith." She smiles at me. I'm telling myself it's not condescending. "This is just the hallway."

I won't let her budge me on. "The light is amazing. All these windows. This would be a great room for glass; you could have changes in tone throughout the room, maybe start lighter by the entrance and have it grow darker by the end."

I find Elijah still watching at the other end. He seems to be smirking. Shooting him a frown, I turn back to his mother. "Sorry, I get distracted."

She claps her hands together. "I have a good feeling about this."

I still need to find out exactly what *this* is, so with that in mind I let her lead me through the next door and see what awaits me there.

My head swims so fast, I struggle to take everything in. So many colours, textures. I'm sweating too. So many steps.

And they think this house is dilapidated.

It's anything but. It shines with fading glory like it's whispering its secrets though crumbled plasterwork and worn wallpaper.

I want to do every room again by myself. Taking my time. Working out what could go where and have the greatest impact.

But my stomach, unrepressed by my lack of nicotine, is growling with hunger, so when Jennings find us and murmurs in a low, discreet voice that lunch is served, I almost faint with relief.

"Come, let's go to the conservatory," Jennifer Fairclough says. We've been talking a lot about the project as we walk, her telling me some of the long history of the building, but I have a feeling lunch will be when the real interview begins.

The conservatory is a large glass affair. Exotic plants cram the space, the air rich with earthy scents. It's heaven—I'm sure. It's not a conservatory. Well, nothing like I've ever seen before.

I thought the ballroom with the star-gilded ceiling would be my favourite. But now I see this barrage of green, living foliage, I think the conservatory wins.

A table is set with pristine white linen and gleaming silverware. Crystal glasses catch the natural light, and I think it should be hot and that I will sweat more in my chiffon, but the air is cool. I glance up and find the domed ceiling is open wide, as windows wrought in old-fashioned metal frames open to the elements. Bird chatter and the hum of insects provides gentle background sound that mixes with the fall of water. I can't see any water, so it must be hidden in the maze of flowers and dark green leaves.

There are two people already sat at the circular table, but only the one with the blue eyes and a dark suit rises when he sees me and pulls out a chair. "Very gentlemanly," I tease, and the eyes crease as he grins.

"Always."

A shorter, more rounded version of Elijah reaches forward with his hand. "Peter Fairclough." He confirms. "It's good of you to come to discuss our project."

I can't help but wonder why he didn't meet me at The Ritz the other day. If he's the one who knows Gerard, surely that would have made sense?

I don't turn but I sense a heavy watchful gaze on my face. "Thanks for having me," I reply, but I'm nervous and uncomfortable. I was happier walking around the house, dreaming big ideas. A formal lunch is not a situation I'm used to. They tend not to be a regular occurrence when growing up in a tattoo shop.

"You know Gerard?" I meet Peter's muted gaze. His eyes are a paler version of his brother's, more Wedgewood than delphinium. Poor Peter.

"Oh, Steers. He's a laugh that one, totally incorrigible."

"Incorrigible? He's a lecturer; my lecturer? He seems quite staid to me." I smile a little. I know Gerard, he's my friend and supporter. Hell, he's the reason I'm here.

"I wouldn't want to be his wife." Peter smirks, and I offer him a tight smile.

"Good thing he's not married then."

"Of course he's married. We went to his wedding, didn't we, Elijah?"

I can't look at the delphinium blues. My heart beats too

fast. Thankfully, Jennings brings a bottle of champagne and fills the flute in front of me. I glug it down quickly, not waiting for decorum to dictate when I should drink. Married? But how? He's always at my place... and we... and we...

I want to close my eyes and hide in an overwhelming tide of bitterness. I trusted him. I trusted him, and he abused it.

I can't believe it.

One dark eyebrow quirks, but the wide lips on the handsome face stay quiet. I shake it off. I can deal with Gerard, the cheating, two-timing scumbag later.

"So, what do you think of the house?" Elijah asks. If he can sense my internal revelations he is kind enough to help steer the conversation. *Thank you.* I silently get myself together.

"It's beautiful." I brush a strand of hair that's stuck across my face. "I still don't understand what you want me to do here. The house is full of so many beautiful things anyway."

Jennifer sips her own champagne and then smiles warmly at Elijah. "It was Elijah's idea really. The house has never been open before, apart the odd open day for charity, but the family have resisted the urge to give The National Trust access, no matter how financially viable it may make the building."

"And now?" I take another sip of my drink and try not to screw my face up in disgust as the sharp bubbles hit the back of my throat. I can't drink too quickly as I haven't eaten, and that's always a recipe for disaster.

Elijah leans forward slightly as if he's closing the space between us across the table and gives me an intent stare. "I thought maybe instead of just opening it up and making money, we could try to give something back to the local area."

"I thought you needed a new roof?"

Peter snorts. "Steers is such a jerk." He coughs and clears his throat as his mother glares at him. I kind of like her despite the fact she's clearly on a different planet to me, let alone in a different class. "Our roof is sound, do not worry about that. Elijah wanted it to be cultural. The idea being we have an artist..." She indicates me by pointing her silver fork, " to stay here and fill the house with wonderful creations, and the public can come and watch, help maybe? You know, get involved."

I stare open mouthed.

I'm sorry. Do what?

It's no good, I'm going to have to ask. "You want me to create sculptures while people I don't know stand and watch?"

The delphinium blues glint and shine. "That's exactly what we want."

Nine

I push my chair back and it scrapes against the tiled floor. If I had the time to stop and look properly, I'd admire the intricate, Victorian—I would hazard a guess—pattern. "That's not an installation." I place my napkin on my empty plate. Lunch hasn't even been served but I already know I shouldn't be here.

Installing art behind closed doors and then walking away before it's seen is one thing. What they're suggesting is something else entirely—and that's not happening.

"I'm sorry. I'm not the right person for this." I turn to Peter, "I suggest you talk to Gerard." *Because I'm never going to talk to the cheating scum again.* "And ask him to give you Meg's contact details. She's highly talented." *And loves an audience.*

I turn to Jennifer. I wish I had pockets to shove my hands in. "Sorry I wasted your time. Thank you for showing me your beautiful home."

A deep sensation of disappointment fills me as I turn away. I can't bear to stop and pretend I'd ever consider staying somewhere working with the public watching me. It's just not viable.

My work is deeply private. It comes straight from my heart, inspired by my scars and yearnings, my feelings.

I think of the cameo, the delicate etching inspired by Elijah. I go to turn back. To say sorry. Sorry for wasting his time. Sorry he took me for that drink and made an effort with me. Sorry I couldn't offer what he wanted. But I don't. I walk away.

"Hey." Firm fingers grab the black chiffon of my sleeve. "Where are you running to?"

I turn with my stomach tangled in knots. Elijah is standing behind me, his hand sliding through his short hair. A deep crease runs between his eyebrows, and his gaze is full of worry. He still looks beautiful though, and it makes me slow my need to run. "I'm sorry, but there is no way I can work in front of people. Gerard knows that. I won't even work in front of him; lectures and workshop time on campus are painful."

"How do you tattoo people's skin then?" His question makes me stop.

"What do you mean?"

"How can you tattoo people's skin if you can't work in front of people? How does that work?"

I frown. His change in direction takes the wind out of my sails. "That's different. That's just instinctive." I pause. "How do you know?"

"I told you. Facebook is a wonderful place."

Jesus, how long did he waste researching Facebook for boring facts about me?

"You need to get a life."

His eyes settle on my face and it gives me an uneasy sensation down in the pit of my tummy. "I have one, thanks."

"You aren't the only one who can research."

His eyebrow rises, and he smirks. I'd punch him if he was one step closer. "What have you been finding out?"

"Like, you're engaged?" *To a skinny social pariah.*

The smirk drops, and he shrugs. "So?"

And *so* I've been obsessed with the colour blue for days, and it annoys the fuck out of me.

"Nothing." I straighten and regain my composure. "Look, I need to go home; I'm going to Brighton tomorrow."

He nods. "Can I show you something first?"

I hesitate. He's kind of hard to say no to. "Okay, but it has to be quick."

I step to the side and he points his hand down one of the fine gravel pathways. "This way."

He leads us around some formal gardens, and through an old red bricked wall, an archway trailing with roses leads us into what seems to be a full and vibrant kitchen garden.

"Where are we going?"

We walk around a bricked low wall and enter what look like old outhouses. He twists a key

on the outside of a white door and pushes it open.

"Is this the cellar where you put naughty guests who don't behave at lunch?"

He rolls his eyes, which I find a little too cute.

As I walk into the room, he hangs back and waits, his eyes on me.

"What is this?" My voice comes out breathless. I fold my hands across my chest to stop my fingers from shaking. Inside the room is a pretty white metal bed with cream bedding. French cream furniture is fitted over grey slate floors. A sheepskin lies on the floor next to the bed. But it's the walls that are making my legs shake. The tone of dusky pink is the exact same as the roses across my skin.

"Is that why you wanted a picture of my tattoos?"

He smiles. "I don't randomly request pictures of women's tattoos. I'm not some weird collector of ink."

I laugh, but it's nervous and awkward. My skin reveals me as the weird collector of ink. Not him.

"How did you get this done?" I stutter. "And why?"

"I did it." He gives me an offhanded shrug. "I just thought you'd like something pretty."

"You thought the girl covered in tattoos would like something pretty?" It's my turn to roll my eyes, but truth is, I love it. It's beautiful. Clean, simple, elegant, and the colour of my roses. My roses. My freedom, my fresh start.

"There's more." He motions back down to the small hallway. The outhouse has a low uneven ceiling crossed with beams. Every so often Elijah has to duck to miss hitting his head. He opens the other doors down the hallway. Inside each one are individual studios. "No one is putting you on display, Faith. You've got your own workspace. It's up to you if you open this up to the public. All we ask,"—he steps closer, the smell of his aftershave is intoxicating in the small space—"is that you come and see our visitors and tell them what you're doing; why you've done what you have."

"That's all?" I tilt my head to the side.

"Can I be honest with you?"

Hell, will someone be honest with me! I burn with chagrin as I think of married Gerard Steers. *Married?*

"My mother would twist this and make it sound something it was never meant to be." I read his face. "She'd make it into some media frenzy, but all I want is to get the local kids in and get them involved with art, give them somewhere to come for free where they can explore and create."

"And you care about kids in art because..."

I'm being harsh. I don't care.

He doesn't answer. He just watches me, evaluating and reading.

"Shall I take you home?" He doesn't meet my eyes.

"Yes, please."

Ten

Warm air rushes through the train. It's sunny, with a clear sky above, and pleasant to be outdoors, but the train is hot and cramped. Lots of people are here to escape from London for a day at the beach on a Sunday morning. In the double seat across from me, a child watches me, her dark eyes sweeping across my skin. She is mesmerised by the ink I have on show. Whirling patterns, leaves, petals, words, secrets. I give her a smile and a small wave, but her mum pulls her close. With a despondent sigh, I stare out of the window and watch the South Downs roll by. Soon we will be by the sea. Thousands of tourists all roasting to pink on the pebble beach, screaming and laughing on the pier.

Abi doesn't know I'm on my way. It's a surprise for her and the kids. Although it's also a guilty retreat for me. I need a day away from London. I need to think.

Elijah Fairclough has managed to worm his way under my skin.

I want to scrape my fingers across thick blue paint.

I also want to kiss him; have his fingers against my ink. My hands in his hair.

What does he care about kids needing something to do

during the holidays, those long summer weeks that stretch out in an endless golden haze? I remember those days.

Days spent reading, listening, sketching. Sketching dreams that would one day take physical form in clay beneath my fingers. Days filled with the hum of ink machines buzzing the air like a swarm of bees. The groans and curses of grown men wishing they'd never laid on the table.

I wished I'd asked Elijah more. I left agitated and confused, and now I don't have the right amount of information to make an informed decision. The ride back to London in his stunning MG crackled with a heavy atmosphere and neither of us attempted to lift it. He seemed frustrated as I exited the car.

I don't know what he wants from me. To create art in front of people? I can't do that. Sometimes I can't even create it for myself.

My phone vibrates, so breaking eye contact with the curious child opposite, I root about in my bag.

Gerard Steers: How did you get on?

I frown. I can't believe what Peter alluded to at lunch… I should just ask him. *Are you married? Because if you are, I'm going to cut your knob off with a Stanley knife.*

I put my phone back. I can't believe he might be married. Not that it matters. Well, it does. But then, what of the other men I've slept with? I've never asked them. But then, I've never even talked to them, nothing more than a few niceties. It's just physical, and most of the time I'm already over it before the act is even finished.

But Gerard's my friend. My confidante. Someone who I trust, within the very limited allowance I give myself to trust.

The train pulls into the station and I'm happy to sit and

wait for everyone to get off and start barging for the beach. There will be a scrum for space. Thank God, I'm not doing that.

When the carriage is empty, I grab my bag and jacket off the floor and step out. The lingering scent of salt and brine fills the air and I breathe in deep.

I can't ever say I miss home because I no longer have a home to miss. Not bricks and mortar anyway. I won't be walking down a pathway and sliding a key into a lock that contains my childhood memories. The house is still there, but the memories are evil demons and I won't allow them to dance in my heart anymore. There is no longer a heart to dance in.

Instead, I turn in the opposite direction, knocking on a smart red door after a short walk through the back lanes.

For a moment, I wonder if there is anyone home, but then I hear the familiar slam of the back door. Abi opens the door, and I love watching her face drop in shock and little tears spring from the corners of her eyes. "You aren't supposed to cry." I smile.

"What the fuck are you doing here?" She grabs me in tight and pulls me over the threshold. Light splatters of water land on my shoulders.

"Hey." I smooth a hand through her brown waves and lean back to check her face. "Are you okay?"

She squeezes me again. "I'm just pleased to see your ugly mug, that's all."

I chuckle, despite the odd wave of emotion that washes over me.

She turns and pulls me into the neat and tidy home. "Adam," she screeches. "Look who's home."

I smile at her use of "home". She's my best friend and she will always be home to me.

"Are you going to stop by and see Al before you get the train back?" Abi puts another mug of tea down in front of me. I stroke Charlotte's curls as she sleeps on my lap. Roger has gone to bed, but Charlotte fought sleep until the last minute, her eyes fluttering shut even as she adamantly told us she wasn't sleepy.

It was cute with a dollop of adorable on top.

A seagull squawks as it flies overhead. It's getting late. The long July evening is stretching out, but I know the train to London is calling. "Do you think he will still be up?" I ask.

"For you? Yes."

I nod, and she points at my mug. "Drink your tea. I'll come with you."

An unsettled, unwelcome pinch pulls on my insides. I'm scared to see Al. What if he's so sick I barely recognise him? What if it's the last time I ever see him? I'm not ready for a last time yet.

Abi walks around the garden table and hangs her arms around Adam's neck, dropping her chin onto his shoulder and kissing his earlobe. He squeezes her joined hands and pecks her cheek. "You take Faith, and I'll sort the kids. We've still got to get the school uniform ready."

Abi rolls her eyes and glares at me. "You see how rock-and-roll my life is, Faith? Bloody school uniform washing is all I have to get excited for at the weekend."

I laugh and shake my head. These two, they are so damn loved up, so bloody perfect. I don't understand how they met so young and made it work. While I fell apart, they found everything. I'm happy for them. I could never be that settled. Inside me, the twisted memories I run from won't ever let me have anything like what they maintain together.

Adam lifts her arms over his head and comes over to where I'm sitting, lifting the sleeping mop-haired angel out of my arms.

I stand unwillingly, my legs moving as if they are wading through sea water thick with seaweed. Why don't I want to see Al? He's been my stabilising force my entire life.

I know why. It's because I'm scared of saying goodbye.

Abi gives me a sympathetic smile and holds out her hand. "Come on, Faith."

The house is in darkness. The flicker of a television screen flashing through the net curtains the only indication someone is home. I knock hesitantly. This is all so foreign. Al used to work all hours, his shop a hive of activity, sometimes until the early hours of the morning. Sometimes all night if his customer could withstand the pain for that long. Now he's in bed? I should have called—announced my intended visit.

The door opens a crack, and I hold in a gasp as Dan peeks his head through the gap. God, he looks so tired. Worn and faded like a pair of much-loved jeans. "Faith?"

"Hey, Dan."

He opens the door and steps forward, grabbing me tight. As close to me as any brother could be, we've grown up side-by-side. His smell washes over me. Strong soap and his hair wax mingle, pulling memories from deep within me.

The scruff on his cheeks scratches my face and his lips brush mine. A simple welcome. "What are you doing here?"

He pushes a hand though his hair, making it stand in a tousled mess. My mind slips to a buzz cut and long fingers scratching through dark hair.

I nod my head behind me. "I came to check on this loser. Thought I'd better stop in and check on the other loser in my life." I grin, but the stretch of my lips is like a dam holding back a torrent of water.

He steps back and makes room for us to enter. Abi slips through after me, closing the door behind her.

The lounge is in darkness. Scattered cans and pizza boxes decorate the coffee table top and some of the floor.

"Keeping the place nice, Dan." I smile up at him and lean down to switch on a lamp. I kind of wish I hadn't as the light illuminates the mess some more.

"Shut your face, Hitchin." He grins though and leans in, wrapping his arms around me in a giant squeeze. "God, I've missed you."

"I've missed you, too." I talk into his neck, and random tears threaten to spill. Once Dan could have been so much more than a lifelong friend. We were on the cusp of experimenting with new emotions and sensations when everything was destroyed.

I love him, though. But much to Al's disappointment, I know the love will never be enough. Not for Dan. He deserves more.

"Want a beer?" He asks, turning for the kitchen. I follow him while Abi hangs behind, giving us some space.

"Yeah, thanks." I slip my hands into the pockets of my denim shorts and lean a hip against the counter. The kitchen is cleaner than the lounge, but I'm not surprised. Clearly, food comes out of cardboard delivery boxes.

He hands me an open bottle and we click the necks

together. "How are you?" I rest my eyes on his face before giving him a full body sweep.

Despite the tiredness smudging soft lines into his face, his body is still impressive. Smooth round muscles covered in ink. His T-shirt is tight, stretched across well-developed pecs.

"I'm okay. It's good to see you." He smiles and pushes his sandy hair out of his face. "I thought you were never going to come back."

"It's only for the day."

He frowns. "It must be nearly the summer holiday. Aren't you coming home?"

I shake my head. "You know I can't, Dan. I don't want to see Dad. We have nothing to say to one another. And I don't want to see..." I trail off. I can't say the name. "I don't want to be gossiped about."

"It's Brighton, it's full of gossiping queens." He pulls the face he always pulls when he thinks I'm being ridiculous. It's all *doh* mixed with a bit of *duh*.

I grin. Sometimes I miss the sheer cattiness of the homosexual community. In London, everything is more proper, and diluted into the vast population.

"Anyway." I change the subject from myself. "How's Al?"

Dan's face freezes for a moment before his lips curve into a smile that's too small to mean anything. "Okay."

"Where is he?"

"Asleep upstairs."

"Would you rather I didn't wake him?" I watch him carefully. "You look like you could do with some sleep yourself."

He smiles that rueful grimace I know so well. "What you saying? Don't I look as handsome as normal?"

"Always." I snigger. "Always."

I place my now empty bottle on the side. Abi is moving around the lounge and I can sense her cleaning—there is no way she can ignore that level of mess. She's probably been desperate to get in here and help for weeks; at least me talking to Dan has given her an opening. "I'm going to pop up and see him."

"Okay." Dan nods but doesn't meet my eyes.

I work my way up the wide stairs. It's a nice house, comfortable but not flashy. Al's done well out of his skill with an ink machine, but he's never been rolling in it. I'm guessing Dan must be earning well, now he's taken over the running of the shop. I don't think I can ask though. I was the one who ran away to London. Not that I had much choice.

I slip into the front bedroom. The sun still hasn't set, but the shadows of dusk creep across the grey carpet, heralding the late hour.

My legs wobble as I see the shape on the bed. It's half the size I remember. The man lying under the thin duvet is a wasted remnant of the person I know. One eye cracks open.

"Figured you'd turn up soon."

I snort and sit on the edge of the bed. "Well, I'm not rushing here because you are about to cark it. It's not a mercy visit."

He smiles but keeps his eyes shut, sighing a little. I grab his hand and will myself not to cry. "Did you decide about Bowsley?" he asks.

Even sick, he still remembers every detail about my life. He's always acted like I'm his daughter, as I've always acted like he's my favourite blood relative, even though there is no blood between us. Just a shit load of love.

"No."

My mind darts to lying scumbag Gerard and then even quicker to Elijah Fairclough in his immaculate black suit, cut to cling to his broad muscles.

"Do it."

"Why?"

"It's the dying wish of an old man."

"Bollocks."

He grins again, eyes still closed. His hand grabs mine and squeezes tight.

"Do it. Then come back and marry Dan. He loves you."

"I am not marrying Dan."

"Why?"

"Because he's like my brother," I stutter over the word. "And I can't break my rules for anyone, especially not your son."

Sometimes I think what it would be like to sink into Dan's familiar embrace. What would it be like to give myself to someone who knows me so well? Is that what Abi and Adam have every night? Comforting familiarity that encompasses every inch of them?

How could I ever tell Dan that I could only love him once? That I would never feel anything. That his touch, his kiss would mean nothing, because deep within me, I don't know how to turn on the emotions and sensations I shut off many, many years ago.

"You're a crazy old man, you know that?"

I settle on the bed and tell him about Bowsley, what they want me to do.

"You see, I'm not a teacher. I don't even have a degree. How can they expect someone to do that?"

Al has his eyes open now; a distant gaze is settled on my face. The skin around his eyes is sunken, and he looks out at me from dark hollows. "They must have seen your work to know it would fit in with their plans."

I shrug. "I don't know where. Most of it is covered in dust in my studio."

His fingers grab mine. "You know the degree and your escape to London will all be for nothing if you never share the things you make."

"But I'm not qualified to teach."

"Was I qualified to teach you? The first time you brushed the pens over Dan's skin, were you qualified?"

"Well, no, but you were watching me like a hawk."

"Rubbish. You just did it."

"It's different."

"How? Just show these kids what it's like to create. That's all they need; to see if the fire to create is within them and if it is, to set it free."

I watch him for a moment before chuckling. "You are such a poetic old man."

He chuckles but soon starts coughing and wheezing.

"Has Dad been to see you?" The question tastes bitter.

He stops coughing. "Yes." There's a pause that speaks louder than any words. "I will never forgive him for what he did."

His eyes shut, and I know I've exhausted him with my talk of stately homes and luxurious conservatories. I lean over and kiss his dry cheek.

"I'll be back," I whisper. *Don't cry, Faith.* Don't let him know this could be it.

It's hard though. I can't walk away.

Dan opens the door and a loud sob rumbles from my chest. I fall into his arms, wetting the stretch of his shirt with my tears. His hand palms my hair, and I breathe in the scent of his soap and wax.

"It's okay."

I look into his face. I must look hideous, but I don't care. "Nothing is okay."

His lips brush a kiss on the tip of my nose, and for the billionth time I wish I wasn't so fucked up, so I could take what was offered right in front of me.

I never will.

But in that moment of untangling myself from his arms I decide my own future.

It's time to move on. Time to get away from people who hurt me. The summer will give me space to breathe.

"Call me." I rush my words and then I run down the stairs so fast I almost slip on the carpet.

Abi and I walk to the station in silence and hug goodbye.

Then I'm on the train. Breathing, crying, mourning my friend who's being stolen from me.

I grab my phone and look at it for the first time all day.

Gerard Steers: Faith, talk to me, what did you decide?

I'll tell you what I decided you cheating bastard.

Faith Hitchin: I'm not finishing my degree. Do not contact me again.

Next, I open my Messenger Inbox. There's a message from Eli Jones. My heart pounds a little, but I try to shut it down.

Eli Jones: I'm not engaged.

I hesitate. Why's he even telling me? What does it even matter? But then I remember I was the one who'd asked the question in some weird uncontrollable blurt of words.

Faith Hitchin: Don't care.
Eli Jones: That's good.

That's good? What does that mean?

Faith Hitchin: Why are you Eli Jones on Facebook?

There is a pause and I wonder where he's gone. Our conversations are random.

Eli Jones: Have you seen my other profile?

What's he talking about? I click out of Messenger and search for Elijah Fairclough on Facebook. There he is—with five thousand friends. I have to double check I've read the figure properly.

Faith Hitchin: I see.
Eli Jones: Have you decided about Bowsley?

I stare out the window at the dark sky and darker trees.

Faith Hitchin: Yes. Can we talk tomorrow?
Eli Jones: Ominous.
Faith Hitchin: Don't be a baby.
Eli Jones: What time tomorrow?
Faith Hitchin: ten am?

Better to get it over and done with. I put my phone in my hobo bag as the train glides into London Victoria. I'm home—for now. But my home is changing, moving, like it always does. I'm tired and I want to sleep, so I swallow the expense and take a taxi home, not even bothering to wash or change before I crash onto my bed.

I can only wait to see what tomorrow brings and where I'll be going next.

Eleven

At nine am, I'm twitching. I can't seem to calm myself down. Elijah will be here, with those blue eyes—here in my apartment.

I hate the way I'm reacting to the prospect of seeing him. I can't stop sweating and have been walking around with tissues wedged under my armpits—this damn heat is going to be the end of me.

Why did he tell me he wasn't engaged? It's no skin off my nose either way. I'm pulling down the swathes of blue material I've hung in my apartment, too, when someone raps a knock against the front door of the apartment.

"Go away, Gerard," I holler. "I'm not interested in your shit."

There's another knock and I groan. "Faith? It's Elijah?"

What the hell? This isn't ten o'clock.

"Hold on." In horror I sweep a glance around. It looks like pigs live here.

"Faith." Another knock. "Faith." Another knock.

Okay, so that's damn annoying.

It's easy to reach the door; the apartment has the same cubic square feet as a hamster cage. "Sorry." I begin unlatching the locks. My fingers are fumbling. I wish they wouldn't.

I pull on the handle and as I do, I can't help wondering which version of Elijah will be standing on the other side. Is it going to be the man in sliders with the easy smile, or will it be the awkward guy in the expensive suit?

The door opens, and I smile. Actually, he's somewhere in between.

And hell does he look hot.

His jeans are faded and fit just fine. His legs are long, and doesn't the denim know just how to fit perfectly around his thighs. A navy T-shirt stretches across his chest. I couldn't comment on the curve and definition of his chest... because I'm not looking.

Who the hell am I kidding? I'm looking.

He's wearing a Quiksilver baseball cap.

And I do believe this is the finest he's looked yet.

"Come in." I open the door wider. "You're early. I've only just got up." I turn and stare with a sinking stomach into the stinking pit that is my home.

"Uh, Faith."

"Yeah?"

He points an index finger at my armpits.

Holy fuck! I'm a sweaty mess anyway, now I'm hanging with Hades in hell.

I remove the crumpled shreds of tissue from under my arms and turn to him sheepishly. "I actually have nothing to say about that."

He laughs. It's the most wondrous chuckle I've ever heard. "Truthfully, you are something else."

And he doesn't even know me yet.

"That's me. One of a kind." I brazen it out and walk

towards the tiny kitchenette. "Would you like a coffee?" I should attempt some civility in the moment.

"Here."

I look at his hands for the first time—that's how wondrous the T-shirt is—I haven't even noticed he's holding two Costa coffee mugs in a cardboard holder in one hand, and a paper bag in the other.

He smiles, his lips lifting on the left, a small dimple appearing. "I decided to play a little game of guess the coffee."

He's got one big mug wedged in the holder and one espresso. His eyes narrow as he runs them over me, sweeping across my skin. Resting on my chest.

Holy fuck. I haven't put a bra on yet. A vest—no bra. It's too hot for a damn bra.

What the hell is wrong with me?

I fold my arms and glare. "Stop looking at my chest."

"Sorry, it's just kind of there." He shakes his head a little and I march away into the small bedroom. I dig out a sports bra and somehow manage to get it over my sticky skin. I walk back out yanking my vest back over my head.

He's watching. There's no hiding it.

"And coffee?" I prompt when he doesn't say anything.

He blinks a little, obviously refocusing. "Here. I went for a short and strong espresso for you."

How did he know?

"Are you a specialist in coffee habits?" I smile a little and hold out my hand for the small cardboard cup.

"It was a guess."

I smile and meet his gaze. Jeez, he's good to look at. Those eyes... honestly, I can't believe he's been walking blinking them at people. How does anyone have a conversation with him without drooling?

"It's perfect, thank you."

I take a sip, pleased to be hit by a strong sweet afternote. "And the sugar?"

"Another guess. Figured it would soften that hardened edge of yours."

"Whatever." I wave my hand to where there's a small cramped sofa under the window. The sash is up, letting in the hum of London from below.

His eyes flick over the place. "This is nice. Must cost a pretty penny though?" He sits on the sofa and makes it look even smaller, stretching his legs in front of him.

This flat is officially too small for him.

I swallow nervously. I'm not often nervous, but I am right now. The future is a myriad of crossroads in front of me and this is the defining moment.

He carries on oblivious to my tongue tie. "I can see why you have the studio, too. There isn't much space in here."

I nod and glance about my flat. I love this place and I'd never give it up, not even for somewhere I could create at home. "The studio is from the university; they have a few of them. Somehow, I managed to get one." I cringe as a moment of realisation hits me. Gerard 'I'm-so-married' Steers wangled it for me. It had nothing to do with my skill, and more to do the with the fact I'd made it very clear early on I was going to sleep with him.

I guess he must have been disappointed I only put out once. That's an expensive shag.

"This place is mine," I add.

He doesn't ask how I can afford a prime piece of real estate in an expensive part of London. Instead he takes a sip of his coffee and I watch his lips cling to the plastic lip. I reckon he's a great kisser.

Faith. For God's sake...

"Here, I grabbed a few pastries, too." He thrusts the bag at me, a small smile sliding across his face. "I got the impression this could be bad news, and I'd need all the pain au chocolat's I could find."

My stomach rumbles as I take the bag. I didn't eat last night when I got back as it was too late, and I'd only managed a snack at Abi's; which means my last full meal was two days ago. It's not like I can't afford groceries, I just can't be bothered to go and get them. Mundane jobs like shopping and laundry don't register with me. Or putting on a bra, that kind of thing.

"Faith, it's really hot in here. You can't possibly breathe in here, surely?" Elijah turns for the windows, but then frowns when he finds they are all open.

"You kinda get used to it," I reply with an offhanded wave of my fingers.

He shakes his head and I'm mesmerised by the flash of his eyes as they twinkle at me.

"Either we go out and drink our coffee somewhere shady, preferably with air con, or you're going to need to find some more tissue paper for me to use under my own armpits."

I scowl and flush a burning red, from my chest to the top of my head.

"There's a park behind, if you fancy a walk?" I suggest, still clutching the bag of goodies. This is odd. Here's this man: gorgeous and refined, standing in my tiny flat, like he can just about fit in it, and I can't stop looking at him.

He's beautiful.

I could become obsessed.

That familiar tingle of longing cruises its way into my consciousness.

I can imagine us hot and sweaty, skin slipping and sliding, hands wandering, limbs tangling.

I bite my lip and consider my options.

But then he might be my boss for the summer, and I don't break my one-time-only rule for anyone. If I allowed my usual obsessive nature to take over, it could ruin everything.

"Sure." He holds his hand in an 'after you' gesture to the door, but then stops. "Wait, Faith. Shall we just do the business talk now, get it over and done with?"

"Why are you so nervous?" I frown at him. "Even if I say no to your project, there are many people who wouldn't. It's not reliant on me."

He gazes at me, his eyes drawing me in. Deep, vibrant blue pools, perfect for diving into and letting go of all restraint. "That's true."

I know he's only agreeing with me, but his words have a sting to their edge.

"But I want you to do it," he continues. As his lips curve into a smile, I'm sure he's aware of every thought I'm having.

"Why?"

"I told you at Bowsley, I have a good vibe."

"About the project?" I ask.

"About you."

Fuck. I get really hot. A sudden rush of sweat simultaneously bursts from every pore on my skin.

His words.

I shove my hands in the pockets of my shorts because I'm scared what they are going to do. I want to slide them over his body, run them through his hair, pull at his clothes and tug them from his skin.

And those things you shouldn't do with your boss. Not ever.

"I'll do it."

The relief that flickers across his expression takes me by surprise and I giggle nervously. "I just hope you aren't disappointed."

He shrugs and for a second, I get a glimpse of the awkward man in the suit I met in The Ritz. This man is complicated: so many sides, so many puzzles.

It's not good. It's makes him all the more intriguing. All the more dangerous. All the more suitable to become the subject of my latest obsession.

"But I have something I need to tell you." A pinch of nerves squeezes my stomach.

"Yes?"

"I'm dropping out of my degree."

There it is. The bombshell.

"Why?"

"I'd rather not say."

His eyes narrow into slits.

"You'd rather not say?"

"Does that affect you wanting to hire me for the project?"

There's a pause, and my heart pounds painfully.

"No." He gives a small shake of his head. "Faith, come let's go find the park and then you can tell me all about it."

"Don't you have work to get to? It's a Monday—or does stuff not happen on a Monday?"

I grin at him and he smiles back. Damn, those eyes are going to melt my panties.

"Stuff is later. Now, I have time for the park."

I grab my keys and we make our way out into the hot and sticky July heat. It's no better outside than in. I don't know what he does, but if 'stuff', whatever that is, means he has time to go to the park with me so I can stare at his beautiful face, then I am all for it.

"You look nice in your cap."

Apparently, I'm now just opening my mouth and shit is coming out of it. He stops my brain from working in a coherent fashion.

"Oh, why, thank you." He grins and takes a sip of his now cold coffee. We are under a tree at the local park. It's nice. A bit too nice. "Sometimes it's easier this way."

I've just bitten into a bit of croissant, but it doesn't stop me asking, "What do you mean?" He grins at me and chuckles.

"Sorry." I wipe the flakes of pastry I've sprayed everywhere—truthfully, it's a good opportunity to touch his arm. It's smooth, warm and firm.

"It's nothing." He shakes his head, but I lean a little closer, watching under the peak of the subject of our conversation.

"Do you get recognised? Are we about to be papped?"

He rolls his eyes, which makes me snort a laugh. The man in the suit right now is far away, and long forgotten. "No, it's just I'd rather people didn't always know what I'm doing."

"And do people always know what you are doing?"

Is it me or are we having a repetitive conversation?

He shrugs.

"Is your brother really in line for the throne?"

He chuckles and his eyes dance. I really wish I didn't notice the way his shoulders lift and his arms flex under his T-shirt. "Peter's an arse."

"Not close then?" I grin.

He shrugs again, but in the moment it's ever so slightly sad, and my chest contracts in response. "It's just family."

"What about your sister?" My questions keep on coming. I don't think I've asked so many questions in my life.

"She's lovely, sweet even." His face lights with a warm smile. "I want to make sure she's happy."

An awful sinking sensation pulls on my stomach twisting it into tangled knots. "It must be nice to be looked after."

Another shrug.

Then those blues snap onto my face and I'm captured under their intensity. "Why the change of direction? From what I understand, you are on track for a First."

I can't look into his eyes and I study the nearest tree. "Things change, and I like it that way. I don't want things to stay the same for too long."

From my peripheral vision, I see him nod.

When our eyes meet, I lose all rational thought.

"Tell me a dream. Something you've never done but want to." He takes a sip of his coffee, but those eyes are still on me like a spotlight, unflinching and all-seeing.

I grin and think of the stupidest thing I can come up with. "Kiss in the rain. You know, like the movies?"

His lips curve into a smile. "That's it? A life dream?"

It's my turn to shrug. "Maybe."

He chuckles and stands from the grass. "I hope it comes true." Holding his hand out, he helps me up from the grass. I take it despite the fact I'm more than capable of getting up by myself. It's sweet, chivalrous—all the many things I'm not used to.

"So, I'm still hired?" We are watching one another, and

around us the air seems to be tightening.

I don't want it to. I can't allow myself to think that way about him. He's a pay check, an opportunity. Not someone I should obsess about and crave until I get what I want and walk away without a backwards glance.

The sun's rays land on his face as he smiles. He truly is beautiful.

"You're still hired." He takes my empty espresso carton, sliding it into his own empty one.

"Thank you." I mean it. He could have so easily have told me the job was no longer mine.

He grins. "Thank *you*."

"What are your plans for the rest of the day?" Small talk's never been a skill I've possessed.

"I'm off to work now."

"What do you do?" We walk the scorching pavement back towards the flat. I don't really want to go back up the stairs.

He shrugs again. "Just stuff." His face is tight.

"Are you a drug baron?"

Laughing, Elijah shakes his head. "Nope."

"Pimp?"

He bursts a shout of laughter and it makes my heart jump. *Stop it, Faith.* "No." His eyes dance and I'm mesmerised. *He's your boss.* "Although I apologise sincerely for being so dull."

The door to the flat is right here, but I'm hovering. "You'd better go."

"I had." Hesitation runs between us until he breaks it. "Would you like me to help you box up the studio? Assuming you don't have anyone else to ask and have to give it back to the University?"

How does he know I don't have anyone else to ask? My

only other London friend is on my Shit List.

"That would be nice."

I don't really care about the studio. I just want to spend more time with him.

And that fact alone is the most dangerous thing I've contemplated in a long time.

He goes to walk away. "Dinner on me, tonight?"

"Tonight?"

"Do you have other plans?"

"Well, no."

He grins. "As I thought."

My eyes narrow to slits. "Rude."

"Hey, don't you be rude, I'm your boss."

A bloom of a chuckle bursts out of my mouth. "Sorry, Boss."

This is dangerous flirting.

I like the Elijah Fairclough who brings pastries and coffee. He's far from the man in the expensive suit with a pensive face.

"Have a good day," he calls as he gets to the corner of the street, and I'm still stood watching him walk away.

With a small wave, I slip into the building.

This is bad. It's so, so bad.

Because Elijah Fairclough is beautiful, and smart, and kind. Elusive and complex. All the things I crave and want.

But I know I'll never break my rules for anyone, and he looks like the kind of guy who wants things just his own way.

I shut the apartment door, resolute. I will stop this. I will stick to my own ways, and no one will ever make me change them.

They keep me safe and that's all that matters.

Twelve

The rose colour walls wink at me as I sit on the white linen. Now I'm here it's surreal. There's a tray of tea things on the side: biscuits, and a teapot with steam coming from the spout. I told Jennings I don't need tea brought to my room, but he didn't seem to take me very seriously.

I've spent the last hour wandering around my various studios. All of them are blank spaces, apart from all the equipment already purchased on my behalf. I've even got a brand-new kiln, not one caked in other people's disasters. All the studios are waiting for me to fill them with ideas, experiments, and a deep vision they hopefully will inspire within me.

I can't believe I'm here. Me. If I think for too long on what I've agreed to do over the summer—to try to teach other people, to guide them, to be put on show—a wave of nausea rises in my stomach. I don't really want to throw up in my pretty room, and the en-suite wet room is too pristine to be sullied with the contents of my stomach, so I keep swallowing it back down and trying very hard not to think at all.

"Knock, knock." I glance up toward the voice on the outside of the closed door.

"Come in."

I smile at Elijah as he pokes his head around the side. It's impossible not to stare at that handsome face. My first assumption that night in the pub garden was correct—he's beautiful.

"Why do you look like you're about to puke?" he asks.

I glare at him, forgetting how lovely he looks as he irritates the hell out of me. "Why do you look like a knob?" I mutter under my breath, but loud enough for him to hear. He chuckles and pushes the door wider open. There is someone behind him who I didn't know was there. That's bloody embarrassing. *Way to go being professional, Faith.*

"Faith, this is Tabitha, my younger sister."

A dark head of hair peeks out from behind his broad shoulders. He's dressed in jeans and a white shirt, the sleeves rolled up to reveal tanned forearms. Not that I'm taking any notice of what he looks like. Much. I am only human, and he is apparently a god of good looks and easy charm.

"Hi." I wave at the petite dark-haired girl behind him. She's younger than me, and much younger than him. That's an age gap of note.

"Hi." I stretch up from the bed and step closer to shake her hand. She's a fragile and delicate version of him. What is a handsome and strong profile on him has been delicately chiselled into fine elfin features on her, but there's a light in her eyes that reminds me what it's like to be a teenager—before life fucks you over.

"I love your work." She smiles nervously. "I'm so excited to see you working here."

I frown. "How have you seen my work already? I haven't done anything yet."

I twitch from foot to foot. It's weird having the tall

hulking shape of Elijah standing in the feminine pink bedroom he painted for me. I glance up at him through my lashes. He's frustratingly elusive, blowing hot and cold. Over the last week, he's been helping me move my stuff out of the studio and transporting it down to one of my rooms here. I've given my studio back to the university—I still haven't spoken to Gerard and nor do I plan to. I've got the weekend to sort myself out here, and then on Monday we are opening the doors to six teenagers who will be here for three weeks. I panicked when I found out it was so soon—but Jennifer assured me the rooms are supposed to be bare, the idea being that I'm supposed to fill them over the summer.

I still don't know if I can perform on request. All I know is I've got to try.

"Eli showed me the pictures from your portfolio," Tabitha says, and I raise an eyebrow at her older brother who somehow is managing to stand there looking completely innocent.

"Did he indeed?"

Elijah shoves his hands into his pockets and stares at the ceiling.

"That's a private portfolio." I glare at him.

Tabitha's eyes widen, and she looks like she might cry. I let it go. Honestly what's the point? "Would you like to see the bits I brought from my studio?" I ask.

"Can I?"

"Sure, why not." I smile at her. She's nothing like her brother who's full of confidence.

Elijah smiles and waves. "Good, you two are getting along. I'll leave you to it."

Jesus. I'm not a bloody babysitter.

He walks off without a backwards glance and I scowl

after him. He's so bloody hot and cold. One minute he's sitting in my apartment and supporting me as I tell him I'm dropping out of my course, clinking a glass against mine as he helps me carefully wrap my work into newspaper, while promising to keep my secret so his mother doesn't change her mind about me.

The next he's looking at me like we've never met.

Well, fine by me. I haven't got time for hot and cold games. I've got an installation to launch.

I force a smile at Tabitha. "Come on. I'll show you where we've stashed it all."

She smiles and falls into step at my side. "I like your tattoos."

I flush. I've decided not to hide them, unless the public are in the house. I shouldn't have to hide anything. The Fairclough's invited me here. They can cope with my artwork, even if it's on my skin. "Thanks."

We walk down the cool passageway to the room I've locked at the end.

"Does it hurt when you get them done?"

I shrug. "A little, I guess, though I think you can become used to that type of discomfort."

Her eyes widen. "I'm not sure I would. I don't like needles."

I laugh. "It's not like a blood test; it just looks like a pen."

Her face lightens. "Really?"

"Uh, yeah, but don't get any ideas. You are far too pretty to cover yourself in thoughts you can't erase."

I turn the key in the lock.

"You are pretty, too," she says, and I find myself blushing.

"Here you go." I pull on the door and allow it to fall open. She steps in and glances at all the boxes.

"It's all boxed up."

"Wanna help me unpack it and work out where it's going?" I smile a little. She's sweet, and if she's here with me, it might stop me thinking of her brother and his broad shoulders and hot and cold games.

"Can I?" She smiles like I've told her she can keep it all.

"Sure." I shrug, "Lets unpack. Sort by colour and material, and then I'll show you what I was thinking for the house."

I'm sure I catch a shadow by the door, but when I turn there is no one there.

"That would be so cool. I don't know what to do with myself, school broke up weeks ago."

"Then would you like to be my assistant?"

"I'd love that."

I stare at her pretty little face with her upturned nose and eyes nearly as deep as her brother's. "I'd like that, too."

She dives headfirst into the boxes, and I sit back watching her reactions. This will be a good gauge of how my audience will receive them.

My phone vibrates in the pocket of my shorts and I pull it out.

Eli Jones: Thank you.

I smile and push the phone back in my pocket. Right, it's time to get to work.

An hour later, when Jennings comes to knock on the door to tell us lunch is ready, we've unpacked everything. I'm not sure if I'll get used to having someone remind me to eat, but my stomach is gurgling and my back aches from being bent and stooped over boxes. The floor in the drying room is covered in discarded newspaper and we crunch over it on our way back to the stone covered hallway.

Jennings clears his throat as we pass him by. "Your grandmother is attending lunch," he says to Tabitha, and her face falls.

"What does that mean?" I ask.

She speaks out of the side of her mouth, but there is no way Jennings can't hear. "It means lunch has become painfully awkward." As we pass my pink bedroom, I quickly duck through the door and grab one of my oversized cotton shirts, pulling it on and buttoning it up.

Lunch is in the dining room and the large gleaming table is set with silverware. It's just Jennifer and a woman with a white bob waiting for us.

I didn't know we were late but neither of them look at us approvingly as we walk in. I say hi to Jennifer who has been milling around most of the morning, organising the staff into cleaning the rooms I think I might need over the next couple of days.

The woman with the white hair looks at me expectantly. It is her house, though; am I supposed to introduce myself?

Finally, after at least five awkward seconds, Tabitha notices us watching one another. "Oh, Grandma, this is Faith. She's here for the installation Elijah and mother planned."

I smile and reach my hand forward.

"So, you're the artist?"

If I thought Jennifer Fairclough was immaculate and together, then she must have inherited the art of being unruffled from her mother. Her silk blouse is tucked into a straight skirt at her slender waist, a row of pearls sit under the collar. Despite the intense and unrelenting heat, she is the epitome of high-class chic. I look like a painter and decorator next to her. I wipe my hands on my loose-fitting shirt.

"I'm a sculptor, really." I always feel I need to explain to people not to expect any masterpiece canvases from me.

'I'm Connie Fairclough."

"Faith Hitchin."

"How's it going?" Jennifer cuts in, reprieving me from the sharp gaze of Grandma Baroness. "I see Tabitha has offered her services."

I nod and reach for a bread roll, before realising no one else has touched the food. I drop the roll and my stomach rumbles in protest. "She's been a godsend. After lunch, we are going to walk the rooms. I've already got some ideas going."

I need to get ideas going. I've got two days.

Tabitha offers me a grateful shy smile, and I smile back. She's cute. We haven't spoken much while we've been working. I sense she's painfully shy, and I can remember a time when I was crippled with anxiety every time I opened my mouth.

Grandma Baroness weaves her hands together and places them in her lap, closing her eyes. What is she doing? "Dear Lord..."

My eyes pop open when I realise lunch is being opened with a prayer. A faint snicker comes from the other side of the table, and I meet Tabitha's amused gaze. I shush her with a glare and then close my own eyes. Where the hell is Elijah? How come he's been wafting around all morning, and now it's time for an awkward lunch he's nowhere in sight?

When we've all said "Amen", I grab for the roll and break it open with my hands, spearing some butter curls on a small white dish and thickly smearing it on the fresh white bread. I don't even care if I look like I've been dragged up in a zoo. I can't remember the last time I ate and it's beginning to show.

Once I've demolished the roll, I look up to find Jenifer watching me with an amused gaze.

"Sorry, I was hungry." I smile apologetically.

"It's almost poetic to have a starving artist in the house again." It's Connie that speaks, and I'm sure I catch an eye roll coming from Jennifer as I turn to face the older woman.

"Sculptor," I remind her with a forced smile.

She ignores me. "You know, this house used to be a retreat for real artists and authors in its heyday?"

Real artists?

"That's nice." I place some cold cuts of meat, and a scoop of salad onto my plate.

"Oh, yes. We had Hemingway here once."

Unfortunately, I've just taken a sip of my iced water which I nearly choke on.

Connie carries on, regardless of my spluttering. "Oh yes, my mother entertained Virginia Woolf here in 1916; they played croquet on that lawn right there." She points with her fork to the immaculate lawn outside the dining room window.

Virginia Woolf… and now what? They have me?

I'm being hit by a wave of loser syndrome.

Connie nods, her mind someplace else. "Ooh, yes, all the greats." Her eyes snap onto me, bright and clear. "Now tell me, dear, which of my grandsons do you plan to fuck?"

"Mother!" Jennifer's face pales, and she holds her hand across her mouth.

What the hell did she just say to me?

I don't know how to react. Tabitha is squirming in her

chair, her pale and pretty face a vibrant red. My mouth flaps open gormless and stupid.

I know it's what people think of me when they see the tattoos. So it's what I give them. It's easier that way then being the woman who lives under the ink.

I shrug nonchalantly. "I really can't decide. I think I may have them both at once."

Tabitha howls with laughter, and Connie stares at me. Her eyes scanning over my face, a small smile lifting her mouth. I push away from the table. "If you'll excuse me, I need to get back to being a pretend artist."

I push from the table and stalk for the door, while my heart pounds wildly in my ribcage.

What a fucking bitch. I'm tempted to screw her grandsons now out of spite.

I slam into my room and throw myself onto the bed. I don't know why her words burn so bad. For the last six years I've been giving people what they see. What difference does it make if some old woman calls me on it?

It matters because Elijah has been good to me. The last week he's helped me, he never asked questions. Never wanted to know why I'm running away from my degree. He's just packed and lifted boxes.

I lift my hips and slide my phone out of my back pocket.

Faith Hitchin: Where were you?

I stare at the ceiling and wait for his answer to vibrate but it doesn't come. I don't know why it hurts.

Unable to lie still and sulk, I roll off the bed and head down to one of my workshop rooms and shut the door firmly behind me. There are rows of materials along a rack of shelves and impulsively I tug out a box of earthenware clay mix. I pool some from a pitcher and mix until the texture is a little on the wet side. My fingers delve into the pliable substance, and I relish the familiarity of it under my fingernails even though I'm in this strange house.

My phone beeps and I glance at it on the side.

Eli Jones: Sorry. I was called to London.

I don't answer. I'm too busy sensing my way around the lump of thickening clay with my fingers.

Eli Jones: Sorry about my grandmother. She's on a different planet to the rest of us.

I scowl at the screen and then turn my back. I close my eyes and let my hands get to work, forgetting where I am and what the hell I'm doing here.

Thirteen

The touch, when it comes, is passing, innocent. For a moment, I'm not sure if I imagined it. My brain tells me it's a hug, nothing more. Hugs are normal in our house; we have them in abundance with lots to share. My hands are in the bubbly water. Foam seeps up to my elbows as I grasp for a slippery plate. I grip the sponge in my other hand; ready to wash away the gravy, and remnants of mash potato. The squeeze starts at my shoulders—a hand on my shoulder, kneading the top of my arm. I smile, grinning. Dinner was good—fun. It's nice when the house is full, and laughter fills the air.

The hand slides down my arm, the grip still firm. Then the thumb grazes along the side of my boob, the small swell of softness.

At first, I think it's an accident. But I can't turn to check. I'm frozen as the hand runs back along the same path.

It's not an accident.

I don't say a thing, just carry on washing the dishes, and after a moment of holding my breath the hand moves.

I wake in sweat, my legs and arms thrashing against unwanted touches, and blankets. It takes a moment for me to remember where I am. To remember that I've run once again; this time, to a room with dusky pink walls.

It takes another moment for my pulse to calm enough so I can sit up, and I push my hair out of my face. It's dark outside, so it must be past ten. I didn't mean to drop off to sleep when I came back into the pink room. I worked for ages with the clay, twisting and turning it, allowing it to morph into an expression of my feelings—my frustration.

I slip my feet into my trainers and pull a baggy sweatshirt over my camisole. The jumper is so big, it covers my shorts as well. I'm hungry. I didn't go to dinner as I couldn't bear the thought of seeing Connie Fairclough and her sharp tongue again.

I open my door and head down the hallway. I'm sure people are still up; not everyone is asleep by eleven o'clock being tormented by their demon nightmares.

I don't see anyone, and I technically don't know where the kitchen is. Irrelevant of my lack of direction, I creep along the silent hallways. This would be the perfect moment to explore; no one else would be around watching my reactions. I stay on track, though. If I'm going to keep skipping dinner due to rude family members, I'd better find out where I can scrounge food.

I follow all the places where I've seen Jennings hovering. He always knows when food is served; I'm guessing he knows where it comes from.

Eventually, when I've headed towards the yet unexplored back of the house, I find a dark wooden door with *Kitchen* written on an enamel nameplate.

Well, that only took about twenty minutes. Just as well I'm not malnourished and on my last legs. I push through, already decided on just getting a quick snack and then going straight on a mission back to my bed.

I stop with a jump when I see someone sitting at a massive wooden kitchen table. At first, I think it's Jennings—maybe he's not allowed to go to bed? But then the delphinium blues lift and rove over my face, my sweatshirt, my legs.

I hesitate in the doorway. I can't help but wonder what's going on. This morning he was here, then he was gone—just in time for me to get insulted by his gran—and now he's back... my gaze drops to the table... back and drunk.

In his hand is a tumbler full of amber liquid, and in front of him—the only thing on the table—is a bottle of whisky with a label I can't pronounce.

I hover, suspended, while his eyes sweep over the tattoos on my thighs. When they rise to my face, I can't decipher the emotion locked within their depths. "Hi," I say.

"Hi."

"Hard day?" I motion at the bottle.

"You could say that." He pauses for a moment, drifting deep into thought. "Want one?"

I shrug and step up to the table and pull out a chair, telling myself he doesn't look all kinds of levels of serious hot. He does. God, he does.

White shirt rolled at the sleeves and pushed up to the elbow, he's wearing a navy waistcoat. God can this man rock a suit. "You look nice," I say, without thinking.

He turns to face me while his eyes wander thoughtfully over my face. Without a word, he gets up from his chair and opens a cupboard, pulling a short glass from within its depths. He doesn't bother with ice, just splashes some of the honey coloured liquid into the glass.

"I'm rather drunk," he announces as I take a tentative sip.

"Any reason why?" I tuck my legs up and pull my sweatshirt down over my knees, balancing the glass on top.

"Family issues."

I let out a dry chuckle. "Now I've met your family that doesn't surprise me at all."

A slow smile lifts one side of his cheek, and that gorgeous dimple flashes. "I can't believe she said that to you."

"She's a character."

He concentrates on the shape of my knees under the material of my jumper. "I can't believe you said that back. Surely you'd pick me instead of Peter?"

I take a moment to check he's only joking. The slow smile and dimple allow me to let out the breath I'm holding. "It was a hard choice, but on the wire, I couldn't decide."

He chuckles and takes a deep sip of his drink.

"So why are you solo drinking in the kitchen?"

He shrugs. "I didn't have anyone else to drink with."

"Don't you have friends you could have gone out with in London? Or, you could have come and asked me." He seems kind of sad and lonely sitting in the kitchen by himself. *I would have sat with him.*

"We aren't friends though, are we?" He twists his glass around, his long fingers rolling it this way and that.

"Well, no." As cryptic as he's been so far, there is something about him that I like. I really like. And I don't say that about many people. My thoughts of him are living under my skin, morphing into my newest obsession. "But we could be... maybe."

"Why did you sleep with Gerard Steers?"

My eyes narrow to slits. "Who said I did?" I shoot back my whisky and swallow as it reaches the back of my throat.

"It was written all over your face at lunch the other week." He taps his head. "It wasn't hard for me to work out why you didn't want to finish your degree."

I drop my face and stare at the table top. "I trusted him, and he lied."

Elijah doesn't answer but pours himself another drink which he then tosses back. He really is on a mission for a headache.

"I don't trust many people." I hesitate before allowing the truth to slip out into the still kitchen. "And he betrayed that."

"By having an affair with his student? I'd say the betrayal was obvious on many levels."

I shake my head, my cheeks flaming. "It wasn't an affair. But I allowed him to stay around, to talk, to be my friend." There goes that word again.

"So why are you so hurt, if it wasn't an affair?"

I nibble on my lip. The whisky burns in my veins and warms me up from the inside out. "I only ever sleep with someone once." I can't believe I've said this out loud, and I smack my hands over my face, covering my lips. He watches me expectantly, like he's expecting me to finish the bombshell I've just dropped—and just like that I do. He pulls it from me with the power of those blues alone. "I don't normally wait around to make small talk and be friends afterwards."

He raises his head to meet my gaze. He's probably judging me, reading between the lines of what I'm saying. I meet his look defiantly.

"You only sleep with someone once." His voice is a low murmur, and it does something to my stomach, making it flip and flop with every word he mutters.

"I think we should focus the conversation on your solo

whisky drinking." My tipple is firing the blood in my veins, and when he pours me a fresh one I know I shouldn't have it. "I haven't eaten enough for this," I say. I tip the glass in his direction.

"Because of my grandmother?"

I shake my head although I'm not going to outright lie and say I was eager to meet her again. "I was working."

"Working?"

He leans forward, his eyebrows lifting. "Am I allowed to see?"

"Possibly." I smile slightly, my throat burning from the drink.

"Why are you scared of intimacy?" His change of conversational direction again floors me. We never seem to be talking about the same thing for longer than two minutes.

"I'm not." I bristle, taking another sip of my drink. I'm going to be outrageously drunk soon and then I might dive straight into those deep blues and never surface again. *Shut up, Faith, you bloody idiot.*

A shudder crawls over my skin at the word "intimacy". All I can think of is inappropriate touches and hands I can't escape from. The hairs on my arms stand on end and Elijah watches them transfixed.

"But you only sleep with people once. How do you learn them? Enjoy them?"

His question blindsides me. "What's to enjoy?" I blurt.

He frowns, his dark brows knitting together. Slowly, his eyes focus on my face and he lifts a hand to trace a finger along the edge of my cheek. "That's an incredibly sad statement."

"Don't judge me." I bat his hand away. "I don't know you and you don't know me. I'm just hired by your family for a couple of weeks. I'm not here to be laughed at."

There's a small shake of his head and an even smaller smile. "I'm not laughing." He drops his hand and falls back in his seat, reaching for the bottle. "What do you want to know? I'm an open book."

I snort and pour myself another ill-advised drink once he's let go of the bottle. "An open book? You are not even close. I don't know a single thing about you, apart from the fact you restored a classic MG."

"Maybe it's because it's all so very dull, it's not worth telling." His lip curls into a sneer, but I know it's internalised and not directed at me.

I sit forward a little, close enough that his whisky breath fans across my face. "I doubt that." I wave my hand at the room but meaning the house outside of the room. "Wasn't this your idea? Didn't you want to set something up for the community?"

He snorts and his gaze levels with mine. "People like us should give something back."

"People like who?" He's not making much sense, but I don't know if it's because he's drunk or I am. The alcohol burns my stomach and I tug my sweatshirt down lower. He stares at my legs, his eyes drawn to the ink spread across my skin.

"What do you do?" My question is a whisper. "You said before you did 'stuff'."

"I'm a lawyer."

I nearly choke on a swallow of fiery liquid. "That's not 'stuff'." I wipe at my face with the back of my hand in case I've dribbled whisky.

That so explains the expensive and beautifully cut suits.
"And you work where?"
His lips tighten. "In the city."
"What sort of lawyering?" That's not a word. The

alcohol is making up words now. I giggle and slump in my seat a little. My body is heavy, and my head wants to rest on the table.

He flashes me a quick smile. "While lawyering, I work for a corporate firm."

I make a loud snoring noise, and he chuckles, his shoulders dropping as he shakes his head in what I hope is mock pity at me. "Is that why you walk around looking so pained and uptight all the time?" I ask with a cheeky smirk.

"I don't look uptight. We can't all be freewheeling, tattooed artists, like you."

Something about his words tickles my sixth sense. "Oh my god," I'm on the verge of slurring. "That's why you want the art thing here. You don't want to help local kids; you want to play with the clay and paints yourself."

I knock my hand against his shoulder and he catches my fingers, turning my wrist up to investigate my lightning bolt.

"Sometimes I take pro bono cases. If I've got to do this boring career chosen for me by my family, then I want to help others as much as I can..." he trails off with a shrug, while I stare at him like a lunatic.

My mouth dries as I sweep my gaze across him in his waistcoat and shirt. His jaw flexes as he thinks and his long fingers turn the whisky glass.

He is a good guy. I shake my head a little, muddled. Didn't I know that last week when he helped me pack up without question? Not once mentioning he might have an important job... people waiting for him... clients who needed him. No, instead, he sat on my studio floor and wrapped ceramics in paper, ignoring my heavy and stewed silence.

"And the art?"

I watch in silence as his lips set into a straight line, my

wrist still in his hand. "A forgotten dream."

I hate the fact I want to know more. That tingle of inquisitiveness creeps under my skin. Didn't it start like that with Gerard Steers? Aren't I like that with everything? It's an obsession, a chase—until I get it and then I don't ever want it again.

"You could get involved here. Maybe rebuild the dream?" *Why am I saying this?* His handsome face stretches into a tired smile. His eyes are bleary, tired, and red with drink. "Maybe then you won't sit in the kitchen getting drunk by yourself."

His index finger traces the zigzag of the lightning bolt and my heart accelerates in my chest. "I need to be in London."

I try to ignore my stomach plummeting when I realise he's not going to be here.

"Oh."

"Oh?" His fingers still skim over my skin, delicately following the trail of ink.

"I should go back to my room."

But I don't want to. I want to sit in the kitchen and drink whisky with him until the sun comes up and I'm probably too drunk to see it.

I can't remember the last time I wanted to chat with someone of the opposite sex. Apart from Dan, but he's different—he's family.

It's like he knows my mind has wandered. His next question takes me by surprise. "Why did you run from Brighton?"

For a moment, I'm wordless. "What makes you think I ran?"

"It's what you do."

"You've known me two weeks." He's so not wrong. It is

what I do. But because it was forced into me as a necessity. I can't trust anyone. There is no such thing as trust. Only lies and deceit.

"You ran from Gerard. Did you even speak to him to tell him you knew the truth?"

"No," I snap. My hands let go of my knees and I pull my hand away from his touch and push out of the kitchen chair. "I think I should go to bed."

I march for the kitchen door. Damn, I never did get my snack.

"Wait." He gets up from his seat, stretching slightly. He's something else to look at in that suit; tall and powerful but without being dominating and too huge. Bulging muscles just do nothing for me. Stereotypical artistic types have always attracted me, sleek and defined. He's some place in between, even with his lawyer suit on.

He staggers a little as he walks towards me. The whisky bottle is empty, and I only helped with a few shorts. Someone will have a headache tomorrow... who am I kidding? I will have a headache, too. I drank neat spirits on a stomach lined only with a dinner roll. "I'll walk you." His deep rumble of a command doesn't sound that drunk.

"It's fine."

His fingers grip my elbow. "Not a chance. Peter will be out looking for you after hearing what you said to Gran."

My eyes widen in alarm, but he winks. "Joking. But it wouldn't be very gentlemanly to let you wander around in the dark by yourself."

"Are you always a gentleman?"

My eyes meet his. I'm rooted to the spot.

"I try."

He can read me like a fricking book, and it's unnerving. I try to push the thought to the back of my mind as I take in the sight of this man who's been drinking by himself. The lawyer who takes on cases for free, the man who wants to help local kids. The man who couldn't follow his artistic dream—I still need get that full story.

On a whim, I stretch out my hand. "I'm Faith, and I'm your new best friend."

He hesitates for a moment and a small break in his expression pulls at my heart. "Eli, a gentleman at your service."

"Guide me home, Eli." I chuckle a little. The drink makes my legs a little weak.

He looks up and down the corridors. "It's that way, I think," he decides after a moment.

I snort and tug on the crisp sleeve of his shirt. "I think I've got some paracetamol packed somewhere."

"Thank God. My head hurts already."

"Knew it would," I tease as we meander down the corridor, my new friend and me.

Fourteen

I wake to my phone vibrating a message. With a deep groan, I roll over and bash my hand on the bedside table. My tongue has the most awful taste, like a cat curled up and went to sleep in there.

Eli Jones: What happened to my head?

I snicker and roll back over, holding my phone above my head as I type.

Faith Hitchin: You lost it in an attack of loser syndrome. You should recover by midday.

I smile—this is dangerous. Smiling leads to obsessive thoughts until I get what I want, and last night I promised I'd be his friend. Friends don't fuck and walk away.

Eli Jones: Oh good. So, my memory is a little hazy. I walked you back to your room. Guess we dodged Peter the Lurker?

Faith Hitchin: Peter the Lurker was nowhere to be seen.

Eli Jones: And I didn't… embarrass myself?

Fuck, I'm grinning like a lunatic.

Faith Hitchin: Well you did use my studio basin as a urinal.

Eli Jones: I did not. That's not funny.

Faith Hitchin: It is a little bit, come on.

Eli Jones: My head hurts too much for this.

Faith Hitchin: Are you coming to breakfast to protect me from your evil grandmother? Is she a wolf dressed up as a sweet old lady, ready to gobble us all up?

Eli Jones: lol

Faith Hitchin: Are we lol'ing now? We must be friends.

Eli Jones: I'm in London. I hope to be back later.

No. My stomach drops. S*top doing that. It's not good.*

Faith Hitchin: Okay, have a great day being a corporate high flyer.

Eli Jones: Thanks, I won't.

Faith Hitchin: Hey, it's Sunday.

Eli Jones: The law stops for no man.

Faith Hitchin: Loser syndrome, I told you.

Eli Jones: It's a free case. I've got to work it on my own time. I'll see you later.

I stare at my phone. Is that it now? Are we friends? Are we going to act like we've known each other forever?

He doesn't know a thing about me, and if he did, he'd run for the hills and never look back. I push down the blanket and raise my arm, keeping my gaze studiously turned away from the lightning bolt Elijah had touched last night. Instead I look at the Māori decorations I have weaving along my right bicep. Feminine but powerful, they remind me of a time when I thought I could fight. After three weeks in New Zealand, spending some bonus money

Al had given me for a large set of sketches I'd done him, I'd decided to have them inked before my return. I wanted to come back a Māori warrior, ready to defeat my enemy and achieve freedom.

I nibble on my lip. The battle hadn't been won.

Can I be that woman again, the one who fights?

I sit on the edge of the bed, throwing back the duvet. My head aches, my stomach is turning, but hell am I going to let some old woman with a vicious tongue keep me penned in my room. I pull on some clothes, put my hair up in a bun, and decide to go to war over the breakfast table. I need to eat to absorb the alcohol still sloshing around my stomach. I can't work with my brain foggy and distracted. And I want to work. I resist the urge to go and see my stoneware creation of yesterday. Bacon first. Then work.

Tabitha's at the table and I nearly fall at her feet with joy. Nearly, but then she says, "Jeez, you stink of booze."

I glare at her and grab the jug of organic juice in the centre of the table, pouring it into a ridiculously small glass that can only hold about two sips.

Jennifer is sitting behind a broadsheet. Either something's very interesting, or she doesn't want to make eye contact with me. I slide into a seat next to Tabitha.

"What did you do yesterday, Faith?" Tabitha asks, her cheeks tingeing with pink just from making conversation with me.

I offer her a smile and a wink. "After your grandmother was mortally rude to me and accused me of being a slut?"

Tabitha catches on quick. I can see us being friends. Exactly how many Faircloughs do I plan to be friends with?

"Mm, she put you on the spot asking you to choose like that."

I pick up a bread roll, although I know I have to manage

to eat more than that today. "I know, I mean it's such a tough choice. On one hand you've got Peter..." I pick off a piece of bread. "You know he's in line to the throne so that's in his favour, but let's be honest he doesn't look anywhere near as fu—"

"Okay, that's enough." Jennifer puts her paper down onto the space in front of her. She doesn't have a plate with pastries and jam. Just a black coffee.

Tabitha giggles and Jennifer levels her with a stare. "Honestly, so childish." Her daughter sits up straighter and drops her laughter, and I glare at the immaculate shape of Baroness Fairclough.

She meets my gaze with cool disdain. "I'm sorry for my mother's behaviour yesterday. Hopefully we can move on. She can speak without thinking and has a razor-edged tongue."

It's an apology. The 'S' word has been muttered, so being the bigger person, I nod my head. "It's forgotten about."

Jennifer offers me a tight smile. "Thank you." She takes a sip of her coffee. "Are you prepared for tomorrow? Have you thought about the rooms?"

I nod and lift my knife and fork as a plate of crispy bacon is miraculously put in front of me. I turn to Jennings (is he always working?) and raise a questioning eyebrow. "I haven't ordered anything yet."

"Master Fairclough called ahead and said you would require bacon."

Oh God. My cheeks burn with the heat of a thousand suns. "What if I was a vegetarian?" I think the best way to handle this is to brazen it out.

Jennifer's face is frozen, and Tabitha is rocking back and forth with glee.

Jennings goes to remove the plate. "I'll tell cook you are happy with a bread roll."

"No, no, no. I'll keep that." I tug the plate out of his grip.

"As I thought." He would make a fantastic poker player. He turns and goes to the sideboard picking up the coffee pot. It's only when he turns back around and I'm the only one paying him any attention that he cracks a smirk.

"So." Jennifer pulls my attention. "Do you have everything you need to start?"

I nod around a mouthful of bacon. "Yes, although I think I'm going to start with the glass work for the hallway. It makes sense to me that we create a flow through the house."

She nods, but I can see it holds no interest for her. Elijah wasn't wrong. She's just after exposure.

"How do you plan to get lots of people involved in glass work?"

If I could fist bump myself without looking ridiculous I would. "I'm going to make mosaic tiles, something easy and colourful. It will be a wonderful effect."

"A mosaic?" She sounds disappointed—like she expected the girl with the tattoos to have something better than the ancient medium of tiling.

I never said I was making a mosaic.

I finish the bacon and clatter my knife and fork onto the plate just as the shining white bob of evil grandmother gleams into view.

"That's me out of here." I slide back my chair and slip out of the space. I smile at Tabitha. "You coming to help me, or have you got some grown up stuff to do?"

Jennifer tuts, but doesn't say anything.

I'm beginning to realise why Elijah is a lawyer and not an artist.

"I'm coming."

I stop by Jennings who looks up at me in surprise. "Thanks for the bacon," I say.

"You're welcome, Miss Hitchin."

"Faith. I'm Faith." I remind him with a smile.

"Can I get you anything else."

I grin, though it's more of a grimace. "Coffee and lots of it down to the studios? Also, I need to get some wire, are you able to organise that?"

Another tut from Jennifer, and she mumbles under her breath about offering.

"You find the one you want, and I'll organise it."

"Thank you." I grin at him and turn for the door, my head held high in the air and my nose pointed in the opposite direction to the Wicked Witch of the West.

We work our way down the endless plush carpets to what I'm realising is the old staff quarters out back. Every so often, I stop to stare at one of the dark and foreboding portraits on the walls.

"It's like they're watching you, isn't it?" Tabitha says.

"It's bloody creepy." I point to one plump woman in black. "She looks like she's eaten her husband and is mourning her last meal."

Tabitha chuckles and I cast a curious glance over her.

"Have you ever been in a portrait?" I ask. I wonder if somewhere around here there's a gilt framed canvas hanging with Elijah on it.

"When we were kids." She shrugs.

"I have to see." I turn, looking closer at the wall hangings. "Where is it?"

"Faith, shouldn't we be sorting out the studio? People are going to be here tomorrow."

She's right, I need to stay focused. This is all I have at

the moment. There is nothing for me to run back to or run forward to.

We turn to the left, leaving the main house behind. "Do you think Elijah will be here tomorrow?" I attempt nonchalance, but I don't miss her small smile. "I think he should be, seeing it's his project."

She nods, but then her pretty face fall serious. "I hope so, but I don't know. He's working on a horrible case at the moment."

"What?" We are nearly at the outhouses, but I slow my steps down. "What do you mean horrible?"

Her face crumples with agitation. "I don't know much about it; the family always treat me like a baby, Elijah especially. He wants to protect me."

"Well that's stupid, how old are you?"

"Eighteen."

I remember what I was like at eighteen. There was nothing innocent left about me, it had all blown away in the sands of time and disappointment.

"Do you not know anything about the case?"

"Only what I've eavesdropped on." She flushes but I hold my hand up for a high five and she giggles. I stare at my palm expectantly. "Top marks for initiative."

"It's the only way I hear anything, it's how I know about Elijah and…" My ears prick up, but she stops herself talking. Her lips jam shut. Elijah and what?

"So, the case?" I push on the door of the studio I worked in yesterday afternoon.

"It's a sexual harassment case."

"What? Why? Wouldn't that be a police matter?"

She shrugs. "That's all I know."

I let it go, ignoring the tightening in my stomach. "Come

and see what I did yesterday." I grab her arm and tug her in. There, in the middle of the room, is my earthenware statue.

She snorts with laughter, stepping closer and peering at it in detail. "Is that my grandmother?"

I laugh and keep my voice innocent. "No, it's Medusa."

Tabitha raises an eyebrow and smirks.

"What can I say? She made me bloody mad."

"And do all the people that annoy you end up as a statue?"

She's being funny. Sadly, they don't. I run away from most people who annoy me or upset me.

I shake off the thought. "What do you know about glass making?"

"Absolutely nothing." There is a gentle tap at the door and Tabitha opens it. Jennings stands there with a tray of cups, some biscuits, and a coffee pot. "I can pour coffee, though."

I grin. "That's a start. Then I'm teaching you how to make glass."

"Really?"

I chuckle. "Sure, why not?" Panic settles in my stomach and makes me want to hurl into the nearest wastepaper bin. "At least then I can work out how terrible tomorrow is going to be."

Tabitha smiles and starts to make the coffee. "It won't be terrible, you're a natural."

I curl my top lip, but I can't even pretend that this whole situation isn't scaring the life out of me.

Fifteen

"Faith!"

I groan and look up from the kiln. I'm trying to get the quantities right for the glass and at the moment I can't make anything other than a shattered pile of dust. I don't know why it's so hard. I've done it hundreds of times. Now it's late, I'm tired and cranky, and in my stomach is a giant knot of tension I can't dissipate no matter how hard I try.

"Go away." I shout back.

"Open up now, you are being completely ridiculous."

I know he's not going to go away, so, throwing my gloves onto the chair, I stomp for the door and swing it open. Red hair and freckles are leant against the door frame. "So, you've quit?"

"So, you're a cheating bastard?"

Gerard scowls at me. "What are you talking about?"

"Ooh like you're married and never told me."

His face falls, but whether it's because I've caught him out and know how much of a cheating bastard he is, I don't know. "Let me guess... Peter?" He scrubs a freckled hand down his face. It's inexplicable, but my mind wanders to the golden skin of Elijah.

"It doesn't matter who. The point is I trusted you. And this has nothing to do with sex because we both know I couldn't give a shit about that. I trusted you to be my friend. I let you into a world that, in case you didn't realise, is actually quite small."

"For goodness' sake, Faith, I didn't lie. Ella and I separated three years ago. Peter would have told you that if he wasn't such a complete arse."

I shake my head. "It's not the point. We've been friends for two years and you never once mentioned a wife."

He steps into the room and takes in my pile of dusty mess. It's everywhere, crusted along my legs, under my sandals. "So now you walk away from your degree? All because I didn't want to tell the engaging, vivacious girl who I couldn't believe liked me that I'd once made a silly, childish error and married the wrong girl."

I glare at him. Throwing daggers with my evil side cye. "I can let that go maybe before we slept together, but not the time since when we've been friends."

"Is this because you've told me what happened back in Brighton?"

I hold my hand up. "Never talk to me about it." I step towards him, backing him back towards the door. "Don't ever talk to me again. You've crossed a line with this, Gerard. I was willing to think you wanted to be my friend, that maybe I wasn't on a long list of students you wanted to fuck." My pulse races. "What am I thinking now, hey? That you're a dirty scumbag."

"So what are you going to do, Faith? Start again? Find another degree? Waste more years? I gave you so many opportunities; your work is in galleries because of me."

I can barely speak. Blood is pumping in my veins, my

head throbbing. Every muscle, every tendon, is pulled as tight as an elastic band about to snap.

"I think the lady said she didn't want to talk."

My legs sag a little as Elijah's smooth voice cuts through the static buzzing between my ears.

"Back off, Fairclough," Gerard snaps at the newcomer. "This is between me and Faith, we're friends."

Elijah steps into the room, his body angled close to mine. Despite the turmoil inside, I find comfort from having him step near. I don't look at him. My burning, furious gaze stays on Gerard.

He lets out a sigh of air and pushes his hand through his hair. "Seriously, Faith, you need to grow up. You can't keep running every time someone pisses you off."

"Get out," I screech.

Gerard holds his hand out, and Elijah mutters a low curse. As he gets to the door, Gerard stops. "You've got your quantities wrong, you need less calcium oxide."

"Get out!" I charge forward, but fingers grab mine and pull me back around until I'm staring into deep vibrant blues.

Elijah's face is serious, pensive. "Are you okay?" His voice is low, and it eases the tense ball of nerves and anger.

"No, he's a twat." I'm shaking, and Elijah clutches my fingers.

"What are you doing?" I glance down at our joined hands.

He drops them straightaway. "Sorry."

"How much did you hear?"

"Sorry, what?"

"I said how much did you hear?"

"Nothing, what are you asking?"

"Well, why the hell are you standing outside my door listening to my private conversations?"

His face hardens. "I came along because I felt bad for leaving you today. I want to check you were okay, or if you needed any help." His face is pinched, his body rigid. "And if you don't want people to hear your conversations, Faith, you shouldn't have them so damn loud."

He spins on his heel, turning for the door.

Shit.

Gah, what is it with this guy? I've never stopped anyone walking away before, but I grab his hand and stop him. "Wait."

"Forget it, Faith."

"No, I'm sorry." I breathe through my nose like I'm fighting off a panic attack. Which I am. Torn between letting Elijah walk away, because I shouldn't give a shit, and asking him to wait, so I can explain. "I just..." I don't know what to say.

His blues graze across my face. "It's okay."

I give a small shake of my head. "It's not, I shouldn't be rude." I close my eyes for a moment and calm my racing pulse. When I open them again, I smile and try to restart our conversation. "How was your day?"

He's standing in navy suit trousers, with a pale-blue slim-fit shirt tucked in. His tie is askew, and his top shirt button open. He looks lovely. I try my hardest not to notice.

"Really, really exhausting."

"Guess the last thing you needed then was to be screamed at by some random harpy of a live-in artist?"

He chuckles and his eyes shine. "True. I'm sorry Steers was here."

"It's okay." I sag a little, the fight leaving me. "I did leave the course without telling him."

"Have you definitely left the course? You could still go back after the summer; tell them you were tired and didn't mean what you said."

I shake my head. "I never go back." A quick glance down reminds me I'm covered in dust and chemicals. I brush my clothes to avoid looking at him, until the silence is too heavy and I peek through my lashes.

He watches me, perplexed.

"So, what are you doing here? I thought you didn't live here?" I crack a sly smile.

"Oh, I know. It's the only reason you agreed to come." He grins. Honestly, it's mesmerising. And the fact he's here, even if he did overhear my row with slimy Steers makes my chest tighten in this odd way.

"I thought you might want supper. I wasn't convinced you'd brave the dining room."

I smirk a little. "I'm a big girl."

His powerful gaze sweeps over my body. "I know. But is the big girl hungry?"

I notice he's holding a stripy picnic bag. "What's in there?"

"Wine, bread, and cheese."

My smile stretches. "Three of my favourite things."

"Come on. I know just the place."

I'm surprised when he leads us to the conservatory where we had lunch the first time I came here. It's quite exposed, and really I could do without the Wicked Witch of the West thinking I was stealing one of her grandsons. He steps forward confidently, not looking at who else might be around. The conservatory is surprisingly, and wonderfully empty. The lights are low solar bulbs lining the walkways, so we can see where we are going. The insects are quiet, and even the flowers seem to be sleeping.

"What time is it?" I hadn't even thought to check what inconvenient hour Gerard had decided to bombard Bowsley Hall and come knocking on my studio door.

"About ten, I think."

"Ten? Have you just got back from work on a Sunday?" This sounds awful. Even at the ink shop in the height of summer, with drunk idiots begging to be inked, we'd always walk away at 5pm. It was one of my dad's rules. Al would be the one working into the night.

I close my mind to thoughts of my dad. How did he creep in? I slam the door to my memory vault firmly in place.

"I'm trying to help a family."

My ears prick up. His voice lowers. Does he not want anyone else to hear? I continue to follow him and his stripy bag through the dimly lit pathways of the conservatory. How big is this place? It's like being in the jungle. "Tabitha mentioned you are working on a sexual harassment case."

His shoulder straightens under the fine blue shirt. "Yes."

Okay. Maybe we aren't allowed to talk about it.

"Here." He motions with his hand, and I see we have stumbled into a small pebbled area. I stand open mouthed. This place can't be real, surely?

We are in a circular clearing. Pathways converge from different sides of the large conservatory. But we must be against a far wall because right in front of us, gushing from the roof is an indoor waterfall.

Momentarily, I'm lost for words. "This is a-amazing," I finally manage to stutter.

He smiles, and it glimmers in the light of the moon and dances with the glow of the solar lamps. "It's special even in daylight, but it's something else at night. I love sitting here and thinking."

"Doesn't everyone sit here? I'd never be able to leave this place if this was my home." God, it is like standing on an island of heaven. Even the air is dense and sweet, filled with pungent natural scents that remind me of places I haven't even been. It takes me to the places I used to shut my eyes and dream about.

"No, I'm the only one who spends any time here."

"Not even Tabitha?" I'm surprised. She's shown remarkable ability with all the tricky little jobs I've given her today. Somewhere under her pale and slender exterior, is a rebel artist desperate to get out.

I watch Elijah. In the moonlight he looks something else. His straight, perfect nose is highlighted with silvery tones. The short hair on his head glows a little with the natural back-light. And those shoulders in that shirt.

Okay, I need to stop this right now.

He shakes a picnic blanket out and motions for me to sit down. "Not even Tabitha," he continues, answering my long-forgotten question as I became distracted by the handsome sight of him.

"Why? She seems to be unsure of what interests her. She can't wander around this house all day."

"The family haven't decided what she's going to be yet, so until they do, she just has to hang around here being nothing."

I stare at him in confusion, ignoring his immediate presence as he sits close to me on the blanket. "What do you mean the family haven't decided?"

He stares up at the glass ceiling. "The family way is the only way."

"Meaning what?" I press.

His eyes fall on my face; even in the growing depth of night they are piercing and tempting.

Like he doesn't even know what he's doing, his finger lifts and trails along the string of roses I have across my collarbone. "What I mean is that what the family says is what happens."

"You make it sound like the Mafia."

He chuckles. Is he really close, or is it my imagination? It's like he's absorbing the air around me. "It's worse —far worse."

"How?"

I thought I had the worst family in existence.

"Everything is for the Fairclough name. *Everything*."

"That's why you're a lawyer?"

"Yes, although I do like helping people."

"Like the family you're helping now?"

His face darkens a fraction, and it isn't a cloud drifting over the moon causing it.

"So what else do your family say?"

His thumb rubs across the peach and pink rose petals as if he's mesmerised by their existence. "So, I don't have any tattoos, and it's nothing about being scared of pain."

"So why?"

I sit up a little straighter, pulling away from his touch. As if awakened from a dream, he realises what he's doing and busies himself getting the wine out of the bag, along with two glasses.

"This is a very deep conversation for a late evening glass of wine." He hands me a glass and disarms me with a smile. I won't be deterred though. I want to know what's under that exterior. Once again, I think of the two sides of Elijah Fairclough. There's the businessman I met in the Ritz and the guy in sliders who knocked on my door to apologise.

I don't know who's the stronger. Or even if he wants one of them to win over the other. Although I know I want to see more of the guy in the sliders. He's charming and deep. I can sense it.

"It's disapproved. What if someone were to see? What if we were on a holiday and the press caught a picture of it? What if it offended someone?"

I snort my wine everywhere. "That's ridiculous. Ink is an expression of individuality." I've known this since a young age. I've known it since I first picked up a pencil and a scrap of paper and put the two together, creating an alchemy of magic that spilled onto the paper. My sixth sense, the one jingling now during my conversation with Elijah, is one of my strongest personality traits. It's what people say to me that helps me sketch for them what they want on their skin. It's their voice. Their thoughts.

I want to know what he looks like under his clothes. Under the gorgeous blue shirt, loose at the collar is a canvas of bare beautiful skin.

"So, what about Tabitha?"

"I think she wanted to be a vet." He smiles and takes a sip of his wine. "She was always saving things when she was little. There was always some poor animal hidden out in a stable that needed her attention."

I chuckle and take a sip of the chilled wine. It's delicious and smooth.

"Yeah, it was great until she coaxed an injured fox into the kitchen and it crapped all over the place. It took months for the smell to go."

"Gross."

His eyes shine, all thoughts of his "family" problems seem to be forgotten. "Here, have some cheese." He slides over a small wooden board with a curved knife.

"This is all very posh for a late-night picnic."

He grins. It's electric. My tummy tightens no matter how much I don't want it to. Reaching over, he clinks his glass against mine. "Tomorrow."

"Tomorrow." I let a deep breath through my lips. God, I can't even think about it. "I still don't know if I can do it."

He nods. "You can." Where does he gets his confidence in me? In what he's seen in my portfolio? Surely, that's not enough? I want to ask, but instead he says. "So, tell me about the mosaic."

Chuckling, I groan. "Your mother is such a blabbermouth."

"Yep."

"It's not a mosaic. I just let her think that because she was so rude." I settle back onto the picnic blanket staring at the stars through the domed glass roof of the conservatory.

He settles down next to me. It should be weird. It isn't. That familiar surge of obsession tingles beneath my skin.

He's wonderful.

I grin and stretch as his eyes travel over the stories on my skin. "It's going to be so much better than a mosaic."

Before he has a chance to answer. Before I have time to sweep my gaze over his shape, the curve of muscles. Before I have the chance to think that maybe I do like him after all, even if he isn't always the guy in sliders. Before I wonder what he would taste like; we are showered with water from overhead.

With a shriek, I leap to my feet as sprinklers flood the foliage and pathways with large droplets of water.

"Shit! I forgot about the water system." He shouts over the crash of water landing on gravel. He leaps to my side and we both gather the stuff. Wine spills everywhere, soggy bread and cheese goes back in the picnic bag.

My hair is splattered to my head, my face as wet as if I were in the shower. An irrepressible giggle builds inside my chest.

His hands clutch onto me as the deluge continues to pour down. We are soaked. His pale blue shirt is dark and clinging to his chest. My vest top has disintegrated into a useless rag. I stretch the material and try to lift it away from my bra but it's pointless, it's see-through.

I start to laugh, the water sliding off my face, falling into my lips. Then he laughs, and we cling to one another, an upturned lifeboat in a single moment of perfection.

"Was this a ploy to see my bra?" I grin, staring up at him through the droplets falling from my eyelashes. He looks amazing, breathtaking. Unlike any piece of art I could ever hope to create. He steals the air from around me. His hair is damp, droplets clinging to short spikes. His face and eyes shine with laughter. The man in the suit evaporating with the sprinkler system.

Then he's kissing me. His mouth hot. I gasp, shifting forward, sliding my fingers through the wet strands of his hair. His lips are firm, delicious, teasing. And I open my mouth as his warm tongue probes between my teeth, pushing mine for a response. A deep and furious fire lights me from the inside out.

I want to die. I want to combust into a million perfect pieces, spinning in the moment forever.

One of his hands lifts into my hair, tugging on the end of my ponytail and working its way until his fingers are against my scalp, while the other hand cradles my chin, his thumb brushing along the skin at the edge of my jaw.

Fibres of snapping electricity fuse the air between us and I never want the kiss to end.

It does. But his lips gently brush mine, teasing the moment for one long drawn out second.

"You're all wet." His voice is a low murmur.

"So are you."

My heart pounds, crashing in my chest, and in my head and heart, the seeds of an irrepressible need root themselves and come to life.

Sixteen

I haven't slept, and it's nothing to do with the nerves of what today will bring, what the youngsters turning up will be like, or if I ever get my glass mixture to not smash into a million pieces.

It's him.

Thoughts of the kiss looped around my head all night.

He kissed me.

Why?

Doesn't he realise I'm not like other girls? You'd think the tattoos would have been a warning enough.

But of course, he doesn't. He doesn't understand the way I am. The way I will now want him—need him more than anything I've ever had—but then after, I will walk away.

He's like nothing I've ever tasted.

He shouldn't have kissed me.

There's a knock on my door and I roll over in bed. I want to hide under the pillow, not show people how to make mosaic tiles with glass.

"What?" I grouch. It will be Tabitha, and I'm already hanging my head in shame for being rude. That girl brings out a side of me I didn't know existed. "I'll be up soon. Find Jennings and tell him I need about a hundred espressos."

The door opens, and I give a little shout when Elijah's dark head pokes through the gap.

"I'm not dressed," I squeal. I wish I could be all sultry and seductive. But I can't. I want to dive under the duvet and hide. He kissed me under the sprinklers. Like I need the reminder.

I don't want him to see my skin. For the first time, I want to hide my tattoos. All the strength I had behind them evaporates. His eyes skim along my leg, along my thigh with its patterns and swirls, flowers and thorns.

"I brought you the first of many espressos." He grins, wide and open, happy and relaxed. He clearly hasn't lost sleep running our kiss through his mind all night like an out-of-control video stuck in an old VCR recorder.

"Uh, thanks." I tuck the sheet around my chest. I'm not naked, but I am only wearing a sports bra and briefs. My skin is a mesh of rainbow splashes, black ink, and flesh toned pink. I don't want him to see. The exposure is unsettling. My stomach tightens, and my pulse quickens. "Why aren't you at work?"

"May I?" He motions at the edge of the bed.

Oh, good lord.

"Sure." I cough a little and clear my throat. It doesn't help ease the obstructive lump that's making me hot and bothered.

"I've taken a couple of days leave. I thought you'd like the help."

"And your mother approved?" I don't even know why I just said that.

A flicker of a cloud floats across his features. "Even

lawyers scared of their mothers are entitled to annual leave."

"Elijah, I'm sorry."

His startling blue gaze sweeps across my face, and I blush. That's right. I blush. No way to hide it lying under white bedsheets. His frown morphs into a smirk.

"I'm Eli."

"Eli," I concede. It sounds funny on my lips. Elijah, for some inexplicable reason, seems to put more space between us. If I call him Eli, it means this friends thing is real and that deep down I might want to be more than friends.

I know that's a childish fantasy. I don't do more. Not ever.

I can't go through today without talking about last night. It's better if I just get it out there. I mull around for the words, and he watches me, his smirk growing.

"Stop laughing at me," I snap.

"What?" He hands me my coffee and I take a tentative sip. It's perfect: hot, sweet, strong as fuck, and definitely the rocket fuel I need.

"We need to talk about you kissing me in the greenhouse-thing."

He raises an eyebrow. "It's actually a conservatory."

I glare. "I think you're missing the point."

"I kissed you. You looked beautiful, so I kissed you. It's no big thing."

No big thing... I haven't slept since.

Did he say I looked beautiful?

"Why do you look so shocked?" His voice lowers and warms, and I squirm my feet together as a tingle works up my legs.

I take another sip of coffee. "I don't think anyone's told me I look beautiful before."

His mouth falls open a little. "Well, clearly you've been hanging around with the visually impaired." He leans closer and the scent of soap on his skin and a subtle note of a warm aftershave fills my senses. "Because standing there, laughing, your face shining bright, your hair soaking wet, you were the most beautiful thing I'd ever seen."

"Oh, shut up." I hit him with my hand. "I bet you say that to all your female friends."

He shrugs and gets up from the bed. I want to ask him to stay there a moment longer, so I can blink the image onto my retinas for my memory bank. "I don't have any female friends."

"You don't?"

"Do you have male friends? The type I should be jealous of?"

My mind flashes to Dan dealing with the worst period of his life, and I'm sat here grinning like a fool at some handsome aristocrat. "No."

"That's good."

I don't know what good means, but he leaves me to get dressed and I neck back the rest of my coffee. I need to get my hands on more of that nectar later, but right now I slip into the en-suite wet room where I stand under a hot shower and try to wake up.

By the time I'm out, dry, dressed in baggy linen trousers and a light oversized shirt, I've managed to calm myself down. It was just a kiss.

He's already at the breakfast table when I attempt to face his family again. His eyes dance as I walk in and I know he's staring at me on purpose so I'll blush.

Tabitha pats the space next to her. Her mother doesn't lower the paper to note my arrival. The wicked witch is thankfully absent. Jennings brings me some more potent coffee, and I rip a croissant to shreds.

"How was your evening?" Tabitha asks innocently. "Did you manage to get the glass right?"

I pop a shred of pastry into my mouth. "It was rather dull actually."

Elijah snorts across the table and raises an eyebrow which I dutifully ignore.

"No Peter today?" I haven't seen him since my first lunch, and I'm guessing like Elijah, he stays away from the family crazy as much as possible... although Elijah has been here every night since I have... I lock the thought away. Stop it.

Jennifer lowers her paper and gives me a pointed look. "No, Peter takes his work very seriously."

I don't catch Elijah's eye, but he studies his muesli with great intensity.

With a tight smile sent in Jennifer's direction, I decide that breakfast isn't for me. I've never eaten a lot, but my intake of food has decreased dramatically since taking up residence at Bowsley. I now realise that's why rich people are always so thin; it's because the conversation at mealtimes is so awkward no one wants to eat.

"I'm going to go and prep the studio. I want it to be perfect." God, I'm going to puke. In an hour people will be here watching me turn sand into glass. Let's just hope I bloody can.

We've got the portable kilns all set up, so I need to get them ready. And I want to show people, if they are brave enough to have a go at glass blowing, so I need to make sure we have safe areas.

Why didn't I do more yesterday? What have I been doing with my time?

I'm at the door when I turn and notice Tabitha and Elijah are flanking me. Ha, stick that up your arse Ice Queen.

We walk to the outhouses in companionable silence.

"While I hate to admit it, Gerard was right about my mixture." I'd thought about it a lot on the night; it hasn't helped my insomnia.

"Who's Gerard?" Tabitha quizzes.

"A total tool," I tell her, but even I have to laugh. The burn of shame from allowing myself to trust and be hurt is fading. And it's the man dressed in jeans and a black T-shirt who's making me forget and lower my defences.

We enter what's going to be the glass studio and with no time to waste, I pick up the clear plastic packets of silica sand. I give them both a mask to put over their faces and Elijah chuckles.

"Why do I feel like I'm a surgeon about to enter theatre?"

"This is more fun." I grin back at him from under my mask. "At least there's no chance of you harming anyone here."

"True."

Both him and Tabitha lean over and watch as I tip the sand into a crucible. "This is where I messed up yesterday. I added too much calcium oxide." I put in the calcium and some sodium carbonate.

Then I pick up the jar of cobalt oxide and tip it in with a heavy hand. I know the colour of blue I'm aiming for; it's right in front of me. "So, you can add different chemicals to change the colour," I explain. My eyes meet Elijah's. "Then you melt it on the kiln and hey presto. Then we shape the glass and put it in the kiln to harden."

Hey presto, I've made a mess... let's hope not.

Elijah pulls off his mask and glares at his watch. "We haven't got long. Actually, about fifteen minutes."

I swallow hard as my stomach twists. I can do this.

"Maybe we should have started with pottery?" He offers me a wry smile.

"Nah, if we want people to come back, we need to go in big."

He slides his hands into his jeans and the room seems to shrink. Tabitha may as well not be here.

"You still haven't told me what you are going to do with the glass." He wiggles his eyebrows. He knows exactly what happened to distract me from giving him a full explanation. Tabitha's head swizzles between us.

"Well then, I guess you will be waiting."

He chuckles and turns for the door. "I'm going to go and wait for the new arrivals. You ready?"

"No." I shake my head. "No, I'm not ready for this."

He hesitates, his eyes sliding to where his sister is standing innocently watching us. Hesitation ripples through the air, but then he gives me a small smile. "It's going to be fun."

I turn back and watch the sand start to dissolve. I think Elijah and I have a different idea of what's fun.

I'm almost shaking when he returns half an hour later with a group of six teens. I've been letting Tabitha mix the liquid because I'm genuinely worried I'm going to knock it over and burn the hell out of us all with my shaking hands.

"Here she is." Elijah's smile lights onto my face and I don't know what's making me shake more. Them or his direct appraisal.

"Hi." I give them a small wave; somehow making my fingers stop trembling through the sheer power of will alone.

Elijah doesn't look nervous at all. His body is relaxed as

he gestures them all into the studio. He's grinning and smiling, putting everyone at their ease. "So, this is Faith, and she's an enormously talented artist."

God, my cheeks scorch red.

"I don't know about that."

Sort it out Faith. I don't want to waste this opportunity. I have no idea what my future holds right now. I dig down deep and then turn my smile onto our students for the first day.

"Hey," I start again. "I wasn't always an artist, or a student at university." This isn't the time to add that I'm no longer a student at university. My gaze sweeps across the crowd.

"What do you mean?" One bright eyed blonde asks. She reminds me of Meg, but I decide to give her the benefit of the doubt.

"Well, before went to uni, I worked in a tattoo shop in Brighton."

All of their eyes widen. One of the guys—he's bigger than the others, his stare bold—sweeps his gaze along my arms. "You've got a lot of ink," he says.

I meet his stare. "I sure do."

"So, lets introduce ourselves." I begin to warm up and take over from Elijah who shifts back a little to give me the floor. "I'm Faith, I'm twenty-four, and I'm two years into my degree. I like working with glass as you will see and try this week, but also ceramics. What I'm not good at is paint. Which is weird considering I draw on people's skin." I shrug, and people laugh a little. I relax even more.

I look at the girl with the blonde hair and perky demeanour. She doesn't let me down and launches into an excited spiel about her desire to create museum-worthy sculptures. She introduces herself as Charlotte. I doubt I'll remember their names, but I give it a good try out of politeness.

Dylan is the guy who likes the tatts. His eyes are on them more than the glass we are about to set.

Maisie is small and mousey, with an insanely loud giggle.

They are the only names I can remember. *Well done, Faith.*

"Okay, so we've made some liquid here that in a couple of hours is going to be glass. Does anyone know what makes glass?"

An emo boy at the back groans loudly from under his fringe, muttering something about this being worse than school.

I'm almost entirely sure his school have never let him play with burning hot liquids like this before. He's gangly, at that awkward stage of development where boys suddenly become like Bambi as their limbs grow too quick.

"Up ya come, happiness." I wave him forward, sensing Elijah's smile.

I think the most enthusiastic student in the room is the man who arranged it all. He is watching the pot of liquid blue with eyes filled with amazement.

"So, if you grab the stick and stir the mixture, we will be able to check the density."

The emo looks at me blankly. "You want me to touch that?"

"Preferably not with your fingers."

Everyone shuffles forward and even the kids who'd been hanging back during the introductions lean forward to get a better look.

With a dubious look he lifts the spoon and stirs the

liquid. It's perfect. Runny, glossy, and as blue as delphiniums. To say I'm pleased with myself is an understatement.

I grab a metal tray and hold it out. "Now ladle some into here."

"Like soup?" He asks.

I smile. "Kind of like soup, but we don't want to be greedy. We are making a mosaic for the hallway. So the glass has got to be thick enough to hold shape and colour but delicate enough we can weave all the proceeds together to create something astonishing."

Elijah's stare weighs heavy and hot as he watches me, but I don't meet it.

The youngster with the black hair and clothes looks between the empty tray and the crucible, then slowly and carefully ladles a spoonful. He grabs my hand as he tilts the tray to make the liquid run. "Sorry," he mutters.

"You've got it." Blue shimmering liquid glass spreads across the bottom of the tray, thin enough you can still see the bottom.

Everyone is huddled round. "What now?" Maisie asks.

"Now we bake it in the kiln, and you guys all get a go. Think of what colours we need. I thought it would be great to have a spectrum of colour going from light to dark."

"So we need black," emo boy says.

I chuckle. "Yes, we'll need black."

"Cool."

I nod at Tabitha who pales nervously, but then pulls herself together with miraculous resolve. She moves to another bench where the dried sand is waiting. "Who wants to make their own glass?"

They all step up, apart from emo boy who is still holding his tray.

I wave him over and plan to show him the kiln.

My eyes can't help themselves and search the small crowd for Elijah. I want to know he's happy with what I've done and that I've done a good job. I want to see his eyes and see pride there. To see his handsome face and see it smile.

He's not there, and my stomach lurches. Some support on my first morning.

Bloody great.

Seventeen

Seriously, I can't believe it. Elijah didn't come back. Tabitha and I did the whole morning session by ourselves. We then went and had an awkward-as-fuck lunch—which I couldn't eat, because nerves were eating my stomach instead—with six teenagers, before taking Maisie and Dylan and that crew back in to make even more of a mess.

Fair to say we have a lot of glass sheets.

Fair to say Elijah Fairclough is in my black book of hell.

I'm exhausted and lying on my bed. I can't move. I haven't put in a day of work that hard since my last day in Al's shop.

Thinking of Al, I reach over into the ornate shabby chic bedside table and pull out my phone. I haven't had a chance to look at it all day.

Eli Jones: *I'm sorry, I'll explain later.*

I scowl at my phone. He can kiss my damn arse later.

Ignoring my growing agitation, I tap on my contacts and dial Al. He answers after a few rings, but I struggle to hear him.

"Are you down a wind tunnel?" I ask.

There's a vague chuckle, but it chills my stomach. "Cheeky cow. How's Bowsley?"

I glower at the ceiling. "It was a good first day. We made glass. I think it's going to look good."

There's a pause filled with some heavy breathing. "Of course it will. You did it."

"How are you?"

"Cartwheeling in the garden." He starts to cough, and irrepressible tears slide out of my eyes, running down my face. "Hey, you better not be crying there, Faith. You know how I feel about soggy displays of emotion."

I chuckle and wipe my hand across my face. "No tears."

"That's a good girl." He pauses, and I wait for the familiar sound of him lighting a cigarette. It doesn't come, and it makes me want to cry even more. "So, tell me all about it."

I settle back on my pillows and stare at the ceiling as I hold myself together and tell him about the kids and the hot glass, and how I was lucky I didn't get someone burned, and myself sued. He laughs occasionally but is largely silent.

"You still awake?" I ask when I draw my day to a close.

"Yeah, who pissed you off?"

"What?"

"Who pissed you off?" I can hear the weak amusement in his voice.

"The Faircloughs are strange."

"Of course they are..." He pauses for a wheeze... "Stranger than the Hitchins?"

I hesitate. No one is stranger than my fucked-up family. "Elijah said he wanted to be friends, but friends don't just leave one another in the lurch like that."

"Maybe something came up. You can't keep judging people by your exacting high levels of trust."

I scrunch my face, not that he can see it.

"I mean, come on, Faith, you need to have more than just Dan and Abi as friends. What sort of life is that going to be if it's always just you?"

I sit up and dash my hands at the tears trickling down my face. "You know why I don't trust anyone."

"Yes, and it's shit. It's horrible, but you deserve much more than what you allow yourself to have."

"Hey, I trusted that scumbag lecturer, and it turns out he was bloody married."

"I'm not talking about sex, Faith. It's got nothing to do with physical contact. It's about trusting people who care about you enough to be there."

"Well, Elijah's already proven he's crap at that today."

Al goes to say more, "Your dad—" but then he starts to cough, and cough, and cough.

My chest aches and my stomach churns with every hoarse wheeze he makes. I'm helpless and useless on the other side of the phone.

"Al," I shout. Shit, he's almost struggling for breath.

"Faith," Dan's voice says.

I'm sobbing and manage to squeeze out, "Yes."

"It's okay, he needs to rest."

"This is awful, Dan."

"I know," he whispers, and I want to wrap my arms around him tight and never let go. "I've got to go and sort him out."

"I wish I was there."

There's a pause of silence. "Me too."

The line disconnects, and I sob. Large droplets of water splatter the cotton of the duvet cover.

I don't know what I'm going to do when cancer steals him away. He's been here for every moment. From my earliest memories, through everything. Even when he didn't know why I was acting out and covering myself in ink, he was still there. I still remember the look in his eyes when I told him.

"Hey." Elijah pushes at my door, and his face drops in shock as he takes in my wet face and swollen eyes. "Shit, what's the matter? Was it my bloody grandmother again? I'm going to nail that old woman into a box."

I offer him a lame smile and brush at my cheeks. He perches on the bed and reaches fingers for my face. With a delicate touch, he sweeps at the trails of tears. "No." Oh God, I sob all over again. I hate this weakness. Hate the way it makes me tangle into knots, leaves me aching and shuddering. "My uncle, he's..." I can't even say the word. I pull in a quivering breath, "sick."

Elijah's hand cups my cheek and he tilts my face to his. His eyes are deep pools of blue calm and I wish I could dive straight in and hide from the turmoil around me— from the loss I know is soon approaching. His thumb catches another tear. "I'm sorry."

I shrug, still frozen under his touch. "That's life."

He frowns. "Why do you do that? Hide your feelings?"

He won't let me move. His hand stays firm. "Because they aren't to be trusted."

Leaning forward, he presses his lips to my forehead and I battle another wave of tears. "That's the saddest thing I've ever heard."

"Where did you go?" I brush away my heartache for Al and focus on what I'm supposed to be doing now. Although I can't get over him leaving like that. I push his hand away and this time he lets it fall to his lap.

"I had to make some calls." His expression is frank and open.

"All day?" Jesus, either he's the world's best actor, or he made a hell of a lot of calls—right when he should have been helping me.

He sighs and his shoulders slump. I wiggle my fingers under my leg, so I won't reach out and touch him. "It was a lot of calls, and then I was working on something."

"You left me with all those kids, Elijah."

"Sweet little things, weren't they?" He chuckles, and I find myself softening a little. Damn that dimple and the blue eyes.

His smile warms my insides and I begin to liquefy at his close presence. My body shouts with a loud voice that it wants to be touched. Any connection, no matter how fleeting.

I stare at his face, his lips. The stubble on his cheeks.

I could drown in him and never surface.

He watches me in silence. Can he read my face again? Would it matter? It's just sex. Just once. It could be done and dusted and then I could move on.

Then I remember him in the kitchen the other night. That sheer loneliness that radiated from deep within.

My mouth is dry and I lick my lips.

Friends. Trust.

Two things I don't ever do. For good reason.

"What were your calls about?" How I get my vocal cords to untangle and work I don't know.

"My case." His eyes harden.

"Want to talk about it?"

He shakes his head. "No. Thank you, but no."

We stare at one another again. The silence is tangible. A weight that presses us down, pushing us to places where darkness reigns.

"Want to talk about your uncle?"

I shake my head, a lump lodging in my throat.

"Faith." My name is deep and rich from his tongue. "My life is so complicated."

I go to move away. I don't need him to reject me. I choose when and how, nobody else has that power.

"I don't care what your life is. It's your business not mine."

He catches my fingers. "I want you to care, as wrong as that is."

"Don't friends care?"

He raises an eyebrow, his lips curving just a fraction. "Don't friends trust?"

"That's what I've been told." I glare at him.

In one fluid movement he is off the bed holding his hand out to me. "Come on."

"Where are we going? Are we going to stand under the sprinklers again so you can see my bra?"

His face splits with a huge grin. "No, but maybe later. The sprinklers don't come on... he checks his watch, "for another four hours."

"Four hours, that's a long time to wait."

"Are you throwing yourself at me?"

"You'd know if I was."

Before I can move, or even try to duck out of his grasp, he has me pushed against the bedroom door. His lean and hard body pins me in place. His hands are on the bare skin of my arms, hard enough that if my ink wasn't permanent, it would have smudged.

He smells divine. Soap and musky wood notes. My heart stutters in my chest, banging loudly against my ribcage. My head whirls with his presence in my space.

"I would never want you just once. I'd always want to know more, to discover everything. Because under these."

His fingers trail my ink. "Is a story I'm sure I'd like to know."

I'm lost in his eyes, floating away to some crazy place where his words make sense. I shake my head. "I can't offer that." My response is bitter and broken.

His nose skims my jawline, and I hold my breath. "I know."

I stare at him sadly.

"You wanted to know why I only have five Facebook friends."

"You have five thousand." I quirk an eyebrow. He's still pushed up against me, his breath fanning across my face, making my stomach do crazy flips and my palms sweat.

"The real me," he says.

"Who is the real you, Eli?"

"Come, I'll show you." He shifts his body from mine and surprises me by grabbing my hand and leading me out into the outhouse hallway. He doesn't let go as he leads us through a set of doors back into the main house. I squirm my fingers. I don't want to give anyone any more reason to judge me, but he won't let go. "Relax," he says. "Mum and Gran have retired to their rooms." He sends me a sideways glance and a smirk. "They need a rest after having lots of strangers in their house."

I snort with laughter and he chuckles. His fingers squeeze mine tighter. At least I think they do. I could be imagining it.

We head up the stairs. "Oh my god, are you taking me to your bedroom?"

"Shh." He points at a dark door down at the end of a carpeted corridor. "That's Gran's apartment."

I pale a little. And I thought she'd sleep on a broomstick. We go up another flight of stairs and then another. "Seriously, this is very *Flowers in the Attic.* Are you taking me to where you've been locked up your whole childhood?"

He rolls his eyes. It's cute.

Finally, when we can go no higher and I'm close to suffering a nosebleed, he pushes on a plain wooden door. "Welcome to my room."

"Aha! I knew you were luring me to your room." I'm laughing, my eyes dancing as I walk into the room. I'm so distracted, it takes me a moment to work out what I'm looking at. "Why's this a studio?"

There are a handful of easels. All of them placed in different shafts of light.

I freeze on the spot. "What is this? I thought all my studios were downstairs?"

He leans against the doorframe, arms folded across his chest. "It's not all about you, Miss Hitchin." I gauge his expression, but quickly work out he's teasing.

"I hate to inform you." I've got a stupid smile plastered all over my face. "It's always about me."

I step into the room, spinning on the spot. "What's all this, Eli?" His name still sounds funny, but it's also creeping under my skin. Whispering its sweet nothings inside my skull.

Eli. Eli. Eli.

"Yesterday, I was trying to explain what my family were like. Now I'm making excuses for being so evasive all the time. I figured it was just easier to show you."

He's watching me with a hooded gaze. I step around an easel, my mouth open in total shock.

Hell.

My roses are there again. A bloom of them, beautifully recreated with oil paints. Thick and dense, they lift from the surface of the square canvas. A perfect blend of cream, peach, gold, and brown that together make a perfect dusky hue.

"All this from that photo?"

He shrugs and peels himself away from the doorway, filling the space—brighter, fairer, than all of his paintings. I can sense a spell of obsession weave itself around me. For his smell, for his fingers on my skin, for his kiss. Even worse than wanting all the physical things I know I shouldn't want —I want to know his story.

I'm rooted to the spot. Unable to run.

"Your room was an afterthought." He shoots me a shy smile.

"I'm happy to be an afterthought on this occasion."

"You might as well look at that one." He points to the furthest easel, and for some inexplicable reason, my stomach twists as I walk towards it.

It's me.

In black chiffon.

I've got a frown on my face, my lips pursed in disdain. It sums up our meeting at The Ritz in perfect accuracy.

"I keep thinking about that day." He's close, his breath brushing along the back of my neck.

"Why?" It's nothing more than a whisper.

"Because I was an arse, a complete fucking arse, but the thing is, Faith." He teases me around to stare into his deep blue eyes. "That's what this family does to me."

"So get out. I promise you it's not that hard."

He sweeps a searching gaze over my face and I twist a little, so he can't read me.

"I can't run."

"Why?"

There is no excuse for having your family disallow you from speaking the truth. I want to smack Jennifer over the head with one of the canvases if it will make her see sense. Why is he a bloody lawyer when he's so incredibly talented he could have the art society on their knees? And I'm not exaggerating here. I've never seen paintings like it.

"Because my dad ran, and I have to be more of a man than him."

Eighteen

We are sitting cross-legged on the floor of his once-bedroom-now-secret-studio. "So where did you study?" I ask. It's impossible to keep my eyes away from the dense oil roses. I want to touch them.

"I didn't." He shrugs, his face open and relaxed. Right now, he's only the guy in sliders. His smile is bashful, and he runs long fingers through his hair. "I did my GCSE art and then I was told I needed to focus on a job which would be more appropriate for the Fairclough name."

I shake my head in shock. "I cannot believe that. It sucks."

"Yeah." Another shrug lifts his shoulders. "I guess so. I got over it, did what I was told."

"So how did you manage to wrangle this summer art club idea?"

His lips curve into a delicious smile. "It was a compromise."

"Between what? I can't imagine your mother compromising about anything."

The attic is calm and soothing. The kind of place you could sit for hours and read a book in slanting rays of sunlight, or paint endlessly until the sun dipped down too low for natural lighting. There is something Eli about it. The man in sliders who'd turn up unannounced just to apologise.

That growing intense craving pinches my tummy and I shift my eyes away from his golden skin and spend some time studying the wood floor. It doesn't help. "I was engaged, as you know."

Don't I just. An inexplicable stab of jealousy twists in my chest when I think of him with that stick insect socialite. Someone like Eli, the guy whose heart is smeared in paint all over these canvases will never be happy with a woman like that. I just know it.

Not that he would be happy with me either—that's not the way I work—but he deserves more than someone immaculately groomed and living a veneer of an existence.

Call me judgemental.

"And."

His eyes bore into mine. "It wasn't right. There was discussion about how the situation could be retrieved and I suggested the art camp."

I nod, slowly trying to get the story of this man to sit right in my head.

It's just the two of us, and I like it... I like him. I can't remember the last time I thought that about anyone. Normally it's just a desire for a physical connection. But this is something else. I want to know everything about him. I want to know what makes him who he is. Why he paints what he does. Why he does what he does.

"So you can only date someone who is good for the family name?" I think this is what he's hinting at.

He doesn't move, doesn't nod his confirmation, but it's right there in the depths of his eyes. "That's bollocks," I add. "Even Prince William married a commoner."

He snorts and finally shakes his head, although it's at the wrong moment for my liking. "Rumour is Catherine was groomed from a young age to meet William. Do you think it's a coincidence they met at uni and it was all happily ever after?"

I stare at him in shock. "Really?"

"Course."

"So, has someone been groomed to marry you?"

He waves his hand and chuckles. "No."

"I'm sensing a but..."

"But my family have made it clear, I follow family protocol, or I'm cut off."

"From the money?"

"From everything—out the door, don't come back."

My hands curl into tight fists when I think of the injustice of it. "So you can't make a choice about your job, who you date, what you do in your spare time?"

"What they don't know doesn't hurt them." There's a dangerous twinkle in his eyes. Is he talking about me? My stomach flutters but I beat it down. I'm not even considering that. His situation is even more fucked-up than mine and I've had enough fucked-upness for one lifetime.

"I feel bad for you. And I thought it was crap being dragged up in a tattoo shop in Brighton."

He scoots closer and uses gentle fingers to lift my hand, turning my arm this way and that so he can follow the traces of patterns weaving along my skin. "They really are extraordinary. Did your uncle do them all?"

I follow one creeping chain of flowers which runs along my inner arm. "Most of them. Some I did, but I'm awfully right-handed so it's hard for me to do anything other than on my lower body." I point to the small delicate flowers that create part of the chain. "Some Dan did."

"Who's Dan?" The blues burn my face like a spotlight.

"Dan is Uncle Al's son." I can't help but smile.

"And you two were together?"

Laughing, I shake my head. "No, although Al is determined we will marry. It's his dying wish. Or so he said the other week."

"I don't like this Dan already." Elijah smiles but my heart beats erratically. What does he care if I'm supposed to marry my old childhood friend? Not that I would.

"We grew up together, we had an unconventional childhood. Our fathers owned a shared shop, so Dan and I were just wild over the summer months, running the streets and then eventually when we were old enough, we learned the trade."

"But you wanted more?"

My shutters snap down with a bang. "I don't talk about it."

"Talk about what?"

"Anything."

"Why you ran away from Brighton?"

He confuses me with his quick-fire questions. "No." I shake my head.

"Why you're covered in tattoos?"

"Are my tattoos a problem?" Jeez this guy.

"Not for me, but you are the one who covers them up."

"It's not ladylike to have this many." My cheeks burn.

"You don't strike me as being the kind of woman who worries about being ladylike."

I start to get up. "What do you know about it?" I'd die if he knew about my physical cravings. The way I am when I need to pay an insurmountable price and I'll do it anywhere with anyone.

My breath begins to come in ragged gasps. Panic.

"Why do you only have sex with someone once?" His hand grabs my arm and stops me from running.

"Why do you sit in your kitchen and get drunk by yourself?"

"Why aren't you finishing your degree when you are so talented you could end up anywhere."

That does it. I slice at his grip with my arm, knocking him free. "You don't get to say that. Why don't you fight your family and do what you want?"

"I do what I want. I help people."

I wave my hand at the easels and glorious canvases.

His arms drop to his side. His face when it meets mine makes my heart still. "That's just fairy-tale."

And then I'm flying into his arms, winding my fingers around his neck, pushing my lips against his, hungry and desperate all at once. He groans a little and grabs onto me tight, anchoring me to his firm body. Everything about him is challenging. Electric. He bites on my bottom lip, swiping it after with his tongue, and I groan into his mouth.

"I'm not sleeping with you," he mumbles against my lips.

I go to wrestle away. How dare he presume.

He holds me tight, levering me against his rock-hard body. Even from just one kiss, his desire for me is pressed against my hip. When he's sure I'm not going to run, he releases his hold on my arms and slides his palms down my bare arms. A shudder rumbles deep inside me.

This guy, he confuses me. Makes me want to run, makes me want to stay. Makes me question everything.

His forehead rests against mine, his breath fanning my face. I want him to kiss me again. I also want to smack him over the head with the heaviest object I can find. "I'm not going to sleep with you, because as I said downstairs, I don't think once will be enough. And that's all you offer, right?"

He bends slightly so he can stare me right in the eyes. God, I hate his directness.

"Yes. That's all I can offer."

"Then it's no deal for me." He presses closer, his erection painfully jabbing me in the soft stretch of skin along from my thigh. "Believe me, I want to. I've never met anyone like you. Not ever. You make me challenge everything. I shouldn't even be here right now, but I am, because of you." His eyes won't break contact and I start to squirm. "But once won't be enough. I will want all of you, over and over again until I know you inside out."

"Is that what you said to your fiancée?" My instinctive need to hurt and lash out, to protect myself flares into action.

He grins. He actually grins in my face. "Not working." His lips dip to my neck, kissing along my throat to my ear which he nibbles with sharp teeth. "When you are screaming for more, then I might change my mind."

What a cocky shit!

"You are unbelievable." I push against his chest and slip out of his grasp. My legs are wobbling, but I ignore them. "I suggest you go and be wherever you need to be and leave me alone."

I march past him onto the landing.

"Friends don't run away," he calls after me.

"Friends don't act like arseholes," I shout back.

"Sometimes they do. Look it up, it's part of the friendship definition."

I pause on the landing below, uncaring it's right by the Wicked Witch of the West's wing/ apartment/whatever. "Kiss my arse, Elijah."

He leans over the banister, grinning widely. "I fully intend to, Miss Hitchin."

What! The gall of the man.

I stomp downstairs and out of the building by the nearest door I can find.

This house is crazy.

One of the pathways cutting through the formal gardens leads away from the house and I crunch down the gravel. What is he like? I can't work out if he's just full of it, or if that's just some front he's putting on.

I hate being challenged. I like things safe, at an arm's length, with me in control. But when Elijah is near, he blurs it all with his fast questions and those fricking blue eyes until I'm spinning.

"Hey," a voice calls, and I turn to find Tabitha jogging after me. "Where are you going?"

"Anywhere your brother isn't." I don't stop walking but I do slow my pace, so she can catch up with me.

"Where's the nearest pub? I could do with a bloody strong drink. Do you want to come with me?"

Her face lights up for a moment before dropping in an instant. "I'm not allowed to go out really without my mum knowing where."

"Aren't you eighteen?" I question her with a pointed glance.

"Yes, but Mum's always worried. She doesn't want us to get into trouble."

"What trouble could you get into with me?"

Tabitha sniggers a little. "Who knows?"

I look at my tattoos. "These aren't a statement of a corrupt youth."

"Oh, no, I didn't mean anything by that."

"It's fine, I'm all too aware of what your mother and grandmother probably think of me."

"Well, if I was you I'd take that as a compliment, because they only like the most boring people I've ever had the misfortune to meet."

"I feel much better." I grin and point to the boundary wall. "Come on. This isn't a prison, let's get out of here for an hour. We've got another exhausting day in front of us tomorrow."

"And the day after, and the day after that."

Nineteen

"I think everyone had fun though, right?" I sip my wine, it slides down so nicely. Chilled and crisp, it's the perfect antidote to a long day; a stopper on my emotional overload about Al, and a good way to forget Elijah bloody Fairclough.

"Yeah, they really did. Have you thought about being a teacher when you've graduated?"

I pull a face. "I don't think I'm going to graduate."

Tabitha sips at her own wine. She'd looked dubious when I'd ordered it. I'm guessing that although she's at the legal age, she hasn't had much opportunity for partaking in alcohol. But with every sip, she's warming up to my rebellious tendencies. "Why aren't you going to graduate?"

With a highly unattractive grimace, I take another sip of wine, and then another. "Your big brother Peter let it slip my lecturer was—*is*—married."

"So? What does that matter?"

I have to remind myself I'm not talking to Abi, who's largely desensitised to my extreme behaviour. "Because I had a fling with him, though, admittedly short." I gulp down another mouthful of wine, keeping my attention focused on her shocked face. "But it's not about that." I don't know how many times I'm supposed to keeping saying this. It's getting repetitive even to me.

"What is it about then? Apart from you having sex with your teacher." Her face widens in awe. "That's so cool. Not that I'd ever want to have sex with any of the teachers at St Mary's, they are all female, and all nuns for a start."

"I'm sorry, what?" I shake my head and try to make sense of what she's saying.

"Nuns. You know? They ran our school."

I'm wide-eyed. "Wow."

Tabitha grins. "I'd say wow, it was interesting."

With a wink, I lean over the table and drop my voice. "Was it all Enid Blyton, anchovy paste on toast, and pillow fights?"

"Anchovies on what?" Tabitha makes a gagging noise which causes the woman behind the bar with the big bust to look over with a frown.

"Come on, you must have read Enid Blyton?"

She shakes her head. "It's no wonder he likes you so much. Eli's always talking about books like they are real."

"Really?" I can't help but absorb this little nugget of information.

"Hell yeah, he's such a geek. You know Peter used to bully him so bad when they were kids because Eli always wanted to read, or make stuff indoors, and Peter said he wasn't built like proper boys."

"Well that's cruel." And I can assure Peter that he's built exactly like other boys. I might not have seen what's under the clothing, but I'm highly skilled at judging hidden form.

"Siblings, right?" She shrugs. "I was always out of it because I was so much younger."

"That is a massive age gap."

"Ten years between Eli and I, but he always looked after me. Peter I never really saw. He was off to Prep school and was happy there. Eli was a home bird. He hated Prep and being away from home."

I'm not entirely sure what a Prep school is, but I know it's something rich people go to, and really that's all I need to know. I can imagine Peter there all too well. Then I can see those big blue eyes of Elijah absorbing everything and seeing it in shades of depths of colour. Real, painful, and alive.

"When did your dad leave?" I ask. Without even thinking about it, my gaze drops to the teardrops I have running along the inside of my right wrist.

Her eyes hold mine. "When I was two."

"And you still see him?" Elijah didn't say much in his studio once he'd tried to explain his weird relationship with his family, and I've got to colour in the blanks somehow.

"No."

"What, never?"

She shakes her head and I know to drop it.

"What about you? Do you have any siblings?"

A cold creeping crawl spindles sharp tingly claws down my spine. "No." I drain my glass.

"That's sad."

"Tragic." I motion to her glass. "Want another one?"

She nibbles the inside of her mouth. "We should get back."

"One more and then we will get back for a nice sensible night before tomorrow's fun."

Tabitha squints her eyes and I think I probably should have asked her if she's even drunk before. I guess I just thought all teenagers did. Maybe that's just in Brighton.

Three more wines later and Tabitha has wisely

switched onto orange juice—straight. The wine is flooding my veins, hot molten lava of reckless inhibition. It calls to me, crooning my favourite song. My legs are a little weak and heavy and I'm beginning to think how lovely it would be to touch someone, to have hands on my flushed skin and to lose myself to that one desperate moment of euphoria.

"You know." I lean over the table again, although I don't think my voice is as quiet as it should be—not that I really care. "There's a serious lack of talent in this pub. Is the whole village like this?"

One old man in the corner turns to look at me and tilts his glass. Chuckling, I tip mine back. Yeah, buddy, I'm a bit drunk. I'm not fricking legless.

"I thought you and Eli were having a thing?" Tabitha asks. She sounds innocent and sane. Clearly, she needs to have her head read.

"Why on earth would you think that?"

Okay, so maybe we've kissed twice. Maybe if I would allow myself to think about them, I'd admit that they were probably the most electric and seductive kisses I've ever experienced. But, she doesn't know this. No one knows I think that—especially not Elijah.

"Oh, sorry. I must have misread something."

I narrow my gaze and wave my glass at her, sloshing white wine on the table. "What?"

She shifts, uncomfortable, and studies the puddle of wine on the wood. "Nothing. It's just these days I don't see him much, and he's been here a lot since you came, even though that case he's working on is getting nasty."

"Nasty, how?"

She shakes her head, clearly I'm never going to find out about this case.

"He's here because this is his project." I don't know if

she knows about his painting, so I button up tight. I won't spill secrets. I slump back in my chair and wish I could erase the memory of that hungry kiss and how it felt when his hands ran along my ink, caressing the skin of my arms. "And honestly, if it was just him and I left in Bowsley because the world had been taken over by flesh eating zombies, I still wouldn't consider him."

Tabitha chuckles into her orange juice. "No, why?"

"Why?" I'm getting into this. I gulp another two mouthfuls of wine. "He's obnoxious for a start, I mean seriously how big is his ego? Secondly, he's so hot and cold, it's like he doesn't know who he wants to be, and thirdly." I pause for breath.

"Are you stuck for a third thing, Faith? What a relief."

Holy crap. I spin a little on my wooden stool and see the delectable shape of Elijah behind my shoulder. Oh god. I burn a hundred shades of red all at once.

He looks utterly delicious. Pale ripped jeans cling to his hips and thighs, and a navy T-shirt fits across his chest with a snugness I'd be happy to explore with my fingers. I need to close my mouth and stop staring.

He wasn't wearing that earlier, but hell, does he look good. Best yet, even better than any of the suits.

"Did I mention obnoxious?" I force my gaze away from his smirking mouth and glare at Tabitha. "Nice one. How long was he there for?"

Letting out a pealing laugh she claps her hands together. "Long enough."

"What are you two doing here?" He sits on the spare stool at the table and absorbs all the damn space.

"Getting fucking drunk." Okay, the wine is definitely in charge now, steaming through my body.

"Elijah," the man from the corner calls. "Can you get

rid of her? She doesn't stop talking." He points at me incriminatingly, and I scowl back.

"Just because I'm not *that* drunk, there's no need to be rude."

Tabitha almost howls with laughter, but I'm just staring at the blues, waiting to see what he's going to say next.

He stares at me, one side of his lips hitched in a slight curve. "I'm so not covering your arse when you're hanging like a dog tomorrow."

I down the end of my glass. "I'm a true professional."

He stands and holds out a hand. "Come on, Faith, let's get you guys home."

"No! I like it here. There's no atmosphere at Boring Hall."

He leans down and places hands under my elbows, easily lifting me from the stool. "How about I make sure you're not bored?"

With a circular wave of my hand, I pull a 'yeah, right' face. "All talk and ego."

"Come on." He leads me by the elbow and I wave goodbye to the pub, reassuring them all I will be back to see them soon. He's chuckling as we land on the narrow pavement outside the pub. It's much darker than I thought it would be.

"How did you know where to find us Mr. Killjoy?"

"Tabitha texted me."

"Say whaaaaat?" I glare at his little sister. "Traitor."

I start to laugh and then hold in a breath as Elijah wraps an arm around my waist. "I'm worried you're going to fall down," he whispers in my ear, and my stomach thinks it's a gold medal gymnast flying across the high bars.

"I'm not that drunk," I lie and try to shrug free, but he holds tight.

"Humour me."

Tabitha is staring at the pavement as we walk under limited street lights, pretending she can't see what's playing out next to her. I can't remember the last time someone wrapped their arms around me like this. The last time I walked home with a guy not knowing what was going to happen, butterflies of expectation taking to flight in the pit of my tummy.

Everything unknown.

Everything unexpected.

These are things I don't allow in. I steal a glance up at him in the dark shadows and find him already watching me, his lips curved like he can read every damn thought I'm having.

"Just relax," he murmurs, and goose bumps prickle my skin.

Relax? Is he crazy? I'm drunk and there's a gorgeous man walking me home with his arm around my waist like he can't see all the ink on my skin, like he doesn't think I'm a certain type of girl because of the way I look.

Bowsley isn't far, I think, but then it's kind of hard to tell. The fresh air is turning the white wine into some narcotic concoction and the small lane lined with neat hedgerows is starting to whirl and move. I cling onto Elijah a little tighter. And it's nothing to do with his man smell and the warm hardness of his chest beneath my arms. It's because I'm slowly losing the use of my legs. "Did I even eat today?" I ask no one in particular.

"No," They both say in unison.

"That explains some stuff."

"It's something I will be dealing with tomorrow." Elijah's gaze stays focused on me in the dark.

"What?"

"How many meals have you had since you came to Bowsley?"

I shrug. "I've had a few bread rolls that I can remember."

"That's what I thought."

I pull a face at him and we carry on walking along, me stumbling every few steps, and Elijah guiding the way back.

When we get down the long drive of the Hall, Elijah makes sure Tabitha is safely inside the front door, muttering something low under his breath I don't catch. I slump on the wide stone steps, I can sleep right now and be as happy as if I were in a feather bed.

"Whoa, you can't sleep here."

"It's fine." I bat him away. "I'll move before the kids come tomorrow. They'll never know." I close my eyes. I'm going to dream about kisses and wine and then maybe some more kisses.

He doesn't answer and finally I open my eyes to find him watching me thoughtfully. "What ya doing?"

"Deciding how heavy you are."

"Like an elephant."

He snorts and before I can move, he sweeps me up into his arms, pressing me tight against his chest. "Newborn elephant at the very most."

I whack him with my hand, but then drop my head against his chest as he carries me, lulling me with a wonderful rocking motion with every step he takes.

"You're a funny woman." It surprises me when he speaks and jolts me out of my dozing slumber.

"Funny haha, or funny strange?"

He grins, and it's beautiful, shining in the dark. "Both."

I place my hand on his cheek, holding his face as I stare

at him intently. "I'm totally and utterly fucked-up. And you should beware of damaged goods."

When he shrugs, it squeezes me even tighter against his chest.

I can see the shape of the outhouse looming into focus and my fingers slide around his neck, smoothing into the short hair at the back of his head. Stretching towards him, I place my lips against his, waiting for him to hesitate, to push me away. But he does neither, as the night air and a million possibilities swirl around us.

"Stay," I mutter into the warm skin of his neck, and leaning into the door behind him, he snatches the latch and lets us in.

Twenty

The door closes with a soft click and it's like every second of the past few weeks is screeching to a halt in the very moment.

"You said you weren't going to sleep with me." I'm regretting the last glass of wine, but maybe if I hadn't sunk it down I would never have uttered that four-letter-word.

God, his hands are on me. Warm and firm, they slide up my skin, and I shiver despite the heat burning from his touch. With firm fingers he pulls on the band holding my hair and frees the blonde strands until they frame my face. His dark and deep gaze sweeps along every inch of me.

"I've never seen a picture like you before."

My knees tremble with the intensity of his words and a dark licking flame kindles in the pit of my belly, stoking a fire of desire.

I want him to kiss me like I have never wanted to be kissed before. I want to be consumed with that fire like I was earlier in his studio.

"Wait a minute." I push him away a fraction, although I regret the space between us instantly. "What Elijah have I got here right now?"

He smiles, his head cocked to the side. "There's more than one?"

I grasp his chin with my fingers and hold his face still as I stare deep into his eyes. "You know there is."

"Do you care?" It's a tight question.

"No."

"Sure?"

"Kiss me already."

And he does, consuming every molecule of oxygen in my body as his lips crush against mine, tilting my chin with his fingers and dancing his tongue into the depths of my mouth. It's unreal. No one can kiss that well. Every movement he makes is like I've known it for a million years and never tasted it before, all at once.

He pulls on my bottom lip with his teeth and I groan, throwing my head back so he can have access to my throat. I want him so bad, my legs are shaking. I want him inside me, making all the bad times right. I have this inexplicable understanding in my soul that he could. For every crest I've cruised to an unsatisfied ending, I know he could turn that around—it's all there in his kiss.

He guides me to the bed and pushes me gently down onto the mattress, straddling my waist, and pressing softly on my hips to keep me in place. "Some rules," he says.

Now I know why he's pinned me down. "Rules?" My head's whirling a little. I really shouldn't have had that extra glass of wine.

"Don't get all stroppy, but I'm not sleeping with you tonight."

"Why did you say you'd stay, if you don't want to have sex?" He's not going to do this to me again is he?

"I don't have to have sex with you to enjoy you." He leans down and kisses the end of my nose, then quicker than

I can guess his move—not hard after three large wines—he grabs my hands and pins them above my head.

"Way to make me feel cheap."

His eyes narrow. "There is nothing cheap about you."

I laugh, but it's a disgusted, dirty sound.

He leans closer, his lips skimming mine, before shifting to my neck and running up the sensitive skin to my ear. "Trust me."

I thrash against his hold, but he's solid and I can't shift him, not even an inch. Under his slender but broad frame is a steely strength I hadn't even guessed at. "Trust me," he says again, his blues holding mine.

"I can't. It's not that easy."

His gaze is unflinching, his lips tracing maddening paths across my skin. "Trust me, Faith."

There's something in the way he says my name. Somehow it weaves all the tiny moments we've snatched up until now together. It's him in his suit shaking my hand, it's him in his sliders stood on my doorstep, him drinking in the kitchen alone, and him sitting cross-legged on his studio floor. His secret studio where he hides his soul.

A tear slips out of the corner of my eye. "You don't know what you're asking."

His thumb rubs across my cheek, wiping the trail of water. "I want to set you free, Faith." His words kill me. They slice me clean in half, pulling down my defences and my barriers. "Do you want to be free?"

Another tear escapes. I want to be free of the past, the hurt, the broken promises. I nod, and his mouth meets mine in a hungry kiss, and I allow myself to submit to the moment. He doesn't release my hands and I'm desperate to touch him, to run my hand through his hair, to trace the muscles hiding under that navy shirt. He holds them tight, keeping the pace of our kiss under his control, moving his lips languorously slow, licking and nibbling, exploring my tongue with gentle flicks of his. "You taste so good," he whispers in my ear, and just like that the emotional tidal wave is replaced with a wildfire.

I squirm, writhing my legs together under the weight of his body. He lets go of one of his hands, and I pull, testing his grip, but he still has the other firmly clasped around my wrist. His palm smooths down my arm, torturously slow. I note his eyes are on my ink, drinking them in as they swirl on my pale skin. His thumb runs along the inner edge of my arm and it sends a dart of desire straight to the heat between my legs. The hand smooths along the swell of my breast, his thumb gently circling across my nipple through my vest. I moan at the delicate, barely there touch. It's butterfly soft, the briefest of caresses, but it's more evocative than any touch I've felt in a long time. I arch my back when he lifts my top, exposing my stomach. I hold my breath and wait to see how he reacts to my skin. When he meets my gaze, there is something indescribable in his depths. I want it to be desire, but I can't believe it. It could be worry, disgust.

"Stop thinking." He grins, dipping his head to kiss my stomach, his lips working along the Celtic cross I have on my ribcage, across the butterflies with purple wings that are beating just as hard beneath my skin. He lifts my top and bra until my breast and nipple are exposed, catching the hardened bud in his mouth, gently sucking, and applying the slightest pressure with his teeth until I'm arching my back off the bed.

"Please let me go so I can touch you."

He lifts his head, his dark gaze on my face. "I'll let you go, but this is about you, not me."

"What? no." I begin to pull away, struggling to get him off me. "I can't do that; it's not how it works."

He stops fighting me and does the simplest most beautiful thing anyone has ever done. He lifts my hands and kisses the sensitive skin on my palm. "I'm working out how it normally is for you."

I don't have anything to say and I turn my face away.

"Faith." He turns my face back to his, planting a delicate kiss on my lips.

His kiss unlocks a secret door deep inside, and with a deep shaky breath I lay back on the bed, lifting my arms above my head. I watch as he gives a slow smile and then returns to the pattern of kisses he was planting across my midriff.

I won't move. No matter what happens I won't let myself run away. I close my eyes and give myself over to the sensation of his mouth on my skin. His lips are masterful no matter where they are. The stubble on his chin scratches and it's almost as intoxicating as his kisses. His hand reaches back up for my breast, squeezing it gently, running the nipple under the palm of his hand. When his lips find it again, I stretch up and give him access to pull off my top and unhook my bra. He sweeps a gaze from under hooded lids along the various patterns over my skin and pushes me back down, kissing my other breast, sucking it deep into his mouth until fire shoots down to my core One hand palms down my stomach, unhooking the button on my trousers and slipping under the waistband. Normally, I'd pull away now, but I remember the promise I made to myself and hold my breath as his fingers slip under the band of my knickers, his middle fingers circling around my clit. Oh God. I scrunch the bedsheets in my fists as I fight the need to pull away, with an overriding ache to let him go further.

"Relax." He presses his other hand onto my tummy and pushes me back into the mattress. I didn't even know I'd bucked off the bed.

I close my eyes as he starts to sweep a steady rhythm in a circular motion. Every so often his fingers dip and dive, slipping between my wet folds, and each time he does I lift my hips to meet his touch. But before I can beg him to press deeper, to go some place I've never allowed anyone before, he settles back to a smaller, infuriatingly intense circle right over my clit.

I think I'm going to die. My breath is coming in short pants as I try to keep up with the movement of his hand. I want to fight it off. I also want to drown in the sensations forever.

I lift my hips, begging him silently to push his fingers further. My clit pulses and tingles as it loses his focus, and he dips one long finger inside me and then another.

"Oh God, Eli."

His lips slant over mine and my breath rushes into his mouth in heady gasps. Another finger joins the others and I want to explode, then he twists them, finding a sensitive spot I didn't even know existed. With every thrust he presses on the area and my gasped breaths become pants of exertion as I try to hold myself together.

"Let it go."

I shake my head. "I can't."

His fingers aren't listening, and they won't stop their pounding explorations. I spread my legs wider, against all my own willpower. My body takes over, leading to places I never want to go.

A surging tingle begins in my toes and I push my feet

into the sheets. It sweeps scorching hot up my legs. His tongue is in my mouth, his other hand holding me close as his fierce fingers push me over a vast edge. I cry and grunt at the same time, curling over his hand, clenching it between my legs as I shudder.

I can't look at him, but he won't move his damn hand. It's still jammed up my vagina.

This is the bit when I walk away.

"Okay?"

"Yes."

"Look at me."

Somehow, I force myself to open my eyes. He's close, his breath hot on my face. He smiles slowly, and it calms me just a little, although not enough. My instinct to run is too deep. I wiggle my hips to try to get him to remove his fingers. "Can you move? Please?"

"No."

"What?"

"I said no. You aren't running, Faith."

"Jeez."

He laughs. He actually laughs in my face.

I hate him again even if he did just give me a thunderous orgasm using his fingers.

To my absolute horror, he starts to dip his fingers deep within me again. Even more horrifying is the way my body reignites instantly. The heat which had only been quenched a couple of moments before is back like it never dissipated.

"Have you ever let anyone do that to you before?"

I glare at him, my heart thumping in my chest all the while his fingers lick and stroke, teasing and warming me up from the inside out.

"No. Why are you torturing me like this?"

He frowns, and I regret my choice of words instantly. This is messed up. I'm so messed up.

"Torture?" He lifts an eyebrow. "Torture, really?"

"I'm sorry, I didn't mean that."

His hand is still between my legs. His fingers flex, and I let out a low moan.

"Awful torture. It's downright shitty of me to make you moan like that."

His fingers delve extra deep and he dips his head, edging the waistband of my trousers down, his lips following the exposed skin.

Holy crap, he's not...?

"No. Please, Elijah. Please don't do that."

"Do what?" He lowers further, opening my legs with his elbows. "This? Is it torturous?" His tongue sweeps along the super-sensitive skin of my clit, flicking, and then sucking hard.

"Shit," I bellow, bucking from the bed. He catches me, tilting my pelvis until it's almost a cup he can drink from, as his lips suck and his tongue probes. His thumb slides inside me, massaging the walls of my vagina as I ride it out into his mouth. "Elijah!"

When I've crested the wave of my second orgasm, he pulls back, pecking gentle kisses on every bit of skin he finds. Pulling down my trousers, he places my knickers back into a suitable position, but quickly discards the rest of my clothes onto the floor.

"Come here, my runaway girl."

"I need to pay you back." I look at him in confusion. Does he want to snuggle? Surely, he wants something in return?

"Another night, Sunshine. It's late. Come, we need to sleep."

I settle down next to him, but as his arm wraps around me tight and he slides his chin onto my shoulder, I have to ask. "What are you doing?"

"I'm staying. It's what you wanted."

My heart pounds for the millionth time tonight and I grin. And that's how I go to sleep, breaking every rule I've ever made for myself.

Twenty-One

"Come on, Faith. I don't know why you keep hiding from me."

I won't meet his eyes. "I'm not hiding."

He chuckles and leans in for what seems like a genuine hug. "I'd never hurt you. I love you."

My skin tingles, my faulty flight-or-fight alarm sounds loudly in my brain. "It's not right. I know that now. You need to stay away from me before I-"

There's a painful pause. "Before you what, Faithy? What are you going to do? You're just as much to blame as I am, everyone would know that." His fingers tilt my chin. "Everyone would know you begged me to, because that's the type of girl you are. The type of girl you'll always be."

The alarm in my head and heart screeches like a siren. Run, Faith. Run...

I don't. I'm frozen to the spot. The sirens screeching as my soul burns around me.

"Faith, wake up."

I come around at once, blinking into the darkness. Elijah's face is close, his hands on my face.

"What?"

His thumbs caress my cheeks. Even in the dark I can

sense the intensity in his face and my heart which was pounding as it woke from sleep starts to speed and race.

"You were screaming; shouting in your sleep."

I flush, thankful he can't see it. "It's just a bad dream, I have them all the time."

He shakes his head and his lips kiss the tip of my nose. Such a small action makes my heart squeeze with delight. The foul memories of the past fade away. "That's not a dream, that was a terror."

"And what do you know about terrors?" I reach up and kiss his lips, leading the kiss with a bravery that's easy to find in the darkness. I can't believe he stayed, that he's still here. More than the fact he's still here, is the fact I'm okay with it.

"Tabitha had them as a toddler, right up until school," he says when I release his warm lips. "I used to be in the room next to hers and hearing her scream like that used to make my blood run cold. I'd run into her room and find her just staring through me pointing at things I couldn't see."

I snuggle back down onto the mattress and shyly pull him down alongside me. This is all so odd, but at the same time I wouldn't have it any other way. Elijah Fairclough is turning everything I know on its head. "It was just a dream." I kiss him gently. "Forget about it and go back to sleep."

"Who's Aiden?" His question freezes my insides into sharpened icicles.

"No one." My heart's beating so fast. "Come, let's sleep."

"Still want me to stay?" His question is low and soft, and it melts the ice in my gut.

I grin, a stupid wide smile. "Yes."

My eyelashes flutter shut and try to push the remnants of the dream away. It's not easy and I'm floating in and out of a light sleep when a phone rings. "Al!" I launch myself from the bed. My palms slick with cold sweat as the call I've been dreading arrives.

Elijah catches my hand. "Faith, it's okay. It's my phone." He leans over the edge of the bed and rifles in his pockets to look for his mobile. When he has it in his hand he frowns. His sleep smeared face is illuminated by the glow of the back-lit screen and I watch as he answers and mumbles a hello. My crashing nerves start to settle for a whole two seconds until he jumps from the bed, his lithe athletic frame moving with more speed and grace than I've ever seen. He really is beautiful, even when it's silly o'clock in the morning and he's jumping out of my bed.

"When did this happen?" He's pulling on his jeans and I'm guessing that's the end of my first ever all night snuggle.

I watch silently, sitting on the bed covered in a sheet, as he runs his hands through his hair and tugs on his trainers.

"I'm not in London but I'm leaving in five." He pauses, and I think he's forgotten that I'm actually there because the expression of pain that carves his face steals my breath. "Just wait, I'll get this sorted. Don't let him speak to anyone until I'm there. An hour most."

An hour? Bowsley Hall is more than hour away from London.

He turns to me as he disconnects the call. "I've got to go."

"Really?" My reply is tarter than I intended.

"I'm sorry, something's come up."

"Sure." Something's always coming up. This is what he does. One minute he's here, the next he's gone. He's done it the entire time I've known him. "Want to share? Can I do anything?"

I already know his answer before he says it. "Not now."

He leans down and lifts my face, placing a tender kiss on my lips. "I know you think this is my get out, but it's not. And if you promise to not hold a grudge all day, I'll explain later."

I greedily eat up his kiss despite myself. "Don't worry, you don't owe me anything."

He shakes his head. "Don't do that. Don't make everything about you, some pity parade. I'll be back, and I promise to talk."

"Seriously. I said don't worry, I hate talking anyway."

"Then I'll think of something else to do, but right now I need to go." He's still hesitating, so I make it easier for him by lying down and turning my back. I think he's gone; the door opens and a sliver of dawn slides across the room. But then his lips are on my cheek. "Thank you for last night, Sunshine."

Then he's gone.

And I don't know why he calls me "Sunshine", because in truth it's always been the furthest thing to what I am.

I sleep for a couple more hours and then make my way down to breakfast. It's a full house and I groan inwardly. That last glass of wine and lack of sleep are giving me a headache I could happily live without. I grumble a hello and slouch my way to any empty chair as far away from the perfect shiny white bob of the Wicked Witch of the West. Jennings is hovering with a pot of coffee and the moment I'm in my seat he pours me a cup and bends low to speak into my ear. "I believe you like it strong."

"Hmph." Is my exceptionally mature reply.

He turns and goes, but is back before I've even taken a sip, sliding a plate of crispy bacon towards me. "Master Elijah said you'd need breakfast before the arrivals came."

I go to push the plate away, a sour taste turning my lips

down at the edges, but I am bloody hungry. I can't even ask Jennings how Elijah managed to tell him I'd need breakfast when he left at four in the morning, but he fills in the blanks for me. "Sir called from his office and explained you'd be running today by yourself."

The Wicked Witch of the West tuts. "I knew this would happen. We will have hapless youngsters trapping all over the Persian rugs and Elijah won't be here to take responsibility for them."

I glare at her as I chew a piece of bacon and swallow. "I have responsibility for them. That's my job, what I was hired for."

She gives a dainty snort. What is her problem with me? I've never said more than a few words to her, but she literally hates me on sight.

Jennifer cuts in and pulls my pointed glare away from her mother. "Faith, do you think once the afternoon session is completed we can talk about the summer ball? We need to discuss the ballroom and how you plan to display the art you are going to be producing over the next few weeks."

I stare at her blankly because I don't have a clue what she's talking about. "I'm sorry, summer ball?"

"Yes, The Bowsley Ball. It is held every year in the second week of August, and this year we will be showcasing your project. Elijah hopes it will bring in backing for future events."

"Oh, okay." This is all news, but I can sense the shrewd gaze of the wicked witch on me and I refuse to be flustered. "Any particular theme? I could use it to guide the work I do with the kids." I shrug. It sounds vaguely professional and like I might stand a chance of knowing what I'm talking about.

"Theme is your choice, but I will need to get invites

sent out by next Monday if you could confirm by the weekend?"

"Sure. And this is held after the end of the project, so I don't have to attend?" I nod encouragingly.

"Of course you will attend." Jennifer frowns in confusion. "Elijah wants all the students here, and their families." There's a loud tut from the other side of the table. "The press will love it." Ah, and here we have the real reason why Jennifer is so onboard.

It's not easy to force a smile in her direction as I nod my agreement.

"And Saskia will be able to help you with your dress. The estate will cover the cost of your outfit for the event, it would be only fair."

Oh my god. That's it.

"I can assure you I'm more than happy to purchase my own dress."

Jennifer waves her hand at me as if the conversation isn't worth continuing with, but the wicked witch pipes in with, "It's okay, Saskia is highly skilled. She will find something to cover those tattoos."

I clatter my cup down onto the saucer, and Tabitha, who hasn't even spoken a word, looks at me in alarm.

"Thank you, but that won't be necessary." My chair almost tips again as I push back from the table.

It's not Jennifer who speaks. It's evil Granbaroness. "I can assure you it is."

I begin to walk away. I don't have to deal with this. I'm not part of their family. Their rules don't mean anything to me. She speaks louder. "And could we please ask you don't take Tabitha out into the village without our prior approval?"

I spin on my heel and meet her serene, oddly unlined

face. There is no sweet granny in sight here. "She's eighteen. She can go to the village if she wants."

"You, my dear, may have been allowed to run wild as a child, but that is not how the Fairclough children behave."

Children...?

I have nothing to say to this, so I walk from the dining room and along the plush patterned carpets to the outhouses, where I can breathe, sliding my phone out of my pocket.

Faith Hitchin: Ball? Saskia? Are you all still considered minors?

I don't get a reply until much later. I'm too busy to look anyway before we grab a bite to eat at lunch.

Eli Jones: I was going to mention the ball, I promise.

I stick my tongue out at the phone.

Faith Hitchin: Sure you were

I have another thought.

Faith Hitchin: Does Saskia dress you, too?

Eli Jones: Lol. Only my suits.

Did he just lol me?

Eli Jones: I'll be home later, we can talk.

Faith Hitchin: I thought this wasn't your home?

Eli Jones: It's growing in appeal.

With a grin, I put my phone back in my pocket. I should have asked how his four in the morning emergency went. God, I'm like a selfish teenager who can't see past herself.

I walk into the studio and look at all the tiny little squares of blue glass we've spent the morning cutting. The room is crowded with glass and people, and honestly it's breaking me out in an unladylike sweat. "Okay, who wants to make a sculpture?"

"I thought we were making windows?" Dylan quips.

"For a doll's house?" I shake my head in mock dismay.

He shrugs, and everyone else laughs.

"I'll tell you what we are going to do." They all lean in, ready to do something other than cut squares out. "We are going to make a sculpture so damn awesome Elijah Fairclough won't know what's he's seeing when he gets home later."

There are some claps and loud whoops. Tabitha is grinning at me.

"Grab some wire. I'm going to show you how to weave the glass together."

I have no idea how this is going to turn out. I've got no idea if it can even work. Still, with nothing to lose, there's no harm in trying.

"So what we need to do is to double the wire..."

I brush all thoughts of Eli Fairclough out of my mind and instead turn to my first love: art.

We did it. Hell did we do it. Somehow the eight of us created single-stemmed blue flowers using wire and wrapping around the edges of our blue glass squares. Backbreaking work, but those kids left proud at the end of the day. When we'd finished, we hung around outside for a while, absorbing the late afternoon sunshine while Jennings brought us some cool drinks. It was nice, they are a great bunch.

In my glass studio now sits nearly a hundred blue glass flowers. I created some green leaves which I baked this afternoon, and then I had a rather amusing try at blowing some small glass beads. I've lost the knack of it though so I ended up—after I'd been laughed at by Dylan for ten minutes for not knowing "my shit"—deciding to roll the balls and bake them, too. It's not the exact effect I wanted, but it will suffice.

Now I'm exhausted and soaking in the roll top bath in the wet room. It's heaven under the bubbles, sipping a glass of wine I asked Jennings to locate me as I made a hasty exit from the dining room.

"Faith." There's a gentle rap on my bedroom door.

I sit up in surprise, water flooding everywhere. "Crap."

"You okay?"

"Yes," I call back to Elijah. I recognise his voice instantly—well, my body does. My stomach tightens and a dull ache spreads in the pit of my belly. I thought he would have been back hours ago. "Hold on a minute."

"I'm sleeping on my feet out here, don't rush on my account."

I grin as I step out onto the slippery floor, taking extra care not to slide over and bang my head—now's not the time to aim for a concussion.

Wrapping a towel tight around my body, I unlock the door and peer outside. "Did you check for nosy grandparents?" I tease, but he doesn't seem to find my joke funny and slips quickly inside.

He's in a blue shirt and navy suit trousers, the slim fit shirt tucked into the trim waistband. There's no tie in sight which is a shame because it would have made the picture in front of me perfect.

"Sorry, I didn't know you were bathing."

"Bathing?" I giggle. "You're so funny."

He glares and sits on the edge of my bed. I stare closer

at his face. He looks exhausted. Faint purple rings hollow the skin around his eyes, and that favourite blue of mine isn't shining quite as bright. "You look exhausted."

"It's been a long day." He lifts his face and meets my concerned gaze. When he motions me forward, I don't hesitate. He wraps his arms right around my waist and rests his head on my stomach. I smooth my hands through his short hair, mesmerised by the light tickle the short strands create against my palms.

"What happened?"

He pulls away and tugs at the edge of my towel.

"Hey," I scold and back away. "Talking, you promised talking."

"I suggest you get dressed then because my brain is seriously incapacitated by you in that towel." The heat of his stare is almost palpable as it slips across the patterns on my skin.

"I'll get dressed." Turning for my cupboard where I've just randomly thrown my clothes, I pull out a pair of small sleep shorts and a camisole. I wiggle into them, tugging them against my damp skin. When I turn back around his gaze is burning bright.

"Truthfully, I don't know if that's helping."

"Hold on." I grin and root back through my pile of belongings until I pull out a spotty dressing gown, which I quickly slip over my shoulder and tie at the waist.

"What is that?"

"My dressing gown."

"Take it off. Take it off right now."

Unable to repress my laughter, I slip it back off and then turn to him expectantly. "Now talk."

Twenty-Two

I can't get a grip of what's going on. It seems I've gone from being single and never wanting to have more than a one-night-stand, to cuddling and talking in the dark. Part of me wants to ask Elijah what's going on, but the other part of me realises that if I find out it might scare me, will make that flight instinct take to its wings and I'll ruin whatever this is before it starts. And I think I want it to start... and right now that's the best I can aim for.

So I'll settle for sitting cross-legged on my bed in the room he painted for me and listening.

"I'm working on the Melanie Duncan case." He's focused on his fingers, his thumbs running patterns along my palm.

What's the Melanie Duncan case—it sounds familiar, but...?

I shift uneasily. "Okay, don't judge me, but I'm usually locked in a small place playing with clay."

There's a flash of a smile peeking out from under the tired expanse of his face.

"Melanie Duncan is the woman who blew the whistle on sexual harassment in her workplace." He lifts his head from our joined hands.

"That's brave of her."

"Yes, it was. What she went through…" He hesitates, and my palms tingle with what I know could turn into nervous sweat.

"So you're helping her bring the scum down." My brain wants to lead me on a dark and horrific path down memory lane, but I fight it and stay in the moment with Elijah.

"I'm helping her family."

With a shake of my head, I make my confusion clear.

His fingers grip mine and I love their firm touch covered in soft skin. I want them everywhere: I want his lips on my mouth, his body next to mine. I'm so distracted by the warmth of his hands I almost forget we are in the middle of a conversation.

"She killed herself."

The warm run of liquid anticipation freezes, and I stare into his face in shock. "What, when? Because of what happened?"

"Because at first no one believed her, because she had to explain to her husband what had been happening in what should have been a safe place." He shrugs his shoulders, but deep in the blues I see fierce compassion for a woman now passed, that stills the wild beating of my heart.

"So what are you doing now?"

"I'm helping to get justice for her family. They shouldn't have to be without a wife and mother because of a corrupt society that turns a blind eye to such horrors."

The room seems to become smaller. The universe shrinking as my lonely path crosses with that of Elijah Fairclough and changes everything that I thought I knew. "No, they shouldn't."

"So what happened for you to be called before dawn

this morning?" I ask, swallowing the lump around my throat.

"Lewis, Melanie's son, was arrested for breaking and entering."

"What?" I sit a little straighter.

Elijah shakes his head and lets go of a heavy breath of air. "It was silly, but he's so full of anger."

"What was he doing?"

"He was graffitiing the office block his mother worked in."

"Shit."

"Yeah." The blues settle on my face.

"What now? When is the case due in court?"

"Not until October, and actually that's something I want to talk to you about."

His leading sentence makes me wince. I'm not giving away any secrets about myself, no matter how cosy we are in my pink room.

"What?"

"I've brought Lewis here. He needs to be away from the city, away from the demons chasing him." The blues couldn't read me any harder if they tried. "I was hoping you'd let him hang here with you."

"And Tabitha? Jeez, Elijah, I don't know anything about teenagers. You don't seem to be understanding this."

"Tabitha doesn't think so. She broke house rules following you out yesterday."

"Pfft. House rules... this place seems more like a prison than anything else."

Elijah grins and my God does it do crazy things to my stomach. "As you can imagine, my new guest was not well received."

It's almost impossible not to roll my eyes. "You surprise

me." My fingers pick at the duvet cover while I think. "Really, you and Tabitha, you don't get to make any choices for yourself? What if you wanted to date someone? Someone not chosen by your mother?"

The lengthy silence that spreads between us as Elijah watches my face is at least five seconds too long for my liking. "Then I get cut off."

"And is the money that important?" There's an undeniable sting to my words.

"No. Tabitha is. I won't leave her, not for anyone."

We watch one another, time slowly ticking past.

His words hurt even though I don't want them to. Even if I wanted something with him, it's impossible. That's what he's saying, and he's saying it pretty damn plainly.

So isn't this ironic. The one time I'm interested in someone, the one time I can feel my determination to never let anyone close, begin to crumble. It's an impossible situation. It's like I've sought it out as a self-preservation system.

Then he grins. "Was it my spooning? It's made you want more, right?"

I chuckle and get up from the bed. "I already told you, I don't do relationships."

"Then we are all good."

He catches my hand and wheels me around, pulling me off balance until I land back on the bed, falling into his chest. His hands slide up my back, running under the material of my vest. His lips graze my mouth and I catch my breath. "I'm available for spooning weekends and every other weeknight."

I lean back and stare into his face. What is he saying? That he wants this to be, but I won't be his girlfriend? Isn't that my perfect situation? I get to be obsessed. I get to taste and enjoy, but it doesn't mean anything.

"Every other weeknight? But what would I do the nights you aren't available?"

He kisses me, his lips hungry and demanding. "I've been thinking about kissing you for hours."

"Are you a rampant teenager?"

He chuckles into my neck. "I think you're making me one."

"Really?" His words light sparks with excitement. Am I having the same effect on him as he has on me? I can't believe that? Does he really want me?

"Have you changed your mind about your onetime only rule?"

Using his body as a lever, I edge myself out of his grasp. "No. I can't."

He sighs, his insistent hands tugging me back to his broad chest. I want to undo the buttons on his shirt and discover the skin underneath. I want to explore all of him. "We will have to make out like teenagers then."

Uncontrollable giggles wrack my body. "Don't you want to see what we did today?"

"Later. First, I want to forget about a really long, really shit day."

He grabs me and stops any further talk with his lips, and I allow myself to fall into the dream Elijah Fairclough is able to spin with his hands and lips alone.

"So, this ball? Why didn't you tell me?"

His fingers trail up and down my spine. We really have made out like teenagers. There was possibly some dry humping going on, and I'm grinning so hard my cheeks might split.

"I'm working out with you it's best to drip feed information. That way there's less chance of you bolting."

"I'm not a horse running from a race."

He chuckles and plants his lips against my neck, and an irrepressible shiver of desire tingles through my limbs. "And what a fine filly you are."

"That's so cheesy."

"I know, I practise very hard to perfect the right level of cheese."

Who is this guy? Where is the man with the suits and the worries of the world settled on his broad shoulders? I could stay tangled in this moment forever—I could almost forget I had a no second chance rule in place. I could forget any rule I'd ever made. He's still in his suit trousers, his shirt undone after I unbuttoned each one with deliberate care. I want to dive under his clothes and discover who he really is, but he won't let me. Every time my hand strays too far or I take the initiative, he gently stops me and turns it back around to me.

His hands have been over my clothes, hot under my clothes and I've loved every minute of it.

"So, the ball?" I prompt again.

"Yes, totally boring, well normally it is. This year I'm thinking it could be fun."

"An evening with your grandmother judging me and my tattoos does not sound like fun."

Elijah sits up a little higher, leaning on one elbow. "What's she said?"

I smile but it's bitter. "Only that Saskia will help me to find a dress that will cover them up."

A tut takes the place of what I could imagine are expletive thoughts. "She's a witch."

"I know. And she won't let you bring a date of your choice?"

He chuckles. "I wouldn't have anyone to bring." Ouch, his words cut like a knife.

"Shame for you."

"There is this woman I'd like to take on a date; maybe just something casual, dinner, a drink perhaps, but she's got these crazy rules and I don't know if I can abide by them."

I flush a vibrant pink and try not to grin. "Sounds difficult."

"Oh, she is. So difficult, you wouldn't believe. I might ask if she's free this weekend."

"Good idea."

"Even though I might want her to break her rules?"

"Maybe." I have to look away and face the wall, I'm smiling so much. Could I break my rules for him?

I don't know.

Then I remember what I had planned for the weekend and the smile drops. "I was going to go to see Al this weekend."

His face falls a little, but he nods understandingly.

"It's only Sunday, though. I'm still free Friday and Saturday."

"Hold on a minute." He grabs my hands and rolls me until I'm pinned under his amazing body. His body is hard above me and my rules begin to melt around the edges. "Who said I was asking you on a date?" His teeth pull on my earlobe and I shriek a giggle.

"Don't! I'm ticklish there."

His eyes light with fire. "Now *that* you really shouldn't have told me."

I squeal as he attacks me again, laughing so hard I think I may burst.

Finally, I've managed to convince him to see the glasswork. He's nodding silently as he looks at our blooms of blue flowers.

"Have you nothing to say?" I shift from foot to foot. I kind of expected some reaction, not just dead silence.

"Faith, I can't believe you got this out of them in two days; it's insane."

"Oh, it was easy. It was fun, so they were keen to see what stages came next."

"What's on the agenda for tomorrow?"

"Glassblowing and free form glasswork."

"Sounds hot."

"Have you got any other paintings stashed here?"

His eyes narrow. "No, why?"

"I just wondered where you hid all your little secrets."

"Not here."

We turn back for the door and my chest begins to ache. He's already told me he's driving back to London tonight. It's nearly midnight, and I think he's crazy, but he's got a breakfast meeting at eight. I can't believe he came all this way just to talk to me. Although the silly giddy little girl locked inside me wants to believe he came this way to kiss me too.

"You going to be okay with Lewis?"

"Another messed-up teenager? Sure, I've got that handled."

We are outside my room and he kisses me on the cheek. I inhale the delicious scent of him.

"Drive back safe," I say. What I really want to say is "stay", but I don't.

He smiles, kisses me again, and walks away, and I slip into my room before anyone can see me.

Elijah has made it clear that this can't, and won't, be anything other than just fun between the two of us, and that's okay. It's just how I like it: fun, casual, and simple.

When I wake in the morning, there's a notification on my phone from Messenger.

Eli Jones: I like being a teenager with you.

I grin and swipe the message open.

Faith Hitchin: Don't forget to grow up for work. Hope your breakfast meeting goes well.

I'm surprised when a green dot appears next to his name and I can see dots moving at the bottom of the screen telling me he's writing.

Eli Jones: You remembered my meeting, I'm honoured.

I shake my head, and when I glance up as I think of a response, I find an insane version of myself grinning back at me in the mirror.

Faith Hitchin: I feel somewhat neglected by the lack of overnight spooning.

Eli Jones: you're going to break your rules for me.

Faith Hitchin: don't be so sure. They are unbreakable and have been for a very long time.

Eli Jones: are you free Saturday?

Faith Hitchin: I'm living in your grandmother's museum of a house. I think I might be free.

Eli Jones: got to go, the meeting is starting.

Faith Hitchin: have a great day.

But he's gone. I'm still smiling, and I stretch in my bed.

He's making me a whirlwind of irrational emotions. I'm a walking and talking contradiction. Maybe I should text Abi and check she's okay? I've an uncontrollable urge to talk about Eli. I never talk about the opposite sex with anyone but Abi. Well, let's be real, I never talk about them full stop.

I'm typing out a message when there's a light tap on the door. "Miss Hitchin?"

I sit up and pull the duvet close around me. "Yes, come in."

Jennings, who I'm beginning to think is the master of discretion, manages to walk in and firstly not look at my skin, and secondly not look at all embarrassed.

"I haven't missed breakfast, have I?" I hope not, I'm starving after all that making out.

"Not at all… there's a bit of a scene in the house… I'm hoping you can come and help."

"Scene?"

Maybe the witch's broomstick snapped.

"Yes, ma'am, with the new guest."

Lewis!

Crap! I leap out of bed and Jennings swiftly hands me my dotty dressing gown.

I'm almost entirely sure that what I'm about to find isn't going to be a great start to the day.

Twenty-Three

The shouting meets my ears as I walk along the hallway. The house, so normally calm and tranquil, muted almost in its regal splendour, is being ripped apart with the morning cry of, "You can all go fuck yourselves. I don't know why Elijah brought me here, but it fucking sucks."

Yikes.

I kind of skid into the room, making more of an arrival than I'd want when wearing my spotty dressing gown, with my unbrushed hair, and blatantly bruised lips from kissing too much. Dark burning eyes land on me and I wince at the sheer hatred that flows from them.

"Hey." I think it's a strong opening line.

"What the fuck do you want?" Jeez, this guy. He's young, his face marred with a sneer of scorn, and he's also sporting an angry black eye.

"Wow, how did you get that shiner?" I ignore his question and go with one of my own. I grew up in a tattoo shop frequented by drunks—black eyes are something I know rather a lot about.

"Fucking pigs, heavy-handed bastards."

This isn't the first time I've heard this line before either.

There's a tut from the other side of the room followed

by a grumbled, "Charming." I turn and find the wicked witch standing there with a china cup and saucer poised in her hand.

"I'll organise some ice," I say to Lewis, AKA the boiling bundle of hatred trapped like a wild quarry the other side of the breakfast table.

"Don't bother."

I wave my hand like it's no big deal parading around a national treasure of a house in my fluffy robe. "No bother, up to you if you use it."

Tabitha is cowering at the end of the table and I turn to face her, giving her a warm smile and ignoring the teen with the rage. "All ready for today, Tabs?" I ask.

She nods, her head mechanical as it jerks up and down, but doesn't say a word.

"Honestly, Jennifer," the clear-cut tones of Connie Fairclough slice through the dining room. "Is our home to be a halfway house for delinquents now?"

I round on her and glare although it rolls off her like water off a well-oiled duck. "Not helping."

"Well." The wicked witch makes eye contact with me, her demeanour almost open. Clearly, I am no longer the worst thing under the roof at Bowsley. "This is ridiculous. I mean are we even safe in our beds?"

Lewis looks like he's about to lob the teapot.

I walk towards Jennifer and Connie, who are both cowering and commenting from the safety of the other end of the ridiculously long dining room table. "Can you guys just try not to make a fuss?" I ask.

"Not make a fuss." Jennifer fans herself. It's probably the most ruffled I've seen her. Her normally serene face is showing cracks and lines I didn't know existed. "That child is using the foulest language in my dining room."

"Really, you've never heard foul language in the dining room before?"

I step closer ushering the women towards me. "Listen, Elijah wanted you to help this boy. It's important to him, and he's doing a good thing here."

"Working for free?" Connie snaps.

For a moment I stare at her aghast. "You know what happened to Lewis' mother? You know why he is so angry?"

Jennifer manages to look contrite. "Elijah really cares for this family?"

"Yes, because he's a good man, and he wants to help people. Especially those who haven't had the opportunity to be brought up somewhere like this." I wave a hand at the expanse of excessive splendour which is the dining room alone.

"Can you calm him down? I really can't have him shouting like that."

"Who is going to hear? It's just us here."

"That's not the point."

Knowing I won't win, I back away a little. "Do you want to see what we did yesterday? It's going to look amazing."

She dismisses me with a hand, her eyes still trained on Lewis. "Of course. I shall come along after Viviane and the Colonel have left after cribbage."

I do believe I have just stepped back at least a hundred years in time. I shake my head, repressing the giggle bubbling up my throat, and turn for Lewis. "Shall we go and find a bacon sandwich?"

He looks like he wants to say no. He looks like he wants to fire every expletive under the sun towards me in an arsenal of hatred, but his stomach gurgles loudly and I grin. "Your stomach speaks for itself. Come on, let's get out of here." With a turn of my head, I motion to Tabitha. "Would you like a bacon sandwich, too?"

"I—I," she stutters.

"That's a yes. Come on, let's go."

I'm at the door when I hear Connie's icy tone. "Tabitha, stay where you are. You will not get involved with this tiresome fuss making."

My hand is on the door frame, but I turn to watch Tabitha. Her bottom lip is caught between her teeth and her body poised like she's about to push her chair back. With Connie's words her body sags and she slumps in her seat. My gaze flicks to Jennifer, but her eyes are dropped to the floor.

Instantly, I can see who runs this house, and it isn't the baroness. I give Tabitha a small wave and point at the hallway for Lewis.

This house is unlike any place I've ever experienced, and this family is beyond fucked-up—and that's coming from me, the woman with the most unconventional upbringing in existence. Lewis and I head for the kitchen, him silent, me thinking about Elijah—the man with the big heart and the prison of a family and home.

I want to set him free, but I don't know how.

The kitchen is warm, cosy, and happy. Now I know why Elijah chose to drink in here alone. It's an island of normality in a mansion of weirdness. Elaine the cook insists on cooking the bacon, even though I beg her to let me cook. So I set Lewis to buttering the bread which he is doing with so much gusto and pent-up anger, it's slowly turning to small balls of dough and there might not be any left to put the bacon on.

I'm making tea and coffee for everyone. "You can come back here any time," Elaine tells me as I hand her a mug of sweet tea. A proper mug mind you, not one of those poncy cup and saucer things they have going on in the dining room.

"I'm sure other people make you tea." I smile and look around the kitchen. It's just Elaine and Jennings here. There are cleaners and estate staff who come in as workers, but it's only the two of them who live and breathe Bowsley Hall.

"Elijah does when he's here." Her gaze goes a little misty and she sighs.

"Elijah makes tea?" I try to imagine him bringing me a mug of tea while wearing one of his cut-to-perfection suits, but my mind can only paint me a picture of him standing in a suit handing over a cup of tea, next to a bed which I'm naked on... I'm losing the plot.

"He's the main reason I have to order in so much sugar, that boy's always had a sweet tooth."

"Really?" I don't know why, but I want to file away this piece of information. It's not even interesting or exciting. Definitely not one for the spank bank; but I have an inordinate need to learn everything about Elijah Fairclough.

Things I've learned so far:

He hates his job.

He's an amazing artist.

He's an amazing kisser.

He drives sexy.

Oh, and he's highly skilled at unexpected oral sex.

I'm not going to lie. I stir sugar into the tea and contemplate how on earth I'm going to work through all of this today—with kids arriving for an art day, but also a highly-strung Lewis brewing about the place. My mind should be on plans for the day; for the rest of the week. It's not. Elijah is filling my head, and I'm wondering why the night before he devoured me like a man starved for days, and yet last night we'd made out like teenagers and hands had stayed above clothes—most of the time.

That hot and cold thing he has going on is exhausting. It's constant, but it's not making me want to push him away. It's making me want to delve deep and find out what's under the many faces he hides behind.

"So, Lewis." I pull myself from the complexities of Elijah's personality and face the situation in hand. "You can join in with us today." I shake my head. "It's really boring though, so I doubt you'll like it."

His face drops, but I carry on.

"Yeah, everyone thought it was a drag yesterday. I'll leave it up to you."

My mind skips to Dan at home in Brighton. We'd been kids, and he'd been so timid; nothing like the tattooed beast he is now. *Dan, I heard Eliza Johnson is getting a tattoo. It's just as well you don't have one. She's going to make it look so girly*.

A solid lump forms in my throat but I push around it and carry on talking to Lewis. "I reckon we can get you some jobs to do around here until Elijah has everything sorted in London." I cock an eyebrow. "Unless you want to hang out in the library or something?"

There's a flicker of a smile on Jennings' face as he steps in. "I know Bernard in the garden would love some help. Do you know anything about roses? Or herbs?" He turns a little to Elaine and there's a wave of comforting familiarity about the way they look at each other. "Didn't you need the herb garden weeded?"

"Oh, Trevor, you are right," she chimes in. Lewis is watching us with bewilderment. "You can do that can't you, Lewis?"

He's flabbergasted. "You want me to do what?"

Just as we are about to explain it all again, the kitchen door flies open and Tabitha whirls in. She leans against the closed door, her chest rising and falling. Lewis forgets what he was saying, and his words falter as he stares at her.

"You okay, Tabs?" I ask.

She straightens and smiles, moving away from the door. "Yes, what did I miss?"

I shrug, "Nothing much. We were giving Lewis some ideas to keep himself entertained for the day."

"Oh," she meets his anger filled gaze. "Aren't you going to join us?"

His hands flap at his sides, the wind removed from the sails of his anger by the slender girl in front of him; her cheeks flushed, her hair wild and unkempt from her dash through the long hallways to the corridor.

I motion for the table. "Come, grab some bacon, Tabitha. I'm going to go and ring your brother."

I perch on a stone bench in the formal garden, watching the intricacies of the patterned pathways, my phone in my hand, while I drag on my cigarette. I go to type a message—that's how Elijah and I communicate, so it seems—but I know it will leave me unsatisfied in a completely inexplicable way. So instead I dial his yet un-rung number.

"Mr Fairclough's line," a saccharine voice sings down the line on the third ring.

What the hell? I called his mobile, didn't I? That familiar burn of broken trust simmers under my skin, rushing along my veins.

"Hello," the voice says again.

"I was ringing for Elijah," I say, my tone coloured with hesitancy.

There's a click of nails on a hard surface. "Mr Fairclough is in a meeting. May I take a message?"

I breathe an irrational lungful of air, shaking my head at my own stupidity.

"Could you tell him Miss Hitchin called?" I drag another toke on my smoke.

"The artist, right?" The voice on the other end picks up a little.

"Pardon?"

"Faith Hitchin, the artist?"

"Uh, yes. How do you know that?"

I shake my head and almost smack myself upside my head. Of course, she knows that. I'm sure Elijah might have mentioned his charity project at his huge stately home. "Never mind, can you tell him I called?"

"Oh, hold on, he's coming through now. Please wait."

Why, oh why, is my heart pounding? My palms slick with sweat and I have to grip my mobile tighter.

"Faith?" Oh God, my stomach dips as his voice comes across the line. I need to stamp this out right now. Like, *right* bloody now.

"Hi,"

There's a shift on the other end of the phone, a faint crackle and movement. "Everything okay?"

"Fine," I clip. "I just wanted to let you know Lewis is fine, but your mother and granbaronessy might not be talking to you anymore."

There's a pause. "I've seen a message already."

"Yikes, that was quick."

He snorts a dry laugh. "Anything else I can help you with?" He is distant, cold, and it pinches my insides.

Faith, don't be a fool.

"No."

"Listen," his voice drops. "I don't think I'll get back for a few days."

"Oh." There isn't much else to say.

"Will you manage?"

I'm not sure what he's asking. Will I manage the teenagers I foolishly agreed to help on some summer art camp? Will I cope without seeing him for a few days when he's managed to worm his way into my head?

Didn't he say he wanted a date with me on Saturday? Weren't we last night connecting on some level I never ever anticipated?

"Yes."

"Good."

I hang up, frustrated at the prickle of tears tingling the back of my eyes. No. I won't be weak.

This is what happens when I let people in. They end up letting me down.

Well, more fool me.

Twenty-Four

My mood is foul. I've snapped at everyone, until in the end I left Tabitha to clean up with the group this afternoon. So, I've put on some leggings, a running bra, and my trainers. I may as well run around this estate while I'm here.

I run for nearly forty-five minutes. The formal gardens give way to what must be a deer park lined with a deep and tall brick wall.

I let him in.

I didn't want to. But I did.

Stupid, weak Faith Hitchin.

This isn't how I do things, not anymore. Relationships, physical gratification, they are on my terms—no one else's. Yet, I was foolish enough to believe him when he said he wanted to set me free. I thought he wanted to unbind the shackles I keep myself tightly locked in.

When will I learn?

Trust costs.

When I get back, I evade the main house. I don't want to see Tabitha, to have to explain that her brother put me in a foul mood all because he talked to me like a stranger.

I knew he was going to be like that. He told me he would in no uncertain terms.

So why does it sting?

I slide on some skinny jeans and a vest top which I place an oversized loose knitted V-neck over. It does nothing to hide my tattoos but I don't want to hide them. I want to wear them as my armour.

Deep under the surface of my skin is the familiar need, the ache, the itch that can never be scratched, to lose myself in unfamiliar hands, attachment free: no thoughts, no feelings, no pain, just how I like it.

The village is small, only two pubs to choose from: the one I took Tabitha to, and the other that doesn't look like the kind of place Elijah will be known by name behind the bar. I slip out of Bowsley's gates and make my way down the leafy green, shady, and narrow lanes.

The pub is just like I want. There are no hushed gatherings of middle-aged couples sipping wine, and the jukebox is blaring loud intoxicating tunes. I ask for a double vodka on ice and then sit in a corner seat, happy to just let the world go by. Well the world that is The Angel pub.

My one double vodka turns into four and my blood starts to run warm. I'm at the bar chatting to the girl serving; she's thinking of getting ink and wants to know what I think. After watching her for the last half an hour I'm sketching on a sheet of paper she pulled from under the bar.

There's a guy to the right. His dark eyes are on my skin and from under them I force all thoughts of Elijah from my mind. I shouldn't have let him in—now I'm going to force him out.

It's just sex. Just once. Then move on.

"What about this?" I turn it to the girl with the blonde hair behind the bar. She's delicate but with a no-shit edge. She admired my roses, so I've gone for a flowery theme.

She stares at my sketch. "Jesus, did you just draw that

right now with a biro?" She pulls the lilies closer. I grin and nod.

"Lilies are beautiful, but they are a bitch when they stain your clothes."

"What's that?" She lifts the paper and peers closer.

"It's a bee, buried deep but ready to sting if needed."

It's how I feel. Dangerous.

"This is amazing. Do you mind if I get it done?" She stares at it so close, her nose is almost touching the paper. "I'm Vanessa, by the way."

"Faith." I offer my hand. "Of course, you can. It's yours. You'll have to find the right person though, you need a delicate touch."

She pours me another double—not that I need it. "Would you do it?"

I shake my head and sip my drink, sensing the weight of the guy on the next bar stool weigh down on my skin. "No, I don't have my stuff with me."

"Couldn't you get it?" Vanessa laughs nervously. "Sorry, I'm being pushy, but I'm getting a good vibe from you."

"I can't get my kit." I shake my head firmly. I could get my kit, but I don't want to. Those days are long behind me.

I down my drink and slip off my stool. "I've got to get back. I've another busy day tomorrow." All I can hope, I think to myself, is that I'm in a better mood. My eyes slide to the side and see the guy make a move to leave too. If I can just erase Elijah from my head, I know it will help. I just need to forget.

It's late and dark outside. I don't know how late, but the yellow street lamps are lighting the car park. "Hey, Faith" the man calls, and I whirl around.

Just close your eyes and do it, Faith, then you can get rid of him.

I've been telling myself this for a long time. No one can control me. I choose how and when.

What I haven't realised until this very moment, is that over the last few days my mind has been so full of Elijah I haven't thought of anything else. No bad memories. No cravings to help me forget.

The realisation floors me.

But he doesn't want me...

Lost and frighteningly alone, I contemplate the man in front of me. "Sorry, I've got to get going." I begin to back away.

"Come now, Faith, you've been making eyes at me all night, I know you're keen."

Am I keen? God, I'm so fucking confused, I don't know what I'm doing.

I shake my head, but my hand reaches for the guy's shirt. What my hand is doing, I don't know. I'm torn. Confused.

A flicker to the right makes me turn a searching gaze.

Elijah.

Sat on the table top of one of the pub's picnic benches, he's watching me from under hooded lids. My legs shake a little, my knees wobbling as I lurch a step towards him. "What are you doing here?" I don't give the random from the bar a second look and assume he walks away as my attention is pulled to the place it should be.

"I missed you."

His words unravel every single talking to I've spent the day giving myself. They floor me.

"Are you busy?" There's an element of scorn to his tone and my stomach twists. I have nothing to be guilty about, we are nothing to one another, he's made that clear, but a nibble of unrest bites me inside.

The way he fills my head, his scent, his presence, is all encompassing.

It doesn't erase the disappointment I've felt all day. I step another foot closer. And then another. My heart pounds in my chest, my tongue dry and tingling.

"I'm not busy."

He knows, though. I can sense it. He knows what I was thinking of doing with that stranger, but he will never understand why.

It's my sting, my burn, my protection.

He tugs me closer, his fingers weaving into the knit of my sweater. "What are you doing, Faith?" His question is a low murmur.

My insides coil and tighten, that age old need to run edging me to make a dash for it.

"Nothing," I mumble, but a wave of emotion floods me from the inside out.

"Is this because I was busy this morning and couldn't chat?"

"No." I stare at my sandals.

"Faith?" He tilts my chin, so I look at him.

"No. It's not that."

"What then?" A hardened edge creeps into his words. "Because as far as I can tell, you stink of vodka and were leaving the local with a guy, who honestly doesn't look like he's washed in a couple of days."

I scrunch my face with repulsion, anger coursing through me. My hands smack against his chest, pushing him backwards. "You don't get to judge me, Elijah."

"You're kind of giving me good reasons to do just that."

"Don't you dare judge me, you bloody bastard. We can't all be emotionally cut off like you."

He laughs, and it downright infuriates me. My face

floods with heat. "Emotionally cut off? Are you referring to our telephone conversation? Because I was surrounded by my partners after coming out of a crucial five-hour meeting where we bartered concessions with the opposition."

He has me there. I didn't think for one moment maybe he wasn't in a position to speak. I just assumed he was giving me the brush off; that his hot and cold routine was winning out on the side of freezing cold.

"Well, what about the other night? You were all over me like a fucking rash, and then last night it was like we were fifteen and scared to go under the covers."

He grins, and my fist tightens ready to punch his smug face. "You want me," he taunts. One hand snakes out and grabs the waistband of my jeans, tugging me closer, hooking on the belt loop. "Sunshine, I'm just waiting for you to give me the go ahead. You know my stipulation."

His lips skim my throat, scorching a pathway of fire as he reaches my ear and gives a gentle nip with his teeth. "Just waiting for your say."

My skin heats and cools all at the same time. My legs tremble as I try to get a grip on the situation, try to gain some control back. I can't, it's all gone, lost in his touch.

This is Elijah at his most perplexing: hot, determined, and driven. It speaks to a deep, dark part of myself that I've never given the chance to come to light.

He pulls me closer between his legs, clamping his thighs around my hips, tugging me forward until I'm losing balance and falling into his chest and lap. Through the dark material of his jeans his erection rubs against my pelvis, and it does nothing to fight through the static buzzing in my head.

Give in, Faith.

I shake my head and he chuckles. "Do you need a

conversation with yourself? Should I step away and give you some space?"

My eyes screw shut so I can't see his smile, the dancing light in his eyes, his lips I want to kiss so badly.

"I don't let people in." I open my eyes and stare at him openly. My palms stretch across his T-shirt, hard and soft all at the same time.

"And I don't get to be with anyone I want. Maybe somehow this is perfect right now, just for us."

That's it. It's all he has to say. My defences crumble.

"Nothing more than what's in the moment. You can't fix me, Elijah."

"And you can't be my girlfriend."

"I won't want to be." I'm convinced of this. I've never been anyone's girlfriend. I'm not made of the right stuff.

His lips meet my mouth; brushing, caressing, drifting in a heavenly touch. "Tell me you're a rule breaker," he whispers, "please."

I still can't say it. Still can't let go, even though the words are screaming inside my head. "Why are you here? You said you weren't coming back for days."

The blues rest on my face in the dark; reading, absorbing. I want to hide from them, but then I also want to stand proud—this is me in my most fucked-up way and he's still not running away from me screaming.

"I wanted to say hi."

"You drove all the way from London to say hi?"

I kiss him. Stretching onto my tiptoes, I slide my hands around his neck, fixing my mouth to his. Hot and eager, he binds me into his arms. "I'm a rule breaker," I whisper the words into his mouth. In my stomach butterflies take to flight, and across my skin every story I've ever inked is slowly washed away in need and hope.

Twenty-Five

We walk largely in silence to the pink walled outhouse. Anticipation dries my tongue. My fingers are warm in his grasp as our hands swing between us.

Every so often he casts a searching gaze in my direction and grins.

"What?" I ask eventually.

"Nothing."

"No, come on. Something is funny."

"I'm thinking about Gerard Steers."

The warm blood rushing through my veins cools a little. "Why?"

He shakes his head, but his grin grows, and damn does it look mighty fine. "Just schoolboy stuff, don't worry."

I arch an eyebrow. "Are you still a schoolboy, Elijah?"

We are at the door to my room. My heart is pounding, my knees knocking. It's as though this moment is everything all at once. It's nothing, not really, but my head and heart are telling me otherwise—I wish they'd shut up.

His fingers trail along my collarbone, dancing a light as feather touch as they skim up my throat and slide around the back of my neck, his thumb running along my jaw.

Blues sweep across my face. "I've wanted you since the first moment I saw you in The Ritz."

My stomach flips with his words and my legs turn to jelly.

My gaze sweeps up through my lashes, my mouth parting as I breathe in the warm summer air and the hint of his soap. It's a heady concoction which makes my head spin.

When his lips graze mine, it's all encompassing. A brazen fire lights in the pit of my stomach, a needy ache I know won't be quenched, and I'm not even going to try, I'm not going to fight it. I kiss him back, breathing it, living it, giving it everything I have. My fingers slide to their new favourite place, playing with the short hair at the back of his neck. His hands drop from my neck, skimming down my ribcage, anchoring onto the ridge of my hips.

Our tongues tangle, probing and searching; at first gentle and soft, then harder and faster, until our breaths come in shortened gasps. I don't want to breathe if it means ending the kiss. He opens the door, never breaking contact, guiding me in with eager hands, firm and strong.

I'm splintering into hundreds of pieces, all of them desperate for him at the same time. I want my clothes off and his skin on mine. Him warm and strong, burrowing in the darkest places of me. I grab at his shirt, pulling at it, uncaring of the expensive tailoring, catching the buttons and forcing them with unsteady fingers through the holes. He helps, his fingers calmer as he pops them one by one, his lips still on my mouth as he shucks the shirt off his shoulders and it pools by our feet. My hands slide along his hard chest; his smooth, tanned skin gleaming in the dark shadows of the room. He's perfect, toned and lithe, all my favourite things. I kiss the skin I find, trailing my lips across his chest, my hands running down the flat of his stomach to the buckle of his belt. The few moments we've had together he's always focused all the attention on me. Not anymore. Not now I've chosen. I flick my tongue against his nipple, and it buds against my lips as he shivers slightly and groans. I suck, teasing it between my teeth, before I skim my lips to the other side and do the same. His hands hold me tighter, his palms burning through my jeans, gripping my hips.

"Fuck, Faith."

I grin and continue exploring with my mouth and hands. Dropping to my knees, I unbuckle his belt, my fingers working better as I slip the leather through its loop and unhook his suit trousers, tugging them down until they are at his ankles. He kicks off his shoes and manages to hook his toes into his socks, pulling them off with undeniable skill. When he's just in his boxers, I straighten, admiring the sight of him, unable to pull my gaze away from the bulge through the black material of his pants. I rub my palm along his length, and his mouth greedily searches for mine, pulling me tight until we are meshed together.

"You're wearing far too many clothes," he almost growls into my mouth. In a startling move, he sweeps me up, placing me against his chest as he paces for the bed and throws me onto the mattress. His hands are quick, certain and sure as they tug at my jeans, peeling them away from my legs. His hands yank my top off with little ceremony until I'm just in my matching lace underwear. "You are so incredibly beautiful."

I blush and lay back, my whole body burning for him. He lowers towards me, his lips everywhere. His hands are along my sides, then cupping my breasts, and pulling my hair—so many places. I'm falling from one moment to the next like I'm jumping stars. "I need you." Between my legs, a molten river of fire scorches for his touch.

"I want to taste you." He dips his head to travel down my body, but I catch him back up, pulling his mouth to mine.

"Not now."

His eyes meet mine, his hand dipping between us, searching out the places under my drenched knickers. One finger slips swiftly inside, then another, and I arch up to meet his touch. It's not enough though; I need it deeper, fuller, harder.

I grab at his boxers and catch my toes into the waistband, pushing them down while he smirks against my mouth, his lips curving slowly. He turns me, rolling me under his thighs, until I'm face down on the mattress. His fingers trail across the ink on my skin, skimming between the crease in my ass. When he unhooks my bra and slides my knickers down, I'm almost floating above the bed. His fingers never stop trailing, touching, caressing. I spread my legs a little, so they can slip back where I want them the most. It's a guttural groan I let out into the soft pillow as both his fingers slip beneath my clit and enter me, massaging the sensitive spot deep inside.

I'm going to come. It builds and builds until I'm clawing the sheets and he flips me over, pushing my legs wide apart, his eyes sweeping along me. When he lowers his boxers and his erection springs free, I stifle a small cry. I've never wanted anything more, never needed anything as much as I want him right now.

He bends over the side of the bed, one hand searching the pockets of his trousers for his wallet; the other hand teasing and torturing me with delicate strokes. He slips a condom from his wallet and tears the packet open with his teeth. Rolling it on, he positions himself at my entrance and I'm almost bucking off the bed trying to get him inside. His eyes hold mine, never wavering as he slowly pushes in. I sigh a breath as he inches further, deeper and deeper until he's taken me to the hilt. Then he leans down, his lips finding my mouth, our foreheads pressed together as he slowly rotates his hips. It's just the smallest of movements, rolling deep, pressing me to the absolute max. I groan as the friction of our bodies alongside one another rubs my clit. Within me he's stroking the sensitive spot that makes my toes point and stretch.

And then, just when I can't guess how this can be anymore wonderful than being filled to the brim with this deep and strong sensation, he slides in and out. With every drive of his hips, he drills deeper and deeper until our bodies are slinging together, my nails are dragging along his back as an anchor and my hips are lifting from the bed.

Harder and faster he pounds, and I arch myself to meet him, my lips trailing wild kisses across any bit of his skin I can touch. Then, just as I'm cresting a dark tormenting wave of an orgasm, building from my toes and travelling along my legs to where I'm going to explode, he fills me deep again, stopping and waiting. His breath hangs between us as he kisses me deep, his tongue hard and fast. My hips buck against his, willing him to carry on, but he doesn't, and I'm left whimpering on the edge of a dark wilderness. Pushing further and further, I think he's going to split me in two. He moves so slowly, I sob out his name.

"Eli."

His eyes meet mine, his fingers brushing the damp hair from my face. "Scream my name."

And then he's off again, and the orgasm tantalisingly close, held at bay, frozen in the moment, erupts and carries me off and I scream for him. Shouting his name and searing it into my soul forever more.

"Eli. Eli. *Eli*."

He follows, driving hard as he grips my hair, and his hips buck with one final tearing deep thrust.

He collapses across me. My skin is damp. His hair is wet as he kisses along my shoulder, and I'm shuddering and breathing shocked little gasps of air.

I don't want him to ever pull out. I want him to stay there forever, for our sweat to always be mingled, for his body to always be pressed against mine. His lips find mine, soft and gentle, and he leans onto his elbows. His face is frank and open, nothing but beautiful calm. He gives me a slow smile and a strange squeeze presses inside my chest. "Stay there forever," I murmur.

"But you love my spooning." His face lights with mischief and, fuck, it's adorable. This guy is beyond dangerous to be around. Another squeeze tightens my chest and I'm not sure if I'm having a heart attack.

"I do, but I love you more there." I squeeze around him tight.

His gaze holds steady and a moment of silence beats between us. "So, when do you run? When does the rule breaking commence?"

"When can you go again?"

He looks deep in thought, and I giggle. "Give me fifteen."

"Rule breaking commences in fifteen."

He laughs and rolls me over, somehow staying inside me until I'm straddled on top. His eyes skim my skin. Naked and exposed, I allow him to search my patterns, my tales. His thumb runs along the blank space above my heart. "What's this waiting for?"

I shrug. "I've never known."

With a laugh, I shift and allow him to slip out. It's a tragedy, but Elijah is turning me into a rule breaker and I don't want to wait. I pull off the condom, dropping it on the floor and making a mental note to pick it up as soon as I can. Then I shimmy down his body.

"What are you doing?"

"Fifteen minutes is too long."

I hook him up with my fingers and slide my tongue along the length of him. He is soft under my touch, but an instant stirring makes me know I won't have to wait that long. I slip him into my mouth and give two long sucks and, like magic, he firms and hardens. "It's magic." He laughs, and I shake my head focusing on the task in hand.

"So, no spooning then?"

I suck him into my mouth, taking him as deep as I can. All talk of spooning is forgotten about.

I'm exhausted and aching, lying across his chest. The rule is broken, but I know it's going to take more than one night to see it through properly. Elijah is dozing, his arm thrown around me, his breathing regular and comforting.

What am I doing?

I don't even care. This is dangerous and unknown, but I don't care. I can't even protect myself from it.

"What are you thinking about?" A light pressure touches my head and that squeeze tightens my chest again.

"Rules."

"Mm." He snuggles me tighter, his strong arm pulling me in.

"Eli." Changing his name comes easy now. "Will you show me more of your paintings?"

"Mm." His fingers trail along my naked spine. "At the weekend."

I smile in the dark and settle down.

He surprises me when he moves and places a tender kiss along the back of my neck. "Don't be mad when I'm not here in the morning."

"I won't."

I know he has to go to work. I know he has responsibilities, things that I can't even understand. I'll miss him, though. And that fact alone scares the hell out of me.

Twenty-Six

It's mid-morning when my phone rings. Except, I don't know it's my phone, because the ring tone is All Saints *Bootie Call*. I look expectantly at the room, waiting for someone to admit they've got the cheesiest ringtone in the entire universe.

I'm in a good mood and doesn't everyone know it. The studio is a mess of epic proportions. We've broken more glass than we've successfully managed to balloon with hot air, but who the hell cares. The sun's shining, the birds are tweeting; I haven't seen Jennifer or the wicked witch today, and last night I got shagged to oblivion by Eli Fairclough. There is no better day to be had.

"Anyone want to get that?" I snigger and wait for someone to acknowledge the call shame-faced. No one does and the call drops. I lean back over, humming the tune as I pull another strand of molten liquid glass and suspend it in the air. We are trying to make spun glass filaments for our flowers. Not as easy as it sounds.

The phone starts up again and the glass shatters as I jump. "Fuck it," I growl under my breath and scowl at everyone. They all take one step back. Everyone apart from

Lewis who's watching the shattered glass mesmerised, lost in thought.

"Uh, Faith." Tabitha calls my attention and I turn my focus to her. Her hair is pulled up on her head, her cheeks flushed, but then I guess it is quite warm in here. "It's your phone, over there." She nods to where my phone is sitting nearby on the side bench of the studio next to the sink. Eli's name is flashing across the screen along with that god-awful song filling the air. I pounce on it because she can see who's calling. Not that it matters, he is effectively my boss for the summer. But tell that to my cheeks now scorching a vibrant red.

"What did you do to my phone?" I hiss, holding it tight to my ear.

He roars with laughter. "How red are you right now?"

"I'm not," I state and brush my hair out of my face. "What do you want? I am incredibly busy."

He chuckles, and it sends warm licks of anticipation along my insides. "Hold on please, caller."

There's a moment and I can hear the tap of him typing in the background.

There's a beep across the room and Tabitha pulls her phone out of her back pocket. She quickly reads the screen with a furrowed brow and then casts an enquiring glance in my direction before typing on her phone.

"You are red. I have a witness."

"How old are you?" I grumble.

"You weren't complaining about my youthful vitality for life last night." The smirk in his voice is all too evident. I flush even hotter when I think of all the many things I didn't complain about last night.

Tabitha's phone beeps again and she giggles as she types another response.

"Just as I thought," he says. "You've been thinking about rule breaking as much as I have."

I turn my back, so I'm facing the wall. "My rules are very subjective and can be reinstated at any point." He chuckles, and types some more. "Don't you dare message Tabitha again."

"I'm actually working right now."

"Then why are you calling?"

"I wanted to see how Lewis is." My stomach sinks. "And I wanted to hear your voice." God, I'm such a teenager. I grin like a buffoon.

"He's fine, very good at crushing glass into minuscule pieces."

"If he's getting in the way, send him to Jennings to do something useful."

"He's not." I turn around and catch Tabitha showing him how to pull a strand of glass from the kiln. He's watching her intently. "I think he's forgetting why he's here. How did you get on with the lawyers?"

Eli had told me last night between kisses he was attempting to have the charges dropped against Lewis. I don't know how he was managing two cases and driving back and forth to Hampshire. And here I was, smashing glass... the two things didn't compare, not really.

"I think they will drop the charges, they are just making it more complicated to distract me from other things."

"What other things?"

I should be getting back to the glassmaking, but I could also stand here and talk to him all day. I've never known anything like it. I've never wanted to talk to anyone the way I do him. Never wanted to know anyone the way I want to know him.

"Collecting evidence. The team are working on it. Talking to ex-employees, that kind of thing."

"The team?" This is the first I've heard of a team.

"Yeah, just Jess and Roger."

I bite on my bottom lip to stop me from saying anything. It's none of my business anyway.

"Listen, Eli," I keep my voice soft, so he doesn't think I'm having one of the strops it seems he expects from me. "Don't drive back tonight. I don't know if you were planning on it, but I'm worried about you being tired."

"I'm hurt," he mocks. "You don't want my spooning tonight?"

"Hm, well you did only say every other night, so technically you're keeping your promises." An unexpected giggle escapes my lips and I bite it back.

His fingers are hammering keyboard keys in the background and I know he's busy, let alone the fact I've got a roomful of expectant teenagers waiting for some direction.

"I'll see you when you get here. It's all cool. I've got to go, Eli." His name sounds delicious on my tongue.

"Don't break too much glass."

I glare at Tabitha as I hang up and she turns to me and smirks, her eyes dancing. "Cheeky, remember who gives you your workload every day."

She giggles and Lewis looks at her with interest. "What's going on?" he asks.

"Nothing." I sigh, but Tabitha raises her eyebrow and elbows him in the ribs.

"Elijah and Faith are having a thing."

I stare at her horrified. "We are not." My face scorches again. I am so very un-badass.

"Sure." She gives me that look that only an eighteen-year-old can pull off. Part sheer contempt, part uncertainty.

"Hey, I like it. It means I see him more, and that's always a good thing."

I turn and pretend to be uninterested in her assumptions, but inside my heart is beating wildly. The last thing Elijah needs is his awful mother and grandmother finding out about us. He's in their bad books enough as it is.

"Right, let's move this to the hallway. It's time to build this exhibition." I turn to our wonderful creations and split the group up into teams to help move it all. I'm going to make it look so damn good, it will be one less thing for Jennifer Fairclough and her mother to moan about.

I startle when the gentle rap on the bedroom door disturbs my text conversation with Abi. She now knows everything, and honestly, if anyone can squeal while only writing in messages, Abi can.

I told her it's nothing. Nothing for her to get excited about. That she probably won't even meet him, this will all be over soon and then I'll be working out my next plan. Which reminds me, I need to ring the gallery in Whitechapel and see if they've shifted any of my stock. I won't hold my breath.

It's probably Jennings asking if I need anything before he turns in for the night. As far as I can tell, he never has a day off, but I know he and Elaine are liking the fact Lewis and I have taken up residence in the kitchen at meal times. Jennifer didn't bother to come and ask why I was no longer coming to the dining room. I'm guessing she worked it out.

I swing the door open and my stomach tightens and then plummets.

"Turns out I can't stay away."

Eli's blue eyes meet mine and then I'm kissing him, tugging him into the room and slamming the door shut with my foot. "You can't keep driving every day like this," I mumble against his mouth, my tongue alternating between kissing and talking.

Then talking is over, it's just us. I'm tearing the suit and shirt from him, battling cufflinks that seem entirely unnecessary, and waiting for his hands to find my skin.

"Shit, you feel good," he groans as he drops his head, his lips grazing my shoulder, then up and along my neck. We are skin on skin, and I'm on fire.

"It's a long way to come to get naked with someone." I grin at him and it's like I'm slowly morphing into a different person, a person brought about by Eli Fairclough.

"It's two hours." He grabs me up, sliding my legs around his waist. "Believe me, it's worth every damn second." I cling onto him as he walks us to the en-suite. My breasts are pressed tight against his chest, my nipples hardening as they brush his warm skin. He flicks the shower, the jets booming down onto where we stand. "I need to get rid of the city." He kisses my mouth, our lips sliding as the water rushes over our faces. "And then I need you."

He drops me to the floor. My legs are wobbling, but thankfully, he still holds me tight as he rains kisses down on my face. Breaking free, I reach for my lemon soap and lather it in my hand before dropping it back onto the chrome shelf and running my bubble-filled hands along his chest. He shuts his eyes and rolls his neck as the steam rises. His erection grows as my hands drop further down his chest, across his taut abdomen and to the V of his muscles. He's just too much of everything to look at—I've never seen anything like him, never been inspired to stop and look before. But now I'm looking and everything I see is pure perfection. My hand grips his hard on, the remaining soap giving me a silky lubricant. I rub my hand up and down, keeping my grip firm until he groans and one of his hands snakes forward to my hip, tugging me closer. "Every day should end like this."

"Or begin?" I meet his gaze and wink, mesmerised as he grabs the soap and begins to lather it over my skin. God, it's heavenly. He pays extra attention to my breasts until my nipples are standing proud, the darting water from the shower beating down on them. When his hand slips between my legs, delving into soapy wet moistness, I whimper a little. He massages and circles until I'm quivering, my knees opening. He spins me until I'm leant against the tiles of the wet room, his fingers skimming along my buttocks, delving deep. When he positions himself at my entrance, pulling my hips back a little, I'm ready. There's an intense burning tingle right down deep, waiting for him to ease inside. He eases in, slowly and fully, just like last night. Shit, that's good. I cry a little, trying hard to contain myself as he fills me up.

"Fuck," he mutters, his fingers sliding along my back, tracing the patterns of my ink. I push back, grinding my hips in a circle, desperate for more.

He has at it, building it slow and steady until he's pounding deep within me and I'm screaming with every thrust he makes.

"Faith," he groans my name, "please tell me you're close."

Am I?! My legs are trembling, I'm full of a burning need, making me want to push against him until he's torn me open and let the river of need flow free.

I crest the wave, knowing this is normally where it washes flat, leaving me unsatisfied, but not now. Now I'm climbing higher and higher. My hands splay against the tiles, my head resting on the wet surface as I cry a thunderous orgasm.

He follows me, crying out a deep groan into my ear. As soon as he's finished, he pulls away, twisting me in his arms. His mouth lands on mine: hungry, hard, and determined. "I've never wanted anyone more than I want you right now."

My heart crashes in my chest; my pulse thudding in my ears. "Take me to bed," I whisper, and he does, picking me up and stalking with me, water dripping everywhere until we land on the covers and find one another all over again.

Twenty-Seven

"What are you still doing here?" I'm not complaining. His arms are tight and warm, his breath fanning along my skin and I've slept deep and sound.

"I don't have any meetings until lunch."

My toes wiggle as I stretch, and I slide them up his legs. There's a strong chance I never want to move.

He rolls me over though, and I groan in dispute until he slides his hot and firm body over mine. "I didn't get a chance to tell you how amazing the hallway looks."

I grin stupidly. "You like?"

"It's breathtaking." He slides his nose along mine, his mouth fitting my lips perfectly. My body sings with delight, warming and tingling up and down. When he breaks the kiss, I try to pull him back, my hands grasping the back of his neck. "What's the next project?" he asks, ignoring my pleas for more kisses.

"I had an idea for the ballroom."

He lifts an eyebrow; his startling blues focus on my face. "Are you going to share?"

"It's about wild dreams." My heart hammers in my chest, and I nibble my lower lip. "The things we want but can't have."

I want to crumple under the intensity of the blues. There's a lengthy pause. "Sounds dramatic." My stomach twists at his low tone.

A startling rap at the door makes us both jump from the bed. His eyes are wide. "Faith, do you have a minute?" Jennifer's clear-cut call slices through the door.

I motion to the en-suite and point, and Eli pulls the funniest expression as his face scrunches in distaste. I wave my hand at him, shooing him away, and grab my dressing gown, quickly slipping it on.

"Yes?" I open the door, no warmth in my greeting.

"Do you have a moment?" Jennifer asks, not giving me any chance to say no as she steps over the boundary into the room. She frowns at the pink walls and shakes her head. "I can't believe he spent a day painting this pink for you."

"Why? It was a kind gesture to try to make this place feel like home for a while." There is no mistaking my inflection on *this place*.

"Elijah has far more important things to do with his time."

I fold my arms across my chest. "True, he does; such as help people like Lewis."

Her face is carefully neutral as she stares back at me. "Indeed."

"Anyway." I turn and make it look like I'm busy, not lying in bed with her son. "How can I help? I'm about to get dressed for the day."

"I was wondering if you'd thought of any plans for the ball? As I need to get my invites to the printers tomorrow?"

To the printers? Clearly Jennifer Fairclough doesn't nip down to the local stationers for her party invites.

"Yes, I have." I straighten myself up a little. "It's going to be a dream anything theme. People can come as anything they've ever wanted to be."

The glance of derision she casts in my direction makes me want to punch her damn hard. "Really?"

Ignoring her tone, I carry on. "The dress code is optional of course." There's no way Jennifer will do anything other than dress to impress. "The room will be decorated in art that represents the dreams of the people here." I choose my words carefully.

Her face is folded. "Excellent. I shall get on that."

I offer her a tight smile. "Is that all?"

There's a moment of hesitation. "Well," she clears her throat. "It would be nice if you could come back to the dining room for your meals. It doesn't look good for the house to be so fractured."

"And Lewis?"

"Lewis too. I understand he will be with us for the next couple of weeks."

I nod. The last place I want to go back to is that stiff and stuffy dining room with the wicked witch. "Does it really matter how this house appears to be?"

When she turns, her eyes are deep with an inexplicable emotion. "Appearances are everything." She swallows hard. "Which brings me to my next thing. It's been noted that Elijah has been here with you."

A blush creeps from under the neckline of my dressing gown, but I brazen it out and watch her in silence.

"It can't be anything. If he chooses to release his urges with you, then so be it, but it will be nothing more. At the end of the summer, you will be leaving this house and no longer seeing my son."

I pull on the door and hold it open for her. "Don't ever talk to me about my own business again. The rules and games of this family mean nothing to me and I can't wait to leave."

I slam the door and lean against it, hearing Eli pad out of the bathroom. He winds me into his arms. "I'm sorry she's such a bitch. She shouldn't speak to you like that."

For the briefest moment I'm going to ask if he's going to stand up for me, if he's going to tell her she's wrong. But then I remember what we said, the agreement we made, and start to laugh.

"Would you care to release your urges with me?" I wiggle my hips suggestively and he grabs them firmly, anchoring me to him.

"I thought you'd never ask."

Then his mouth is on mine demanding everything and I forget about reality and the sting of words that never truly go away.

We are in the kitchen and I've pushed Elaine out of the way to cook some bacon when my phone rings. When I pull it from my pocket, I wish I'd never heard it, wish I'd never seen it. My heart crashes, my stomach drops, and my hands don't want to work.

Dan.

"Hi." I can sense Eli's curious gaze burn into my back as I push the bacon around the pan.

"You okay, Faithy?" Dan's words slur and run into one another.

"Shit, are you drunk?" I glance at the kitchen clock. It's only quarter to nine. I've got forty-five minutes to eat and say goodbye to Eli before the kids arrive. I turn and slide a hungry glance over to Eli, who's stooped over the table reading the paper, pretending not to listen to my conversation. I'm going to need at least thirty-five minutes to say goodbye to him.

"A little," Dan slurs. "Maybe just a wee bit."

"Why are you drunk in the morning?" I ask, although I have a very good feeling why and my throat begins to tighten. I grip the spatula harder, giving the bacon hell to distract me from emotional overloads.

"He's gone into the hospice, Faith. They took him last night in a private ambulance."

"Why? He was okay the other week."

"Weeks, Faith? This is lung cancer. It's not going to hang around for you to finish making crappy art."

A single tear rolls down my face and splashes into the frying pan. "That's not fair. What happened? And I mean tell me, not just shout at me."

"Yesterday lunch, his lungs..." Dan trails off. "He's not getting enough oxygen, sleeping more and more. I can't get him to eat, to drink, to take painkillers." There's another pause and I hear Dan light a cigarette. I want one too, but then I think of Al and his lungs collapsing, being eaten by a sick cancer that won't stop attacking.

A hand gently takes the spatula and I look up into Eli's face. He wipes away a tear from my face with his thumb and then another and then another. I don't care that Jennings and Elaine are watching us, or that Lewis is bashing about with something noisy and metallic the other side of the room. I care about his touch because it's the only thing I can cling onto. I stare into the blues and my hand shakes as I hold the phone to my ear.

"Have they said how long he will need the respite care for?" I know my lifelong friend won't be leaving the hospice, no one ever does.

"A couple of weeks maybe."

A couple of weeks?

I can't get it to absorb into my brain quite right.

"Listen, Dan. Don't drink anymore. Go have a shower and a sleep, then get back there for him." I flick my eyes over Eli's concerned face. "Then I'll be there. I'll come tonight once the kids have gone home. I might need you or Abi to get me from the station."

"He will kill me for telling you and making you come."

"Nah, tell him to take it up with me when I get there. Can I crash at yours?"

There's a moment of silence. Dan knows Abi's is too cramped, and that there is no other door for me to walk through. "Sure."

"What's wrong?" The skin on the back of my neck prickles.

"Your dad was there when the ambulance came. He's been spending a lot of time at ours."

The bottom of the world just falls away and leaves me suspended, hanging from an endless expanse of sky.

"He can't be there when I get back, you know that right? I never want to see him again. Al knows that." My legs are shaking and not with the delicious warm trembles that Eli creates.

"Faith, this isn't about you."

I want to rip Dan's head off. It's never been about me. But I take a staggered breath and let it go. "I'll see you later. I'll let you know when my train gets in." I go to hang up, but then call him back. "Sober up, Dan, you can be drunk forever afterwards."

I hang up, but my hands are shaking so badly my phone slips out of my hand. Eli is there. Just right there, sweeping it up off the floor, while still maintaining a supportive hold on my elbow. I want to run from his touch, but at the same time I want to bury myself so far under his skin I'll never surface and face reality again.

"Wait," his voice is soft, and the audience I know we have around us melts away. He bends a little until the blues are levelled with my gaze. "Just wait. Talk to me; tell me what you need."

I can't. I need to think, to pace, to breathe air in my lungs. But his hands are on my arms holding me in place. "Al's gone to the hospice."

He nods. "I worked that out. Tell me what you need." I don't understand what he's asking. "What do you need me to do to help?"

His question floors me. I don't think anyone has ever said anything remotely like that to me before. It makes tears tingle along the edge of my eyelashes.

"I don't know. I've got to get there, but I've got to be here today and tomorrow, and I don't know what I'm even thinking or saying..." I trail off as a tidal wave of unspent tears threatens to drown me.

He steers me for a kitchen chair and pushes me gently down, his hands on my shoulders. "Elaine, this woman needs your magic medicine."

Elaine is already bustling around.

"I don't need a sweet tea, Elijah." I shake my head at him, and despite the torn expression on his face, his lips quirk a little.

"Elaine, have you been spilling my tea drinking secrets? No," he turns his focus directly onto me. "No, this is better." Elaine shuffles over with a bottle of the unpronounceable whisky.

"From my cooking stash." She pours me a shot and slides the glass over. "Here."

"Cooking?" I raise an eyebrow and stare at the glass. "I can't drink that, I'm about to teach a bunch of kids how to make vases with clay."

Eli whispers to Elaine and walks away, and without really thinking about it, I pick up the glass and take a little sip. It burns my lips, the peat and smoke flavours dampening the whirlpool of emotions rushing inside me.

While he's gone, I stare at the glass. What am I going to face when I go home? What will Al look like? What will it be like to see him like that? How will I cope? Why is my father there? Why has Al let him back in now, after everything?

Maybe everything is about me just like Dan said?

Before I've taken three sips of fiery liquid, Eli is back in front of me. "Okay, I'm going to be here today, I can help." he crouches down in front of my spot on the kitchen chair. "Not that I know much about vases, but hey, I can make it up." He grins, and a watery tide threatens to wash me away. "Then tonight I'll drive you to Brighton. I don't want you to get the train there and back by yourself."

"Ssh." I frown at the people around us, but Eli shakes his head.

"Don't worry, these guys are my friends."

I stare at him for a moment. Wasn't this the room where I told him I'd be his friend? Maybe this is it, the kitchen and the space, it gives him his centre... I'm losing the plot. I'm thinking crazy unnecessary thoughts to stop thinking about the ones that scare me the most. I don't know where Eli's centre is because I don't even know where he lives—let's keep it real right now.

"And what about your mother? What she's going to say when you're home helping, or taking me to Brighton?" Let's not forget the fact she was only in my bedroom a short while ago reading me the "don't shag my son" riot act.

"I couldn't give a fuck what they think."

He leans forward and kisses me firmly on the mouth, and in the back of my limited sensibilities I hear Elaine sigh and Lewis ask what the hell's going on.

When Eli pulls away, I watch his face and I have a bad feeling. A very, very bad sinking sensation inside me. Because somehow, and I don't know how, he's managed to take awful news and turn it into something that's making my heart soar. And with every bank of wind my soaring heart is climbing on, I know I'm falling deeper and deeper under his spell.

Far enough under I'll accept his lift, just so I can be with him, and take him to that awful place called home.

Twenty-Eight

"You never told me what happened for you to run away from Brighton?" His voice cuts through the silence in the car.

The silence is partly because I'm lost in thought, scared shitless of what the next few days are going to bring, and partly because I'm fricking livid. Eli told me as we loaded overnight bags into the car, under the watchful gaze of his mother, that he's asked Gerard Steers to step in at Bowsley while I go to Brighton.

I send him a total stink eye and fold my arms tighter across my chest. His lips quirk at the edges which just makes me even madder.

"Faith, I wanted to give you some breathing space. Gerard, twat he may be, is an old family friend; it made sense to call him."

I grumble under my breath.

"It was Peter who suggested it, when I told him you needed to take time out."

I raise an eyebrow. Of course it bloody was. I haven't seen Peter since my first lunch here, but I still fondly remember him as being the one who told me the truth about

Steers. Although I suppose knowing the truth is better than being lied to.

"And I'm sure your mother would love to replace me with him on a permanent basis."

He turns as much as his concentration on the heavy evening traffic will allow. "No one is replacing you. This is your job, your gig. The credit it all yours."

"I don't want the credit," I snap. "I want to see it through. I like those kids, they're a good bunch."

"Look, everything will be the same when we get back. Gerard is just going to clear up the awful mess I helped you to create today." His hand grasps my knee and as furious as I am, I can't ignore the little flare of heat that blooms with his touch. "And will you stop changing the subject about Brighton?"

I scowl in his direction, not that he takes any notice. "I'm not spilling my shit to you, Eli. You've got your own family issues." And hell, does he?! His mother looked like she wanted to lie down in front of the wheels of his car when he left with me. "And I've got mine."

I truly hope my dad isn't at Dan's when I get there. I rub at my face. I don't need to worry about make-up; I've washed it away with tears sporadically throughout the day.

My gaze drops to a tattoo on my thigh peeking out from under the ripped edge of my denim shorts. An ancient knot symbolising strength. I wish I could somehow activate it and make it take over my trembling nerves. I'm not as strong as I'd like to be. No matter how shit-kicker my external attitude is, underneath I'm nothing more than a confused teenager who doesn't know what to do.

Eli's fingers trail along the ink on my leg. "What does it mean?"

I pause for a moment steeling myself. "It means strength. At least I hoped it would help."

His thumb rubs across the ink, stretching the skin slightly. "Did it help?"

I shrug and turn my gaze out of the window and we drive the rest of the way in silence.

When we pull up outside Al's, I drag in a deep breath. The front room lights are on, so someone is there. I guess the only way I'm going to find out who, is by getting out the car and taking one step at a time to the front door.

"Faith," Eli's call is soft, and I turn to find him watching me, his hands gripping the steering wheel. "Sorry I've pissed you off."

I shake my head, my anger dissipating under those blues. "I'm sorry your mum knows about us. I would never want to cause problems for you and your family."

He shifts forward, settling his hands on my face and his lips catch mine. His kiss is everything as each and every one of them are. "I can't ignore this feeling I have that all of this is for something. You came into my life and it's like you were set to challenge everything."

My tongue dries. "Like what?"

"I was sleeping, working, existing... and then there was you. A challenge to everything I've ever known."

"This is just for the summer, that's what we said." God, those words hurt, but I can't think of anything more than that. It was my compromise. I'm not the girl who thinks of happily ever after. Eli isn't my prince. He isn't going to swoop in and make the past disappear. He's not going to erase all the many reasons for my ink.

He pulls away slightly. "Yes. That's what we said."

I crumple a little. It's what I want him to say, but my

chest squeezes in such a way that for a moment I forget how to breathe. I don't even know what it means when your chest pushes the air out of your lungs like that. All I know is I want to kiss him, to cling to him, until the summer is over and then I'll go back to how I was before.

"Come, let's go." I pull on the door handle and step out of the car, not giving him a chance to do that gentlemanly thing he does with the door.

He eyes the street as we stand side by side. "So, this is where you grew up?"

I shake my head and point in the direction of a road largely out of sight, a three-minute walk away. "I used to live there. But I spent most my time here with Dan."

The door opens then as if on cue and Dan leans against the door frame, his eyes watching me, analysing Eli and the way his hand is holding mine.

Dan's face is a picture I never want to see again. His eyes blurred, red-rimmed. In his hand is an empty glass. "Dan?" My voice cracks and I fly up the path into his chest and wrap my arms tight around him as though I want to keep us both afloat. I cry into his neck and droplets of tears splatter his T-shirt. "You okay?"

"Yes, yes." He wipes at his nose with the back of his hand and straightens up to meet Eli.

"Hi, I'm sorry to meet you under these circumstances." Eli steps up and holds up his hand. Dan shifts from foot to foot but then shakes his hand.

"Eli, Dan. Dan, Eli." I wave my hand between them and step into the front room. "Fuck, Dan, this place is revolting."

He glares at me. "Because you're the queen of clean." He picks up a pizza box and places it on the table. "I've been busy."

There's movement from the kitchen. Please, God, don't let it be him; I wouldn't able to take it. A girl with dark hair comes out, wringing her hands on a tea towel. "Who the hell are you?" I ask.

It's not a surprise that her gaze narrows into slits and she looks at me with as much warmth as a polar ice cap. I didn't mean to be rude. My expectations were focused on the worst. "JoAnne." She drops the tea towel onto the edge of the sofa. I can see she's not one to tidy either. "Who the hell are you?"

I'm taken aback. Dan and I have always known the ins and outs of each other's lives. We've known all there is to know: every kiss, every fuck, every row. Tighter than family, it's always been us, with Abi as our third wheel until she got all grown up and married. Yet here the two of us stand, both of us flanked by total strangers. "I'm Faith." I step up and hold out my hand. "I'm sorry, I didn't mean to be rude. I thought someone else might be here."

Dan comes close to my side and squeezes my shoulder. JoAnne's gaze zooms to his hand on my skin. "I got rid of the crew. Everyone is taking it in turns to keep him entertained."

"Is he still awake?"

Whether I can walk into that hospice I don't know.

"Not really, Faith." Dan's gaze focuses on Eli. 'So how do you two know each other?"

"Elijah owns the house I'm working at, he drove me here."

I cringe under Eli's hot gaze. What was I supposed to say? He's my boss, but we are embroiled in some forbidden and pointless affair that's going nowhere.

"Thanks." Dan nods at Eli, but thankfully only I spot the faint curve of Eli's lips.

"Always a willing chauffeur to a woman in need."

I glare at him but then turn to JoAnne. "So, you guys are a thing?"

This is so awkward. When did this happen? That life would carry on and things would change without me knowing.

I know when it happened. It was when I ran away.

"Yes." She's not a fan of me; it's not hard to read that headline. What on earth has Dan told her?

Oh well, I haven't got time for this shit now. "Can I go and see Al? Oh and thank you but I don't need a room now. Eli and I are going to stay in a hotel along the sea front." Eli has taken care of everything, which is a good thing because my brain can't handle more than three minutes of the future at a time right now.

Dan nods, "Want me to take you, or is your chauffeur driving you about all day?"

Eli steps up and places a hand on my shoulder. "I've got it, thanks."

Jeez, are we in a pissing contest?

This isn't the time. I glare at them both and stalk back out the door. At the moment, Al is more important than the rest of the world. They can all go to hell. With a deep breath that stretches my lungs, I pull on big girl panties I didn't even know I owned and go to face the worst scenario I could ever consider—saying goodbye to one of my best friends.

The hospice is down and along the sea front. If you've gotta go, and we all do in the end, then the sea view is a nice plus.

Al looks awful: grey, ashen and barely conscious.

I kiss his head and grip his hand tight in mine.

I'm aware of Eli moving around. "Faith, I'll wait

outside."

"No." I look at him with fright. "Please don't leave me."

A frown flickers across his face, but he sits down in the seat positioned in the corner of the room.

"Hey, Uncle Al." I wipe his hair back from his head. It's fine and a little greasy.

I'm surprised when his eyes flutter open.

"I must be dying if you've come home."

"Don't exaggerate, old man. I came back just the other week, remember?"

Al looks at me blankly and I know he doesn't remember my visit the other Sunday.

"I was thinking of my next tattoo." I settle a hip on the bed and stroke his hand with mine.

He shakes his head but then winces and coughs. "No more."

"Say what?" I laugh and notice Eli's eyes on my face.

"No more. Tell me what you're making." He coughs again, and it makes me want to cry. I won't though. Not now. Tears can well later.

Eli steps up from the chair in the corner. "She's making a jolly fine mess at the moment, Sir." He smiles that handsome flash of white teeth at Al. "I'm Elijah." He squeezes Al's hand.

Fuck, I am going to cry.

Bollocks.

Al wheezes. "I see why you took the job."

I roll my eyes and chuckle. "He's a pain in the arse for a boss." I smirk at Eli.

"Worse than me?" Al asks.

"Hell yeah, makes you look like a little old lady in a sweet shop."

Eli pulls up his chair and I sit squarer on the bed and we fill the air with chit chat and inane conversation as the afternoon slowly ticks away.

When the door opens, it's getting late. We've been there for hours watching and talking as Al slowly drifts in and out of sleep. I'll never be able to thank Eli enough for bringing me down here and spending his time here like this with me.

I want the afternoon to last forever.

"Oh, sorry, I didn't realise there was someone here."

The voice makes my blood chill. "What?" I slide off the bed and turn for the door. There's my dad. In all his bastard glory. "GET OUT," I screech.

My skin crawls at the sight of him. My stomach lurches until I could bring up that last cup of tea.

"Faith, please wait and listen."

Ignoring the wheezy pleas of Al from the bed, I glare at the man I used to consider my father. "I have nothing to listen to. You're a bastard and I said I never wanted to see you again."

"Faith, please. We need to talk. I need to ex—"

"Honestly, Dad, I don't know how to explain this in a way you'll understand." I hear Eli's gasp when I say 'Dad' but I ignore it. "So, I'll go old school and tell it to you straight. Go fuck yourself. You're dead to me, and that will never change."

My insides tremble with rage, but I manage to turn my back on the failure of a parent by the door and bend down to give Al a kiss on his forehead. "I'm sorry," I whisper. He responds with a simple nod but the pain in his eyes says it all.

I can't change the way I feel even if a dying man asks me to.

I breeze past my dad and wait for Eli in the corridor of

the hospice. When he comes out and tries to take me in his arms, bending to meet my eyes, I fight him off. "Stop, stop trying to make everything all right."

"I'm not..."

"You are. You're trying to fix me, but you can't."

I turn and run, desperate for the fresh air outside and soothing balm of the sea.

Twenty-Nine

His feet echo after mine along the empty pier. I don't stop, though. I don't even know if I want to talk. I don't even know if I want to breathe. Finally, when I'm over the ocean I sit on the wooden edge, my feet dangling over the sea.

He sits next to me, his hands clasping the metal railing like mine.

"Do you know how many times I've sat here and wanted to dive in down there, to fall into the blackness and never surface again?" My words are low, barely audible over the rush of the waves.

"Why?"

I ignore his question, my gaze focused on the dark horizon. "It's why I understand Lewis' mum. I get what she did."

I watch as his fists tighten on the metal pole of the railings. "You need to talk to me. At the moment all I can envision is the very worst, and it's killing me."

I shake my head. "I can't, Eli." I look up at him though unshed tears. "If I do, you'll never look at me the same again."

"Why?"

"Because you'll finally realise my heart is as black as

that sea. It's why I can't let myself feel anything for anyone." I drop my head against the cool metal. "It's why no matter how my stomach flutters when you knock on my bedroom door at Bowsley; no matter how much I love waking in your arms, I'll never let myself love you."

His head shakes. "This was never about love. You know that; it's what we agreed."

I'm at war with myself. With what I know and what I'll know I'll never have.

"But that doesn't mean I'm not your friend, doesn't mean you can't talk to me," he adds.

A tear slips down my cheek and then another. I watch the waves come and go in silence until finally I break, and with my words I know I'm going to unravel the secret spell of summer magic we have weaved between us.

Because I am darkness itself and I ruin everything —eventually.

"When I was thirteen, Dad told me he had a new girlfriend." I shudder a breath but steel myself with a solid control of iron fisted resolution. "I didn't think much of it. I was always with Dan—it had always been me and Dad, and Dan and Al. Life wasn't conventional.

"I mean I know my dad used to have flings; he was always popular. But mum had never been around, and I was always his number one girl."

Eli reaches a hand and places it on my tattoo of strength.

"It was just before my fourteenth birthday when Sandy and Aiden moved in with us. Aiden was two years above me at school. I thought it would be cool to have an older brother, kind of like Dan, but a real brother. Everything was fine. Sandy was high maintenance, but I quickly learned how to keep out of her way and keep life sweet.

"This is the Aiden you screamed about in your sleep the other night?" Eli uses gentle fingertips to pull my face to his, his eyes searching and deep in the dark.

"Yes," I whisper. "At first I didn't notice what was happening. It was just hugs, touches. Sometimes they would linger longer than I'd expect."

Eli hisses a breath, but I've started now, and I can't stop.

"But you know, I was a teenager, my body was doing its own thing. One Saturday night when Dad and Sandy had gone to bed, he told me to snuggle up while we watched the end of the movie. He kissed me."

I can't look at Eli, but I don't think he can look at me either.

"I told him it was wrong, that we were family, but he said I was being silly and that he knew I enjoyed it.

"He felt me, down there. He grabbed me hard and laughed, told me the body never lies and that I wanted him as much as he wanted me."

"You were just a kid."

I shrug. "I grew up quick." My eyes screw shut against the memories, but they are still there, etched into my memory. "So it carried on, little touches, explorations, and I was always torn between knowing it was wrong and him telling me that I wanted it, that my body was betraying me. That I was naughty and no one would believe I hadn't led him on."

Eli hisses, clenching the metal barrier.

"Then one day he went too far." A snivelling sob works its way from deep within me. "I told him he had to stop, but he didn't, he kept going and going. He groomed me to believe my body wanted it, that because I responded to his touch, it was right." I shut my eyes to the memories, the sting of pain.

"That's why you have the one-time-only rule?"

I nod, a jerky movement. "My body isn't to be trusted."

Eli shakes his head. "So what then?"

"I told my dad. I told Sandy. I'd finally cracked and let all my secrets slide to Dan and Abi. They made me believe it was wrong, that Aiden had taken advantage of me... abused me. And I knew he had. He was older, and he knew what he was doing. It's not like I was in love with him. I hated him touching me, but my body just couldn't fight it. He was always stronger, more convincing." I brush away a tear. "Bloody traitorous body."

"That's why you have so many tattoos—you've been arming yourself."

I shrug. "That or make people think I'm a certain way so they won't expect anything from me other than what I give them—which is nothing." My gaze flicks over him quickly. He who I've given everything to without really knowing it.

"So, anyway. Dad didn't believe me. Sandy told me I was a whore, that I'd tricked her son. At first, she told Dad he had to go with her, away from the lies I was spreading, but eventually she left him. They still live here. Aiden is still walking around like he didn't abuse a teenage girl, and my father and I don't speak."

"Why didn't he believe you?"

I laugh. It's bitter. It hurts. "By this point, Aiden had done his damage. I was sliding down a slippery path to not giving a fuck about anything. Then I slept with one of his friends. I didn't know Aiden had told him what he'd already done with me. I thought he liked me, but then he ridiculed me in front of the school." I point to my lightning bolt. "This was to remind me never to trust anyone more than once." Our eyes meet. Eli broke that rule for me. "Dad heard the rumours. I was helping in the shop by then. He said I must have led Aiden on, that I'd confused myself over what happened.

"So, I screamed at him, told him he'd forced himself on me, that he'd taken my—" I stop. I can't carry on, because that one memory burns more than the others. "But he turned around and said it was only an assault if the other person didn't want it."

Eli's mouth is open. Then he's up off the wooden deck, pacing away, his hands in his hair, his shoulders bunched over. "Fuck!" He screams into the air, and I launch up, going to him, soothing him. Funny that it's me calming him. "I'm going to fucking rip someone's head off."

And I can sense it, it's boiling under him. His hands drop to my face, his thumbs skimming my cheeks. Lips crash onto my mouth, his tongue hot and desperate. "I want to take away every bad thing that's ever happened to you." The intensity radiating from his face, the deep frown etched into his features tells me he means it.

"You already have."

"So that's it. Aiden is still walking around, and you haven't spoken to your dad."

I smile slightly, but a giant wave of tears floods down my face. "And Al saved me. Took me in, believed me, and now he's going to die."

I sob, my tears drenching Eli's T-shirt. His arms tighten around me, holding me so close it's as if we are breathing as one.

"I—" he hesitates.

"You what?" I look up into his beautiful face.

His head shakes. "You've got me churning so many emotions, Faith. I can't make sense of it all. You know the way I was brought up—the Faircloughs aren't allowed to feel. We keep a stiff upper lip and live behind closed doors.

Anything can happen, so long as the rest of the world doesn't know." He shudders a breath, his forehead dropping to mine. "But you've blown open all the damn doors and I don't know how to close them again."

And I know what he means because as he pulls me back in and tangles me tight, holds me, my heart opens up and a wealth of tears begin to fall that could wash away all my stories in ink.

Eventually, we turn back to the hotel. I hold on to the belt of his jeans and follow up him up the steps. We are silent, all words spent.

In the room he turns to me, the tip of his finger trailing down my face and along my roses. "Let me love you," he whispers.

I nod, briefly.

Love. It's something I don't know. An emotion hidden from me, deep within the black of my heart. But I know I want to be with him, hold him, have him. I open my arms, so he can step in, and sweet kisses land on my lips, my cheeks, the tip of my nose.

Slowly, with more care than we've shown one another before, we undress. One garment at a time falls to the floor until we are two people naked and bare for each other to see. His hand slides to my shoulder, running down my arms. My body hums in response, but this time I allow it. I don't think it's a bad thing, I don't try to fight it. I just let it happen, opening my heart and mind to whatever comes next. My nipples harden, and he runs his palms over them in a gentle circular motion. It links directly to the growing heat aching in the pit of my tummy.

"Does it seem crazy we've only known each other a few weeks?" I ask, my head falling back so he can kiss my neck.

"No. What's crazy is I haven't known you before."

With his words, he lifts me to the bed and holds himself above me. There's no wild frenzy of discovery. It's slow and sweet and he keeps his eyes on me the whole time as he slowly fills me up and rocks me into a rhythm that has my heart pounding gently in my chest. I cling to him when I come, clenching myself around him, and when he groans my name into my ear, I kiss his neck, his shoulders, his mouth. He's still here despite what I told him on the pier. Despite what I told him my body allowed me to do. For years I never let myself believe I was a victim. But right there and then, with his gentle lovemaking, he showed me acutely how it is meant to be. That's how a first time is meant to be. It's supposed to fill you up, allow your heart and soul to bloom and to leave you in a place from where you grow and develop, blossoming into someone else, someone better.

He just gave that to me.

I stare at him. Unspoken words run between us.

I allowed him to love me.

And it's the most dangerous thing I've ever done.

It's the depth of night. Morning hasn't yet stolen its clear and bright fingers of sunlight into the corners of the hotel rooms. Eli's breath is regular, his chest rising and falling, and I'm laid across it, my arms around him tight, my fingers playing with the light smattering of hair across his wonderful chest. But I can't sleep. I'm thinking of everything. All the things to be lost, all the things to be found. I know I've got to walk away from Eli in a couple of weeks. It's what we always said. So why does thinking about it hurt me as much as the thought of Al in that hospice bed? Why, when I think of it does all thoughts of the future and any plans I should be making evaporate, leaving me on an empty precipice of nothing?

I can't come back to Brighton, I know that now. Life has moved on here without me, and that's fine. I need to see what's happening with my exhibits at the gallery. Maybe I should call them later and find out if there has been any success.

I'm dreading facing Jennifer at Bowsley, and the wicked witch. She will know I've done the one thing she guessed right back on that very first morning and fucked her grandson.

"What are you thinking of?" Gentle lips press against my forehead and I snuggle deeper.

"Your grandmother."

He chuckles, his chest rocking me gently. "Not what I want you to be thinking of right now."

I snigger. "Better than a whole host of other things."

He wiggles down until we are eye-to-eye and his thumb brushes against my cheek. It makes my heart beat wildly. "I'm glad you shared with me."

I nod. It's good to be open, and honest.

"What happens when we go back to Bowsley? I don't want to get you in trouble, Eli. I really don't."

His gaze is steady and for a moment he's silent. "I don't know."

"What happened with your dad?" I snuggle into his side, loving the way the warmth of his skin sinks into me.

His fingers trail up and down my arm. "He was never my gran's choice; my mother insisted on following her own path." His voice is clipped. "He had money, but it wasn't the right money for Gran. But Mother insisted she loved him. She got pregnant with Peter quickly—too quickly—and the marriage was rushed through before any scandal could arise."

"She was pregnant before they got married? Wow." I

can't imagine the infallible Jennifer ever allowing that to happen.

His fingers continue their journey. "I had a happy childhood, actually. There was always laughter. Dad was fun. He loved music, art, and drama."

"Did he paint, too?"

"Yeah, but then slowly it all got shifted to one small corner of the house, and then eventually time was swallowed, and he never used to do anything like that. The music stopped."

"That's why you paint in the attic?"

"It's not a suitable career, I told you."

"Yet, you've convinced your family to open up the house to art all summer. So it's not exactly dead is it?"

"I had to fight hard for that."

"And it got you out of your engagement." There's a beat of silence that chills my stomach. "Did you ever love her, the girl you said you'd marry?"

His lips kiss my forehead again and then the tip of my nose. "Love is a luxury I've never been allowed. When Dad left, it all went with him."

"And you're that worried about Tabitha?" I know this is it. It's her he's staying for, like the true and honest big brother he is.

"Yes. I don't want them to just marry her off."

"But she's only eighteen."

"So? That means nothing when it comes to society and the success of the Fairclough name."

"All this for a name?"

He nods, his lips straight.

"Yikes, it makes growing up in the shop seem like a dream."

He offers me a small sigh.

"Do you ever hear from your dad?" I ask.

He shakes his head. "No. He made his choice and left."

I nod. We both have parents who made choices and who hurt us with them. It's another tangled thread that binds us together.

"I've been thinking." He smiles, and it warms my tummy.

"Dangerous."

I chuckle as he pounces on me, kissing along my tickling throat, holding my hands above my head.

"What have you been thinking?" I prompt, when I can catch a breath.

"I want you to ink me."

The blues are dead serious.

"But you don't have any tattoos?" He doesn't. His perfect smooth and golden skin is flawless.

"And I want you to give me my first."

I hesitate. I don't do that anymore, I left it behind. "Eli, I'm not sure. You will be stuck forever with something by me on your skin that you won't ever be able to remove."

He kisses me, deep and hard. "And that's exactly why I want it."

His words slice me deep, because I know that we made an agreement, and I know our time will end. But I also know that we are both encountering emotions we've never experienced before. But it means nothing. Nothing at all.

Thirty

The sun is high in the sky when I sit back and admire my work. "You've been remarkably brave."

He winces as he sits up from lying face down on the bed in Al's shop. We let ourselves into Al's home at three, not long after he asked me, borrowed his keys and let ourselves into the shop.

"That bloody hurts."

With a roll of my eyes I chuckle and give him some space.

I start tidying, trying not to watch him as he walks to the mirror and turns his back.

He gave me free reign. Told me to do whatever I thought would be best. At first, I didn't have a clue, but then when I put the machine on it came to me.

Eli is two people, two halves, a battle that never ends. Two desires that won't ever meet. The man in the suit, the guy in the sliders. So I did him a yin-yang made from waves, vibrant with blues and purple instead of the obligatory black.

"What do you think?" I ask when he doesn't say a word.

"I think it's perfect." He comes over, his chest still bare

and kisses me, pulling me into his arms. I'm careful not to touch his back despite the longing I have to hug him tight.

"Come, let's go get ice cream." I grin at him widely.

"Ice cream?" His eyes widen in shock. "But what about my figure?"

I'm giggling and launching myself around him, my hands in his hair, when the door opens and we both turn to find Dan watching us. "What are you guys doing here?"

"Getting ice-cream." I laugh, and I never want to stop.

I never want this to end. Because when it does it will all be gone.

We've had ice cream, kissed with our toes in the sea, and I've done the hardest thing I've ever faced. I've said goodbye to Al.

"Create something, Faith, always create." He squeezed my fingers and tears stole down my face, but then I looked at Eli and he captured them all. Al watched us, smiling. I'm glad I left him knowing I was happy at last. Even if it's short lived.

I didn't see Dad again, and that I can live with for all eternity.

My tears keep coming and going. Eli squeezes my leg every time he hears me give a gentle sob. The car ride has been largely silent.

When we pull up through the gates at Bowsley, he turns to me, his fingers sliding through my hair. "You okay? Can you do this?"

"I want to. Al wanted me to."

"You know Steers will be here?"

I nod. It's okay, the last couple of days have weakened my anger. I know now my anger is at myself, my body, my disgust. He's just a man who didn't tell me the whole truth.

We won't be friends again, but I'm not going to throw anything at him—that I know of.

He goes to open the door. "Eli, I..." I trail off. There isn't a word that can adequately describe how I feel. How grateful I am, how inexplicably shaken to the foundations of my existence I am by his presence and the way he makes me feel.

He nods, and it's all we need.

We stand by the car and stare at the doors of the house. "I don't know if I'm more worried about your mother, or the mess of clay they've probably all made."

His hand slips into mine and takes me by surprise. "Let's take one at a time."

He holds my hand right up to the front door and into the beautifully decorated hallway with the glass flowers. I try to pull away, but he won't let me; sending me a wide smile instead that tells me we are in this together, whatever that means.

"Oh my god, the prodigal son returns." Why does Peter the Arse have to be here now? We step through into the sitting room. I've barely been in this pale-coloured room, all the furniture a brocade stripe of pale green. It seems the sort of place I would dirty just by being there.

"Shut up, Peter." Elijah growls. He's still holding my hand and I'm visibly sweating. I wish I had his quiet confidence, but I don't.

Gerard is there, and he jumps up when he sees me, placing down his glass of something short and dark on the table. "Faith, are you okay? How was it at home?"

I nod. "Fine, thank you. How did you get on with the groups?"

He looks a little crestfallen at my stiff answer—but really, what else was he expecting? I've been to Brighton for a couple of days, not to Mars for a brain lobotomy. He's still a lying bastard.

"Good. You've got them so excited. I wish half my students on my degree course were that enthusiastic."

I send him a tight smile. "Do we have any ceramics to show for it?"

"Yeah, Tabitha was a little loose on the description, but she said it was for use with the ball." Gerard pushes his glasses back up his nose.

It's good to be talking art again and I slowly relax. Eli leans over and kisses me on the cheek and Peter almost chokes on his drink. "I'm going to go find Mother. Are you okay here?"

I raise an eyebrow. "I'd rather be here with these losers than facing down your mother."

He chuckles, his eyes drifting affectionately across my face. "That's what I thought." He steps away and our time away is officially over.

"How's Lewis?" I ask Gerard—ignoring Peter, mainly because he's a twat.

"Fine, fine, he's been okay. He had an outburst yesterday after his dad called but he seems settled again now."

Reluctantly, I give Gerard a smile. "Thanks."

I go to grab my bags to head back to my rooms and Gerard drops into step at my side. "So, you and Elijah, right?"

"Are you gossiping, Gerard?"

He grabs my arm, holding me still. "No, but hell, Faith, I don't want to see you get hurt."

"But you hurt me, so how does that work?"

"I hurt you because I was an idiot and didn't tell you the

whole truth. This family will tear you apart. You can't trust them."

"I can't trust anyone, can I?" I glare at him.

"Me?" He shrugs and smiles optimistically.

"Yeah, right."

I try to ignore him and head to the outhouses. It's strangely comforting returning to them after the couple of days in Brighton.

I fling bags inside the pink room and then head straight for the room I'd set out for pottery.

Laughter seeps through the door, and I send Gerard a quizzical look. He just holds his hands up. I turn the door knob and the laughter stops. With a push, I open the door.

Tabitha is one side of a brown clay-dust clouded table, Lewis is the other. Lewis has a streak of red dust through his hair. Tabitha looks like she's been rolling in the stuff. "Everything okay in here?" I ask.

Tabs flushes a little and nods, stepping towards me. "It's good to see you. How was your friend?"

"Ill." I brush at some of the clay debris in her hair. "Really ill, but we said goodbye." I give her a small smile, suddenly aware of the atmosphere in the tiny studio. "It was as good as it could be, I guess."

She turns her back on Lewis and I don't miss the flicker of annoyance crossing his face.

I'll have to talk to him. If there's something going on here, it needs to be stopped immediately. Tabitha is the baby of the Faircloughs. I can only imagine what major shit would brew into a storm if she had a fling with a wild teenager Eli brought home.

"So, we need to get ready for this ball. I've had some ideas while I've been away." I realise Gerard is still in the room and look at him expectantly. "Off you go, Steers. Thanks for helping, but we are all good now."

He grins, and I don't like it. "Actually, Jennifer has asked me to stay to help, just in case you get called away again."

"Are you fricking kidding me?" I spin for the door just as Eli walks in. He's still in his casual clothes, but his body is rigid and hard. He doesn't meet my eye.

"He's staying, Faith," he says, and the distance in his voice kills me, just downright slices me in half.

I glare at him. "Not a chance."

He steps closer, his body close but not close enough. "Faith, let it go."

I stare into his face, searching for some familiarity there from our weekend, or the car, or all the many moments I've etched into my brain but it's not there. "Like bloody hell, I will." With a shove of my elbow, I push past him and march for the house looking for Jennifer, finding her in a room I haven't seen before. Containing a Regency desk and decorated in pale pastels and paler wood, it's the most feminine study I've ever seen. Jennifer sits behind the desk reading some papers, a cup of tea steaming in front of her.

"Why have you asked Steers to stay?" I ask and plant myself directly in front of her.

She sighs and glances up at me. "What are you talking about?"

"Gerard told me you'd asked him to stay and work the project, and Eli—Elijah's just confirmed it, but why?"

"There's a lot to do, can you really do it by yourself?"

"A lot to do for what?"

"For my ball, of course."

I glare at her in bewilderment. "When I took this job, no one told me anything about a ball or the fact this was all leading to one. Is this what Elijah wanted when he arranged this? I don't think so. Why are you making it all about some social event now?"

She stands, her slender hip perching against the desk. "I don't expect you to understand, but everything we do is for some ulterior purpose. Elijah knew when he arranged his art outreach project that it would be to bring attention to Bowsley; to open it to the public eye, to get interest so we can earn an income from the property."

"No, it wasn't." I shake my head. "He did it because he loves art and he wants to help others less fortunate."

She chuckles and shakes her head like I'm some naughty, but cheeky young child.

"Work with Gerard, make it beneficial. Who knows what press and gallery acquisitions buyers will be here for the ball; maybe it will be worth your while as much as ours."

I'm simmering, every cuss I know stinging the tip of my tongue.

With a turn, I flounce for the door.

"Oh, Faith," she calls me back.

"Yes." My hands are clenched into fists.

"I've told Elijah that whatever this is you think you have going on between you, it's over. As of now." She eyes me coolly while I seethe inside. "Have your weekend, take from that what you may. But Elijah is returning to London and you will leave him alone if you value your future here on this project."

"And you think the project is more important because?"

"I've had confirmation the acquisitions director of the Tate Modern is coming to our little summer ball. She's even seen some of your work already."

My stomach drops away. "How?"

"I sent her one of your flowers."

She did what? "Why?"

Jennifer settles back into her chair. "Because contrary to popular belief I'm not a complete bitch. You are talented."

I don't know what to say.

Is she bribing me to say away from Elijah by dangling the biggest carrot in the art world under my nose?

Well, fuck that. I straighten myself up tall. "Elijah wants me. Maybe that's something you are just going to have to deal with, but I know he won't let me down."

I walk out without a backward glance and head back to my room.

Is Elijah really going to London and staying away? Staying away from me and his project, his dream? I can't believe what she said. She's wrong. I just know it.

He's sat on my bed, his head in his hands. I snort when I see him and slam the door shut. "What happened to taking one at a time together?"

When his eyes meet my own, my heart cracks a little. "I told you, Faith, this family is fucked-up"

She was right. He is going to leave, and the last couple of days have been for nothing. "So you are giving up. Running back to London with your tail between your legs?"

"It's not running away, it's called going to work."

"What did she say? Did she threaten Tabitha?"

He shakes his head. When he steps from the bed, his tall powerful body dwarfs mine. His hands hold my skin, his lips a brush away from mine. "I'm sorry, Faith, but it's over." It's nothing more than a whisper and then he's gone.

And inside I want to die. I told him everything. Gave him everything, broke every rule.

This was never meant to be anything, so why the hell does this hurt so much?

Thirty-One

"I'm just putting this out there." Abi gives me one of her *I know all the shit* stares down the camera. Even fuzzy and held with a shaking hand her glare is powerful.

"What?" I groan and roll back onto the grass. It's been a long day. It's been a long few days. The afternoon session is finished and after a quick clean up with Steers, Lewis, and Tabs, I've headed out for some alone time. This house is an unhealthy place to be.

"I think he's protecting you. If his dragon of a mother is teasing your future prospects, saying that someone's coming to see your work from the fucking Tate. I mean come on, Faith, it's the Tate Modern—you drool in that place for hours—then I'm gonna put money on the fact he's trying not to ruin that for you."

I shake my head. "He's saving himself from being cut off. That's all."

"I don't believe it. That guy was so hot on you, he was almost melting the room. That stare, those eyes. Jeez, he was melting my panties just being in the same room."

"Abs!"

She pokes her tongue out but grins. "It's true. Hey,

Adam, Elijah was melting your jocks too wasn't he with those swoon intense eyes."

The camera spins until I'm facing Adam who's sprawled on the sofa clutching a bottle of beer. "Totally. Faith, us dudes don't talk about this stuff, but that guy had it bad."

"You two are really bloody annoying." I scowl and drag on my cigarette. It seems that while my uncle and father-figure dying of cancer is enough to put me off smoking, Elijah Fairclough leaving me without a backwards glance is beyond the limits of my willpower.

I blow smoke and stare at the clouds. "So now I'm stuck here, in this hellish prison."

Abi laughs, the phone shaking even more until my stomach rolls like I'm on a ship at sea. "A prison? It's a fucking castle, Faith, get a grip."

"You wait. Which reminds me, would you two be able to get a babysitter for the 18th of August?"

"Why?" She sits up a little straighter. "Don't get me all excited here, Faith."

A wide grin spreads across my face, despite the gaping hole that seems to be residing on a permanent basis in my chest. "I thought you might like to come to the ball? I could do with some friendly back up."

Abi squeals but then squints at me. "You don't need back up, although of course we are coming. You're Faith Hitchin, you survive everything, even being in that place."

I nod. She's kind, too kind to me really, considering I'm such a stroppy bitch. "That I do." Flicking the screen of my phone, I check the time. "Speaking of which, I'm going to ring that gallery who had some of my stuff, see if they've made any sales."

Abi nods and waves her fingers at the camera. "See you.

I'm going to look for a ball dress. What sort of thing are you wearing?"

I hesitate. Jennifer had said that Saskia woman would take care of it. Whether that was still happening after I slept with her son I didn't know.

Oh well. I can dress myself.

I hang up and then double check the time before calling another number. It's answered on the fifth ring. "Whitlocks."

"Oh, hello, is Damien there?"

There's a muffle down the phone and then the sound of someone passing it over. "Damien speaking."

"Hi Damien, it's Faith Hitchin. I was calling to see if you'd managed to move any of my pieces?"

"Oh Faith, so thrilled you called." Damien's voice is high and rings like he's singing.

"Really, why?"

"We need more sculptures from you."

"More? But I gave you five."

He squeals a little and his hands reverberate in a clap in the background. "I know. We sold all of them about two months ago. I did put a call in to Gerard Steers, but he obviously didn't pass the message on."

"No, he didn't." Why the hell hadn't he told me? Two months ago? Then I would never have taken this job. I could have escaped the painful drama that's unfolded around me.

But then I wouldn't have met Eli... My chest squeezes again, and it hurts more than I can bear.

"Okay." I scrabble around in my head to try to think clearly. I can't believe they've sold them. Not to undermine my own work, it's totally kick ass, but Whitlocks are well known—they have a huge clientele, all who know what they want.

Would someone want my work over the others? Wow.

"I'm doing an installation at Bowsley Hall. I won't be able to get anything to you by the end of the summer. Hopefully, they might be able to let me sell some of this on after it's finished."

"That's a great idea. It would be fantastic publicity for us and them."

His response causes me to pause for thought. "You know Bowsley Hall?"

"Yes, of course, the Faircloughs."

Was there anywhere the influence of this family didn't reach?

Then I remember back at The Ritz, the first day I met Elijah when he looked like he'd fallen off the cover of GQ Magazine in his navy suit, but had a major stick stuck up his arse. *'Yes, I've bought a few bits from there'*.

"Would you like to come to the summer ball? You could see the exhibitions and hopefully if you like them make first bid for them?"

"What a wonderful idea. I'll get Elena and Frances to ring Bowsley and express our interest."

I pause and take a deep breath. "So, you want more then?"

"Darling, yes, of course. Frances wants to talk to you about an exhibition here at the gallery, maybe when you've finished swanning around with one of the richest families in the country you will come by, so we can talk?"

One of the what?

My hands shake holding the phone and I mutter a distracted goodbye, telling Damien I'll hopefully see him at the ball.

No one told me they were the richest family in the country? What, richer than the bloody Queen? Seriously, that can't be right?

Does it matter?

One thing is making more and more sense by the minute. I can totally understand why Jennifer forced Eli and I apart. Him and I, things like that just aren't meant to be outside the pages of a fairy tale.

And I know why he said it could never be anything, and why he was able to walk away like it was nothing.

But then what about what Abi said?

What about the fact I can't stop thinking about him, and it hurts so bad I don't know what to do with myself?

What about the fact I've broken my one true rule and now it cuts so deep I no longer want to breathe, because I know what Elijah did in that hotel room in Brighton. He made me love him.

Tears burn my eyes just as my phone vibrates right on time.

Eli Jones: Did today go okay?

My phone shakes in my hand and tears splash on the screen.

Faith Hitchin: Yes.

And that's it. Every communication we've had in the last four days has been the same. Five little words that hurt.

A giggle stops my pity parade, and I swipe at my face with the back of my hands. Lewis comes around the corner, but unless he's lost his balls overnight the giggle wasn't his.

Tabitha.

They are holding hands as they wander in the garden, lost in a conversation I can't hear. She's glowing, and his eyes are staring at her like he's seeing the stars for the first time.

Shit.

Her eyes fall on me and she jumps in shock. "Faith, are you okay?" Stepping up quick and letting go of his hand with a blush, she drops onto the grass by my side.

"I'm just peachy." I give her a smile.

"Is it my mother? What's she done this time?"

With a laugh, I shake my head. My laughter doesn't sound quite right, but then truthfully when has it ever? "No, it's just been a big few days, you know with my uncle being so ill and, and..."

"Elijah leaving?"

I nod, a lump sticking in my throat.

She nods understandably. "He was pretty mad, but I know he's made headway with Lewis' mother's case." She squeezes his hand and the little gesture makes my chest ache more. "So that's good, right?"

"Sure. And we have created a wonderful mess."

They both laugh. Lewis' eyes don't leave her... and that's what Abi said Eli was like with me at the weekend. Why didn't I see it?

"Listen, you two." I wag my finger at the both of them and they both attempt innocence. "Be careful. Tabitha. I don't know what messed-up shit goes on in your family, but I'd hate to see you both hurt."

His hand falls onto her shoulder. "We're fine," he says, and I eye them both sceptically.

"Okay." I hold my hands up and laugh. "Consider my warning given. If either of you need anything." I look pointedly at Tabitha, "then you know where I am."

"Eli texted me." Her change of direction takes me by surprise.

"Yeah?" I attempt nonchalance.

"He wants to make sure you are following up the theme for the ball."

I roll my eyes, which is all kinds of childish, but I don't care. "And he can't talk to me about it himself?"

She shrugs, and I get up with a huff. "I need to talk to Gerard anyway."

Hell, I bloody do. He's going to tell me exactly why he didn't tell me about my work being sold before I came to this godforsaken place.

I jump from the lawn, brushing away the dried grass stuck to my skin and march for the house. As I leave, I hear Lewis mutter about "Gerard needing back up," followed by Tabitha giggling.

Lewis is going to be kicked out of the house by the time the ball comes around if they don't watch it.

Jennifer is watching me run up the steps. "Everything okay?"

"Hunky dory." I breeze past her and head towards the drawing room where I know Gerard will be, drinking scotch he can't afford normally, and talking utter bollocks with Peter. I've seen Peter more this week than I have since arriving, and as much as I'm hurt by Eli, I'm relieved that I did in fact pick the less twatty brother.

"Hey." I launch into the room not bothering to knock. Jennings is serving drinks, and he gives me a small smile when he can. I'm still hanging out in the kitchen with Lewis, to hell with Jennifer and her false appearances. Elaine and Jennings have been looking after me, making sure I eat and rest, drink enough water, etc. Who knows why they're making such a fuss, but it's appreciated.

"Faith, lovely for you to join us. What fireworks can we expect today?" Peter smirks with his greeting. I will punch him soon, purely for the fact he's breathing and annoying me.

"Shut it." I scowl and turn to Gerard. "Why didn't you tell me my pieces had sold at Whitlocks?"

"That dump," I hear Peter grumble, but I'm not giving him the time of day.

Gerard hold his hands up, but the look on his face tells me he can't believe it took me this long to ask the question. "I didn't want you to ditch your degree because you started making money."

I step closer, toe-to-toe with my once friend. "You didn't want what?"

"Come on, Faith. You would have sold a few pieces and then been offered more contracts. I knew you'd decide to drop out."

"How did that work out for you?" I sneer in his face. "I left anyway, because of you."

"Yes, well, I'm still hoping you might come back."

My head shakes with a force of its own. "I'm not coming back. I don't trust you, no matter what you say. Even more so now, I can't believe that, Gerard."

"You didn't need the money anyway, you've got all that tattoo money tied up in that apartment of yours." I sense Peter's attention sweep in my direction.

"Money's got nothing to do with it." I throw my hands in the air. "It would have been good to know someone wanted my work, that somewhere, something I created was sitting on a mantlepiece being admired."

Gerard places a hand on my arm. "Faith, your work is appreciated everywhere. Why do you think you haven't been turfed out of here yet?"

"Yet," Peter snipes, but we both turn to him and shout.

"Shut up," in unison.

Gerard tries to make eye contact with me, but I won't meet his gaze. "It's because you are ridiculously bloody talented. The Faircloughs need you here because when they have the national press descend at the end of their little art project they need the finest work possible waiting for them. It's why I wanted you to take this job—not Meg, or anyone else." He catches my fingers and holds them up until I look at them. "These are gifted. And if I've done wrong by you, then I'm sorry."

Bollocks. The guy's got that hangdog thing going.

"I'm so fricking furious, Gerard." I sigh a breath. "This place is messed-up; it's not healthy." It's not healthy for my heart I know that.

"And when the acquisitions buyer from The Tate Modern is staring at something amazing you created, on the night of the ball, how messed up will it be then?"

More messed up than I can contemplate.

"I'd better give them something amazing then." I turn to leave. I need to go and think, to clear my head.

"What's the theme again?"

I turn at the door but can't quite raise a smile. My emotions have been through the ringer these last few days. "Dreams."

As I walk the stairs up to Elijah's secret attic studio, I wonder what I would dream for if I could have anything my heart desired.

My hand turns the handle and with a sinking dismay I know the answer. Him.

Thirty-Two

Everything is covered in a fine layer of dust, but the paintings are still as wonderfully vibrant as the first time I saw them. I wonder how much someone would pay for one of these. As I turn to the roses, so thick and lush and beautiful, I can imagine them sitting in a gilt frame on some swanky Burlington Arcade gallery, stark and bright against a black background.

I step closer to run my fingers across the thick paint and then I see the envelope tucked against the edge of the easel. What is that? I pick it up and see my name scrawled across it. It's heavy and lumpy. Tearing it open, I tip the contents into my palm—the MG ignition key landing on my hand. "What the hell?" My voice reverberates back from the bare walls. A card slips out into my hand. It's a business card: Elijah Fairclough, Barrister, imprinted in embossed ink on the thick vellum card stock. I frown at it and then turn it over. An address in Kensington is scrawled in biro across the back.

My heart—it near on takes to flight.

Did he leave this for me days ago? Have I been sending him one-word answers to his messages while he's been waiting for me to come up here and find a car key and a card with an address?

Does he want me to go?

I slip on the stairs, my pulse raising. Connie's door is open as I fly past, but I don't even care. I run to the outhouses hoping I'll find Tabitha.

"I've got to go to an urgent meeting," I shout as I launch into the clay studio. She and Lewis are doing a really shit job at pretending to be busy and not kissing. I haven't got time for it now. "Elijah's leant me his car, where is the MG parked?"

She smiles. "He parks at the gatehouse normally. That way he can come and go unaccountable to Gran and Mum."

I'm about to run for the gates when I have a thought, remembering Connie's doors opening and knowing she would have seen me coming down the stairs. "Guys, can you do me a favour? Upstairs there are some paintings, in the top room on the top flight of stairs. Can you bring them down? They are imperative for the ball."

"What are they?" Tabitha asks.

"Dreams," I shout back, but I'm already running, desperate to find out if my own dream has wings to fly.

The traffic is awful, but the worst of it is coming away from town, not into it. I use my GPS on my phone to guide me through the streets until I find a small mews marked *Private*. There's a man in a box, in charge of a barrier, but when he sees the MG, he waves me through. I give him a thank you and then park up.

It's half-eight, and starting to get dark now summer is halfway through her peak. It's now I glance down and realise I'm still wearing the cut-off dungarees and vest I wore to the group session. Crap. Too late now. I left Bowsley with nothing.

I walk up to the door numbered twenty-one in brass and give a gentle knock. There's a chance my insides are going to twist into a knot and I'm going to puke. I manage to hold it together as footsteps land the other side of the door.

When he opens it up, the breath steals from my throat. He looks like something not even made on this earth. Wide blue eyes, hair trimmed short, and built like an Adonis under a soft grey T-shirt and black jeans—barefoot.

Holy crap.

"Take your time why don't you, Faith?" He leans against the door frame, a slow smile spreading across his face.

"What? I don't understand?"

As quick as a whip he reaches out and pulls me in. "Fuck, I've missed you." He buries his face in my hair and the skin of my neck, inhaling deeply. "I need you."

My legs quiver as I slide my hands around his neck and plant my mouth against his. "And I need you." I need him more than I've ever needed anything in my whole damn life and I'm struggling to stay afloat while the unknown emotions threaten to pull me down.

Then we are in his hallway. I don't even look at his home. All I see is him, holding him as he swoops me up and stalks me to a room upstairs.

I close my eyes and shiver with anticipation as we fall together, fast and hard, burrowing deep until there's just the two of us and the rest of the world ceases to exist.

I'm face down, hugging the pillow, Eli's fingers trail along the exposed skin of my spine. His eyes are closed, his face serene and content, and a warm glow evolves inside my chest when I realise it's me who's given him that expression.

"Still, I can't believe it took you four days to find that envelope."

I'm in shock that this has happened. I was sure it was over between us. I'd resigned myself to it. "You made it seem very real, Eli."

His lashes flutter open and his deep gaze settles on my face with a heartfelt plea. "It had to be. I won't have my mother ruin your prospects."

"Maybe you should let me decide?"

He shakes his head, face serious, lips pressed into a line. "No."

I sigh and roll over onto my back, facing the ceiling. "Why does this feel like it's getting messy? I know that's not what we agreed."

His fingers turn my chin. "None of this is what I expected."

"What do you mean?" I still can't believe I'm here, back in his arms. When I think of that chest crushing ache that's resided within me the last few days, it's like I've allowed myself to be weak. But, here by his side, the furthest thing I feel is weak. I'm brave. Free.

A deep sigh pushes from his chest. "Nothing is what it should be. Things are clean-cut, simple. I do what I'm told, and I get an easy life for it."

"I'm sensing a but?" My fingers drift over his warm skin, relishing every touch.

"But nothing is clean-cut with you, and nothing's easy."

I snicker. "See, this is what I'm talking about; there is nothing easy about me despite what people think." It's a crass joke and it doesn't make him laugh.

His hand reaches for mine and he sits up, pulling me along with him. Between his brows a deep line mars his beautiful face. "What you told me in Brighton, about Aiden and your father..."

"Don't make me regret sharing, I hate pity."

"You'd rather be angry and constantly run?"

"Me, run? You're the one who ran from his home the other day."

He palms a hand through his hair. "Nothing is simple with you."

"Sorry I'm not as pliable as you'd like."

He shakes his head and gives a rueful laugh. "Pliable? You are the exact opposite. It's why I'm crazy about you. Why I've been unable to focus for days. Why I can't stop thinking about that bastard hurting you, and your father letting you down."

What did he just say? He doesn't give me a chance to process.

"It's why I want you to speak to the authorities about what happened to you."

And now what did he say?

I shake my head. "If my own father doesn't believe me, I won't hold my breath on the police."

"But I believe you. Al does, Abi does, and Dan." Eli's eyes darken a little at the mention of Dan.

"Don't you like Dan?" I watch him closely.

"Yeah, sure. He seems a stand up guy."

"See, your mouth's saying the words, but your face isn't agreeing."

He groans and falls back on the mattress and I can't help but greedily absorb the naked sight of him. "You can't blame me for being jealous of the guy you've spent your whole life with."

His words floor me. We aren't supposed to be jealous, because this is nothing. It's just a summer fling until we walk away.

We stare at one another long and hard and we both know. This isn't nothing.

There's a good chance it could be everything.

With a flash of a smile he leans up and kisses me swiftly on the lips. "Are you hungry?"

"No."

"Have you been eating properly?"

Ah—Jennings and Elaine—it all makes sense. "Did you ask Elaine to feed me up?"

His fingers grab for my ribs and he laughs as I squeal. "You are very skinny, you need fattening up."

"Better feed me then," I say, but I don't mean with food.

A broad smile lights his face. "Come."

His little Kensington mews house is something close to wonderful. Open plan and all echoes of black, white, and grey. It's sleek and masculine without being testosterone fuelled. It's also impeccably clean—not a pizza box in sight. And nothing like Bowsley.

Stood in the kitchen and lounge area, I turn and take it all in.

"You like?" he asks, rummaging around at the kitchen island. He's pulling open cupboards and peering inside. Dressed in only a pair of grey joggers which are hanging low on his hips, he's looking probably finer than he ever has. I think the joggers and bare chest win over the suit—just.

"It's smart." I send him a smile. "Now I feel pretty daft taking you to the hovels in Brighton."

"I loved that."

I smile, but the difference in our paths is glaring me smack in the face.

"How's Al?"

I step towards a wall of shelving holding books and CD's. I can even see some old vinyl—now, I definitely want to know what's on them.

"Same." A deep huff of breath escapes me. "I'm going to

try to get back this weekend, just in case. We've still got the rest of this week and next before the ball."

I can't believe it's gone so quickly. Earlier this week I couldn't wait for it to be over, but now I want August to stretch on forever.

"How's it going? And don't give me a one worded reply."

"Fine?" I grin, but then I'm distracted by a shelf on the right. "What the hell?" My feet carry me forward, my heart giving a boom. He's watching me I can tell. "Why have you got my sculptures here? These are the ones from Whitlocks."

He shrugs and carries on rooting about for something to eat.

I pick up the ornament that's caught my eye. Largely experimental, it was a mixture of plaster and cement plaster suspended on wire and then painted with bright shades of red and orange. When I'd made it, it had reminded me of the sun coming up over the pier at home.

"Have you bought these since you've known me?"

But I know he can't have done. Damien said they were sold months ago. My eyes search Elijah who can no longer pretend to be busy. "Start talking."

"I bought them a while back, before we met." He runs a hand through his hair. "I mentioned them to Mother and decided to find out who you were to see if you'd be interested in working at Bowsley." He nods at the piece in my hand. "I liked them, they were fun and fresh. I wanted them on my shelves and I knew I'd like whoever made them to do the installation."

"So your mother never approached Gerard to ask for a recommendation?"

Eli has the sense to look shamefaced. "Well, sort of, but we knew who we wanted."

"Is this that royal we again?"

"I." His eyes are bold and bright. "I knew who I wanted."

I look at the knickknack in my hand. "Really?"

Padding barefoot across the wooden floor, he comes and takes it out of my hand. "You don't seem to realise how talented you are. Those glass flowers in the hallway at the house are beyond anything I expected."

"Really?" I repeat. "They are just flowers."

He raises an eyebrow and looks all kinds of cute. "Sure, just flowers made of glass." He reaches a hand for my hip and pulls me in. I'm dressed in only one of his work shirts and doesn't my body know it. His lips skim my throat and I tilt my neck to give him better access. "It's why I can't let my mother ruin everything for you. It's why I'm here instead of spooning in that pink room of yours."

My hands slide into his hair. My mouth hot on his. He lifts me, and I wrap my legs around his waist, my arms clinging around his neck. "Turns out I don't have any food other than strawberries and cream," he murmurs against my lips.

"Sounds like heaven." My body scorches like dry tinder. Even though we've already been together since I knocked on his door, it's not enough. I want more. I want to drown in him.

With a gentle bump, he places me on the island. It's cool against my bare skin, but it does nothing to calm down the inferno inside my body. His fingers unbutton the shirt, his hands dipping inside the material, easing it back from my body. He pushes me back a little and spreads my knees, so he can slide between them. His lips trail kisses from my collarbone down the valley between my breasts. When he reaches my navel, he pushes me back until I'm bared on the marble. His mouth drifts lower, his teeth nibbling the inside of my thigh. I want him there, right there with his tongue currently trailing lazy circles on the tender skin of my inner thigh. I grasp at his hair and push him in the right direction. My breath catches in my throat as he strokes long firm licks along my lips and delves deep. His hands lift my ass and I splay my fingers against the marble as I groan and writhe under his mouth.

"Fuck, I love that," the words escape; I'm unable to control them.

He burrows deeper, one finger pushing inside and then another, his mouth and tongue never stopping licking and sucking until I'm bucking my hips and pushing myself into his mouth.

"Scream my name."

His mouth returns, his tongue delving in deep as his thumb presses at my other opening. Then as he pushes it in slowly, spinning me out some place in the universe where the stars and sun shine at the same time. I scream his name so loud it imprints into my heart.

Thirty-Three

"Paints." I motion to the array of different types and colours. "You've all got a canvas each."

"Each?" Dylan eyes the wall of canvases. I've grown to like him, and actually out of all the of the kids we've seen, he's the one with the most natural talent. I'm going to talk to Gerard about him—which reminds me I need to do that.

"Yes." I nod. "So, the idea is—and you've all got to use your imagination for this—we are going to fill the walls of the ballroom with our dreams. I want you to use the canvas, use the paints in any way you like to create a replica of a dream or the thing you want most."

"If I want a Fiat 500?" quips Maisie.

"If that's your biggest dream in life, then yes." I smirk at her, but it's wasted. "Here's the thing." I add, making sure I have all their attention. "There are no paintbrushes, no sponges, nothing but your fingers and body."

Stunned faces meet mine. "Like we're supposed to get dirty?" A small brunette near the back, and who's always at the back, pipes up.

"Hell, yes. Dirty as can be." I flush a little. Last night I was definitely dirty, in a way that can't be replicated on a canvas, even by an artist as skilled at Eli.

I grab an easel and pull it over to the centre of the room, and then grab some tubes of acrylic paint.

"Why is everything she does blue?" Dylan mutters, but someone shushes him as I unscrew the top and smear some directly onto the canvas. It's a giant splurge but then I start to spread it with my fingers. It's wet and cool beneath my touch and there is something incredibly pleasurable about making the finger spread mess, and I don't even like painting.

"What are you all waiting for?" I ask. "Get stuck in."

I grin and turn back for the canvas. My idea for the big dream ball is quite simple. We will provide the backdrop—Elijah will provide the centrepieces, and I'll make sure every person there knows he's the true artist, not me.

I don't know how long we've all been in here, when the door open and Tabitha slips in. Her face is blotchy: pale in places, bright red in others, like she's fallen into a pot of jam. I drop my paints and wipe my hands on an oil rag. "What's going on?"

"Nothing." She gives a small shake of her head.

"Well that's a big fat lie."

Red-rimmed eyes meet mine. "Nothing."

"Where's Lewis?" I'm not stupid, there can be only one reason she's crying like this.

She shudders a breath. "He's gone."

"Where?"

I only saw Eli last night, and he didn't mention Lewis being able to go back to the city.

She shrugs, and alarm bells sound in my brain. "Wait here." I walk out into the outhouse hallway and take my phone out of my back pocket. I know Eli and I aren't communicating in public, but this is work—sort of. He answers on the second ring.

"Where's Lewis?" I ask, ignoring the little stab of desire that darts through me at hearing his voice.

"What do you mean, where is Lewis?" He has his business voice on and I know he isn't alone.

"He's not here. Tabitha says he's gone."

"Not that I'm aware of." He pauses. "This isn't good. There's been a development on his mother's case."

My stomach clenches. "And?"

"The other witness... she isn't willing to give evidence."

"So what now?"

There's a hefty pause and I can all too clearly visualise him rubbing his hand through his hair. "Now I think again."

"Okay." I want to ask him if I'm going to see him later—if somehow we are going to manage to find a way to be together—but I don't. "I'm going to find your mother. Maybe she knows where Lewis is."

"Ah crap, I hope you survive."

I chuckle, even though the sound is leaden and heavy. "I'll lick my wounds later."

"Bye, Faith."

"Bye, Elijah."

I hang up and find Elaine watching me clutching a tray of tea and biscuits. "I was bringing a snack for you all."

I smile at her gratefully. "It's a mess in there."

She chuckles and bustles past me. "I'm getting used to that with you around."

I turn for the main house. If anyone will know where Lewis is, it's going to be the Baroness.

The door to her study is open. She's sitting at her desk reading some paperwork. A warm smile curves her lips as I knock. "Have you got a minute?" I ask, although for a moment I wonder if she's lost her sensibilities—she seems almost pleased to see me.

"I do, I do, come in." She motions for the visitor chair. "How are things going? Gerard tells me you are moving onto paints and canvases this week. I can't wait to see what you create."

It's impossible. I shake my head and stare at her in confusion. "I'm sorry, are we friends now because Elijah saw sense and pulled out of our little fling?"

Her smile tightens. "It's for the best. We all want you to succeed, and this way you can."

I sag a little in my seat. It doesn't matter that Eli and I met last night, it doesn't matter what I feel for him—which is scarily close to everything. It will still never be. Because of her.

"Anyway, I'm here about Lewis. What have you done to him?"

"Lewis? That vulgar young boy?"

"Yes, you know, Elijah's client."

"No idea. I'm staying out of the way of all your visitors."

I eye her speculatively. "Until the ball, and then you will pretend to the press that the whole thing has been your idea."

Her lips press together tight and she leans onto her fingers, resting her chin. "And there will be a lot of press. I've had confirmation today that Sky Arts are attending with a film crew. It's possible they will think of televising this whole project if we run it again next year."

I stare at her in alarm. "I can't be involved in that." The idea is awful. Imagine all the people who know my darker side seeing my tattoos on television.

"Whatever, dear, although I believe Elijah has different ideas."

Her carefully calculated words pull the world from under my feet. What does she mean?

Is Eli expecting me to come back next year? Has he been planning this? Does he think this is going on beyond our two-week agreement? But how?

My heart hammers and vibrates in my chest.

"Care to elaborate?" I try to keep my voice even.

"Not right now." She waves her hand at the door and dismisses me.

This woman has such a wonderful way of making me feel like complete shit. How she produced someone as wonderful and kind as Eli I have no idea. I push out of the plush seat and stomp for the door. "So, you haven't seen Lewis?" I double check.

"No, thank goodness."

I open my mouth to tell her she's a bitch of the highest order, but what's the point? I'd just be wasting hot air.

Back in the hallway, I pull my phone out of my pocket again and call Eli back. "I don't know where he is. I'm going to search the grounds."

"I'm coming back; just finishing some urgent files."

"No, don't."

"I'm coming back." His tone is firm.

"Okay. I've got to get looking."

"Faith." He calls me back as I'm about to hang up.

"Yep."

"I was coming back anyway."

A small smile creeps along my face. Stick that up your arse, Baroness.

Before I head outside, I pop to the kitchen and track down Jennings who is talking to a guy in a suit I don't recognise.

"What's going on?"

"Security for the ball." Jennings gives me a wink and I motion him forward with my hand.

"Lewis has gone missing, have you seen him?"

He shakes his head and my stomach drops.

"I'm going to go look for him."

It's muggy outside, the oppressive heat that's been building the last few weeks is pooling into threatening dense clouds. I head up the first gravel pathway and tell myself I'm going to take each section of the garden in turn. It's a bloody big garden though if you include the deer park as well.

Lewis has got to be here somewhere.

It takes me two hours to find him sitting in an abandoned and decrepit building. "Lewis, for God's sake. I've walked half a marathon looking for you."

I drop, exhausted, onto the floor by his side. His face is pale, his eyes rimmed with red.

"What's going on?"

His head shakes, and he kicks his feet into the ground, stubbing the toe of his trainer into the dirt.

"I've got a search party out looking for you, and you're totally missing the chance to create the biggest mess with paint the world has ever seen."

I don't look at him, keeping my focus turned away. I remember when Dan and I were kids and he used to hate it when I knew he'd been crying.

"What's on your canvas?" he turns for me a little, and the breakable fragility glaring at me through red-rimmed eyes makes my stomach ache.

"Blue. Lots of it." I shrug.

"For Elijah?"

I give him another shrug. "Maybe. I don't think that's a dream I get to have though, not really."

"You like him though, right?" Lewis pays close attention to the dirt at his feet.

"Sometimes." I give a little smile, my cheeks heating. Last night I liked him a lot—a lot. "But it's not straightforward, you know. It's complicated. This family here in this house, they might look like they have everything, but I don't think they do."

He makes a huffing noise.

"What's going on with you and Tabitha? You seem to like each other."

He shrugs, which is one of my favourite forms of communication and I shrug straight back at him.

"What do you dream of, Lewis?"

A heart-breaking silence floats around us until a small voice, owned by a lost little boy says, "My mum."

I nudge his shoulder with mine. "I get that. Are you angry with her?"

He nods his head and I watch, silently, as a tear rolls down his cheek. "I'm angry that she didn't fight. Didn't stay with us."

My mind skims back to Eli's words last night. "Sometimes fighting is the hardest thing to consider."

"What do you know about it?"

"Everything. I run from everything and everyone." I stare at the vibrant splashes of green above us in the trees. Birds are chirping, summer lengthening and holding on to its glory before autumn comes to steal it. What am I going to do when this is over? What am I going to do when I repack my small bag and leave Eli and this place?

"Once," I continue. "Someone hurt me, real bad. I didn't tell anyone for the longest time, until the truth was living like a monster inside me: on my skin, in every molecule that makes me what I am."

Lewis' bloodshot eyes land on me. "What happened?"

My head shakes. "It's in the past now."

"What are you going to do?"

I stand from the dirt and hold my hand out to him. He uses it to pull himself up, but then drops it quickly as he watches me expectantly. "I'm going to stop running."

I fill my lungs with air. I'm going to stop running, and it's going to start right now.

"Are you ready to go back? I know a girl who's pretty worried about you."

He nods, and I point to the path I took to find him.

It's time.

Thirty-Four

First things first, I called Eli and told him I'd found Lewis and there was no need to drive back. I also told him about Lewis and Tabitha—call me a wimp but it was much easier on the phone than face-to-face. I'm not sure whether my art leader/teenage babysitter role was supposed to prevent that happening, but if so I failed.

After I'd done that I told Gerard I needed to go and get my stuff ready for the ball and that I'd be leaving straight after the afternoon session. Then I asked Jennifer is she could fit me in with Saskia. I didn't want the Fairclough's to pay for a damn thing towards my outfit for the ball, but some help in finding the perfect dress would be fun.

I get to Knightsbridge just after six. Lucky for me it's late night shopping. I can see Saskia from the other end of the street—not that I know what she looks like. I can just tell it's her. She's six foot, and skinny as a clothes rail, with choppy and stylish ink-coloured hair.

Her eyes fall on my tattoos with no effort to disguise her reaction. "Wowee." She steps closer, her hand reaching for my arm like she expects to be able to feel the ink not just see them.

"Hi, I'm Faith." I cough awkwardly.

"Oh yeah, sorry. I'm Saskia."

We shake hands and she seems genuine enough. I try to relax a little. "I'm hoping you will help me find something for the Fairclough Ball, only Connie wants my tattoos covered up."

Saskia shakes her head. "Connie's a bitch, and no way, these are gorgeous." She meets my gaze with an impish smile. "I reckon we can find the perfect dress, though, in there."

I look at the shop behind her, the green and gold window shades are legendary. "I don't think they approve of my sort in Harrods."

"Believe me, darling, they let everyone in if you can afford it. Let's get champagne and then go dress shopping." She links her hand though my arm. Apart from Tabitha, she's the friendliest person I've met in weeks. "You aren't driving, are you?"

I grimace a little. "No, I drove down, but I'll go back in the morning. I've got my college lecturer helping me now, so I don't have to rush back."

"We can make that a bottle of champagne then. Come on, this is going to be fun." We are at the door where the doorman—wearing his long coat and hat—opens up for us, although right until I'm through the door I'm expecting to get bounced straight back out again. People look at us, but Saskia doesn't even give them a second glance as she glides towards the food hall. "Do you like oysters, Faith?"

"Never had one." I don't add I've never had one because in my humble opinion oysters look like alien brains.

"Oh gosh, you're going to love them."

"If you say so." I chuckle and let her lead me to the champagne and oyster bar.

An hour and a half later I'm stood in front of the long

mirror. "Are you sure?" I've only tried on two dresses. And Saskia is almost swooning over this one. It's clinging to everything I own, which isn't very much. My angled hip bones are poking through the sheer white satin.

"Yes, completely. It makes your ink stand out so beautifully."

I give a rueful laugh. I don't think the secrets inked on my skin are beautiful, but it amuses me the six-foot supermodel in front of me thinks so.

The dress is Gucci. With a Gucci price tag.

"What colour do you think Elijah will wear?" There is no way I can even ask this question without being obvious, so I just put it out there.

"Mm, he always wears black to formal events."

"Black." Okay, I'm disappointed. I love him in navy best of all.

"Believe me, it's a sight to behold." Saskia winks, and I flush a little.

"Will you be coming to the ball?" I ask.

She nods eagerly. "One of the perks of being Jennifer's personal assistant."

"Personal assistant? How come I haven't seen you around the house that much?"

Saskia arches a perfect eyebrow. "I work from an office here in London. Bowsley is, well it's..."

"Nuts?" I add for her when she's run out of words.

"Yeah, sometimes." She gives me a sad small smile. "It makes me kind of sad, because they are all so miserable."

"I can't believe Jennifer would quash her children's dreams and desires like she does. I mean, my own dad is a prize arsehole, but he would never have not let me do anything."

Saskia looks in shock. "Darling, it's not Jennifer, it's

Connie. Even Jennifer doesn't get to live her life. Come on, can't you see it? Jennifer is only in her early sixties, and she's an attractive woman. So ask yourself why hasn't she made another great catch?"

I shrug. "I figured it was because she was a mega bitch."

With a shake of her head, Saskia plays with holding my hair up, exposing the ink on my collarbones and the back of my neck. "No, it's because she's not allowed. It wouldn't be good for the family name."

"Aren't they related to the royal family? I mean come on even Prince Charles married his mistress eventually."

Saskia chuckles. "That's because the queen isn't Connie. She's a fluffy duckling in comparison."

"So everything is Connie. Elijah is a barrister instead of an artist because of his grandmother?"

"Listen, I don't know all of this for a fact, it's just stuff I've picked up over the last few years."

"So when Connie dies they will all get to live?"

"When? That woman is going to live forever. She won't allow herself to die because that way she won't be in control anymore."

We both lapse into silence while I stare at myself in the mirror. Never have I felt more heartache for anyone than I do the Faircloughs right now. People who have everything, but at the same time who have nothing.

My phone vibrates and I jump on it.

Eli Jones: Why is my car parked outside my house but there is no you in sight?

I grin. It sneaks up on my face until my cheeks are close to splitting.

Faith Hitchin: I didn't want to be presumptuous.

Eli Jones: Please always be presumptuous.
Faith Hitchin: How about a date?
Eli Jones: Meet me in half an hour.

I'm grinning like a buffoon when I turn to face Saskia. "I need to get out of this dress." She gives a small smile.

"Are we buying this one?" She fishes into her bag for her Hermes purse.

Nodding, I flash her a smile. "I'm buying this one. Connie Fairclough isn't touching my visit to the ball."

"I'm feeling like a fairy godmother right now."

"Do you turn pumpkins into black cabs, because I've got to get to Kensington?"

Saskia puts her fingers in her ears. "Don't tell me anything, it's better I don't know."

I pass her the dress as I step out of it. "Deal."

In the end, I manage to get to Kensington in twenty minutes. I'm paying the taxi driver and battling my bags when I see Eli's door open. My heart hammers, my palms slicking against the handles of the bags. It's been less than twenty-four hours, but I'm hungry for him again. What happens next week when I don't get to see him anymore? I shove the thought to the back of my mind. It's not worth wasting time on right now.

I'm stepping forward when I see the fact it's not him walking out of his door. A woman with dark hair and olive skin is coming out. She's smiling. She's beautiful—so beautiful I can't believe it's possible for someone to look like that in the flesh. And I know who she is. I know who she is because I've seen her before when I first Googled Elijah Fairclough and found out he was engaged to a socialite.

She stops and reaches onto her tiptoes, kissing him on the cheek. He smiles at her and gives a small wave as she steps down onto the pathway.

What am I going to do?

Inside my stomach a knife is twisting.

I'm frozen to the spot.

Does it matter he's been with her? Is it any of my business? Well no and yes, but then also yes and no. For a moment, I hesitate, but then swallowing my pride I step forward and make my presence known. He gives me a genuine warm smile, like he truly is pleased to see me. He's casual, wearing those grey tracksuit pants he makes look so damn sexy, and his feet are bare again. God, he's gorgeous, and he's been with her who's also gorgeous. "Faith, you're here already?" he says. I wait to see if he will lean in and kiss me or hug me, but he doesn't.

"Sorry, I'm early." It sounds like a question and I want to bitch slap myself. What happened to the girl who used to fuck for fun? Who had one-night-stands on a regular basis just to scratch an itch.

I know what happened to her. Elijah Fairclough.

A pulse of anger spears me.

"Sienna, this is Faith. She's been helping me with the art project."

Sienna smiles warmly. Fuck, she looks like she should be on TV. Maybe even the big screen. Her eyes are a warm chocolate brown and there isn't a single thing about her which isn't painfully perfect. And here I am in ripped jeans and an old V-neck vest showing all my many, many mistakes.

I know it shouldn't, but Eli introducing me as the help stings deep and hard. He's watching me though with an amused smile teasing the edge of his lips.

"Nice to meet you, Faith." She turns for Eli and places her hand on his arm. "Elijah, I hope the files are what you wanted. If you need anything, let me know." With a smile at us both she steps away. "I'll see you at the ball next week."

She's attending the ball? Well, fuck me.

Still, she doesn't know what I have planned—no one does.

She steps down off his front doorstep and beeps the key fob in her hand, a small silver Mercedes lighting up at her touch. Even her car is beautiful.

When she's gone, and he's given her a small wave goodbye, he turns to me expectantly and nods at the bags in my hand. "Been shopping?"

I'm stuck. Torn. I'm as jealous as hell to have found her here, and I want to ask him why she was there, in his home. In the space I had magnificent sex with him in just last night. But, then it's not my business.

We are walking away next weekend.

I can't breathe when I think about it. My throat tightens.

His fingers slide to my neck, brushing along the back of it. "I'm pleased to see you."

"And me."

My heart pounds. It's impossible to worry about the future when his lips are hovering above mine and his hands are sliding along my skin.

So I don't.

I dive straight in and then I scream his name.

Thirty-Five

Isn't it the truth that when things go right in one area of life it falls apart in another. Tabs looks at me as I wander into the dining room and give everyone a cheery wave. I can't lie, I've already had five very strong coffees in the kitchen. Five, that's right. Now I'm buzzing.

I grin at Elijah who's sat staring at the newspaper across his empty plate. "Good morning, Mr Fairclough," I sing-song.

"Good morning, Miss Hitchin."

I take a seat and dig into the pastries piled in the middle of the table. I'm starving; all this driving long distances and shagging is tiring me out. Except last night Eli drove to the gate house and then we both walked hand-in-hand under the shadows until we separated, and I went to the outhouse and he went inside the mansion of terror.

"Are you ready to help me move furniture?" I ask around some buttery goodness.

Jennifer looks up over her coffee cup. "Moving furniture? Who is moving furniture?"

Elijah meets her scrutiny. "I am. I've taken time off from the office until the ball."

"And pray what furniture are you moving?" Jennifer sounds almost exhausted.

Eli grins. "Everything."

Connie sweeps into the room: immaculate, icy, and controlled. Even Jennifer flinches. "Try not to make too much mess with this rabble of youths you've allowed into the house."

Eli straightens his shoulders. "And does the hallway look a mess? I can't believe the amazing job Faith has done."

"Hm."

But Eli doesn't let it go. "You should be thanking Faith and hoping that she lets the house keep the work she's created."

My cheeks flame pink although I can't lie I'm basking under his compliments. Even I need my ego stroked every so often.

"Not quite the big statement pieces we were expecting, though," Connie murmurs. "And for the trouble she's caused, I'm not sure."

Jennifer clatters her cup onto its saucer. "That's enough," she snaps.

We all stop and stare at her. Tabitha has her mouth hanging open.

"When the ball arrives, and we have the doors open and the press here, it will all be worth it." Jennifer looks at me, her expression calm. "And I'm sure Faith has something spectacular planned as a centrepiece."

I need to ask Jennings for some tips of the perfect poker face because I don't have one and it shows.

"Of course," I agree. "Spectacular."

I wonder if I can put my Connie Fairclough Medusa head on display in the centre of the ballroom? Nah, it's supposed to be about dreams not nightmares.

I grab some croissants and get back up from the table. Eli sends me a royal smirk but doesn't say anything. "Got to go," I announce. "Super busy."

Before I head back to the outhouse to bang my head against the wall for not checking to see if I myself was supposed to be making anything, let alone the students, I head to the ballroom.

This room is just beyond anything I could ever have imagined. With its arched white and gilt roof, to the double staircase which leads down with marble stairs from a long mezzanine gallery, to its black and white tiled marble floor, it oozes classical Renaissance splendour. The room is filled with spectacular pieces already. Truthfully, it's like walking through the Victoria and Albert Museum. Pedestals dot along the tiled floors holding Renaissance busts and vases. They are going to have to be moved.

My plan is to have the canvases the kids are creating on easels, natural and relaxed dotted throughout the room, creating a fluid movement which will send people to where the orchestra will be positioned.

I grin as I slide my phone out and call Damien at Whitlocks. "Is it too early?"

There's a chuckle from the other end. "Lucky for you we are unpacking a new shipment."

"Should I be jealous?"

There's a louder chuckle. "No, not when Frances hasn't stopped talking about the Bowsley Ball and how Sky Arts are going to be there."

I rub at my face. This is going to be awful. There will be a ballroom with no centrepiece.

"I was ringing for a favour actually."

"For you, anything right now."

"I need one of those elaborate gilt frames. You know the type, something monstrous and gaudy."

"You do?"

"Uh, yes."

"What's it for?"

I chuckle. "You'll see next week. Listen, can I text you the measurements? If I give you my number, will you send me yours quick?"

"Definitely."

I reel off my number and then hang up, turning to find Eli standing behind me. "What are you up to?"

"Nothing." I shrug.

His eyes gaze about the room and I turn to take in the sight with him. I want to move over and hold his hand.

I've never wanted to hold someone's hand before. It's a first in the life of Faith Hitchin.

I don't. If we could get through these next few days without a trauma with his family, it would make the end of this... this... whatever this is, so much better.

My eyes greedily slide over him. I'll be walking away in a few days. Summer over, four weeks of my life gone.

Four weeks in which I have changed. I've broken my rules, knowing that it was going to hurt. It's the best thing I've ever done.

"Why are you grinning like a crazy person?" He steps closer and despite the fact his family are lurking, despite the fact someone under the roof is clearly snitching on us, he kisses me, right under the domed and gold ceiling.

I love you.

The words I've never spoken before dart into my head.

I don't love him.

It's just four weeks?

Just a fling.

But his hands cradle my face, his thumbs sweeping across my cheeks and my heart beats fast and erratic.

My head swims with him; his smell, his touch, the sense of his body next to mine.

And then in a moment of clarity I know what my centrepiece is going to be.

It's what I want to give him. My heart.

"I've got to go to the studio."

"What are you doing?"

"Can you deal with the painting today?"

His eyes narrow, his hands still tenderly placed on my cheeks. "No, I don't know anything about that."

He knows more about painting than I ever will. He's innately talented, a talent that's been squandered by his family.

My gaze holds his, intense, I'm hoping he can comprehend every emotion I can't express. "Yes, you do. It's all about dreaming."

I go to pull away, but his lips are back on mine, his tongue sweeping into my mouth, my body melting against his.

When he breaks the kiss, my blood is singing in my veins. Hot and fluid, it hums and burns. "Have a good day." His voice is low and intense and my stomach pinches.

"I will."

And then I leave before I give in to my carnal desires on the ballroom floor. I believe the Wicked Witch of the West would have something to say about that—and so would the cleaners.

I lock myself into the glass studio, stripping off my top and tying on an apron, and then I set to work. I don't even know if what I've envisioned is possible. But I'm sure as hell going to give it a go.

"Sweet mother of God." I wipe at the beads of sweat gathering across my forehead. When am I going to learn to think things through?

In the small kiln is a swirling pool of ruby red liquid. I clutch at the small bellow and then using a metal hook I spread the material, blowing it gently to make it spread across the metal sheet spread on the desk top. The swirls I make look like nothing more than half-hearted question marks, but I know once they are finished and fitted together where the head of one links with the tail of another it will create what I want—a ying and yang.

When the first batch is done, I put them into the kiln to bake, and then start on the next lot. I'm going to need a lot of question marks that's for sure.

Funny that my life and my future all come down to a question mark.

It epitomises the moment I'm in. The past is fractured behind me, and unexpectedly Elijah has helped to set me free from the burning hatred and regret.

In front of me is a future I can't yet see.

In a couple of days my work will be in front of the press. Sky Arts will be here, and they will know I created this—that all of this is mine.

The future could be anything.

Then I think of Eli, marked with my ink. The man torn between what he wants and who he's been made to be.

The man I feel more for than I ever even considered possible.

I want to go and hunt him down; to touch him, inhale his breath, and absorb his skin and smell. But I want to honour him more, so I keep working, and leave conscious thought behind me as I throw myself into creating yet more and more glass.

It's getting dark when I find my way to the ballroom. Everything has been moved, and the room is now a cavernous blank canvas. Exactly how I wanted it.

"Are you going to tell me what you have planned?" I shiver as I hear his voice and place my hands on my hips. When I turn, I find a wide grin on his face. The blues dance like the sea under the sun.

"Nope, not until the night. I want it to blow you away."

He steps closer, his hands finding a purchase against the skin of my stomach. "You always blow me away, everything you've done here is extraordinary."

His tugs me closer, his breath fanning across my skin. I melt and allow myself to absorb into him. His mouth grazes across mine, my breath catches and a shiver of deep anticipation runs through me.

"But what about your mother and grandbaronessy?" I smile against his mouth.

"Honestly, who gives a fuck?" He hikes me up and I wrap my legs tight around his waist. He walks us to a room on the East wing. His mouth on mine, his hands firm and tight.

The door kicks shut behind us, and his gaze reads my face. "Let me love you, Faith."

He's said this before.

And I want to tell him that I want him to love me, just as I think I might possibly love him—as inconceivable as that emotion may be to me.

I don't say a word when he settles me back on the bed. Instead I lay down and offer myself silently to him, praying that he can feel it even if I don't say it.

Thirty-Six

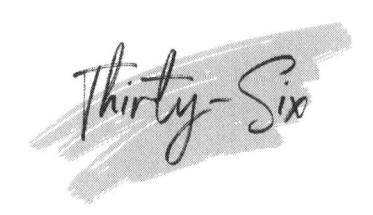

I'm lying on my back, my eyes focused on the ceiling. I can't believe this is about to end. Tomorrow is the final day. The day of the Bowsley Ball. RSVP's have been returned, caterers are in, and there's a small army of staff milling around the house getting it ready. Some areas are being roped off—mainly the East wing where Eli took me the night before last. It shows how little I know about him that until that evening I didn't know he slept in a guest room when he came here, apart from of course when he's in my pink walled room with me, which he has been every night he's been home.

But then, don't I know how he tastes, feels? Don't I know the way he moves in the dark, and the emotions that live under the surface of his skin?

We haven't talked about what happens after tomorrow.

I said two weeks and then I'd walk away.

That now seems impossible.

It's more impossible than when I faced down the Everest of marble in my studio all those weeks ago before turning it into a cameo of Eli's face.

I don't think I can walk away.

There's a gentle rap, one I recognise and my body responds to, before the door is even open.

And there he is, beautiful and blue-eyed.

"Busy?" He smirks a little as he comes into the room and settles next to me on the bed. His lips seek mine and I fall into the silence as his kiss whisks me away to a land where bad things don't happen.

When I pull away, his eyes dance. "I'm hoping your failure to come to dinner means you're hungry."

My fingers trail along the outline of his jaw and scratch against his dark stubble. He's wearing a favourite outfit of mine: tatty old jeans and a T-shirt. This is the Baroness' son at his most attractive.

His lips against mine, he slides across me until his weight is pinning me to the mattress and my body sings with delight. "I've missed you today." He pecks kisses amongst his words. "When am I going to see this secret you've been creating?"

"Tomorrow."

I grin against his mouth and run my hands down his shoulder blades. "Did you say something about food?" I kiss him harder, faster, and slide my tongue into his mouth until it tangles with his. Our kisses are hotter and more desperate than anything I've ever tasted.

"Food," he breaks his lips to ask, "or this?"

I chuckle as he rolls us over until I'm on top and his hands are running along my spine and ribs. My top rides up and the tops of his fingers graze across my skin. "I hope you've washed all the paint off."

He rolls us again. "Are you complaining?"

"Maybe," I squeal as his fingers delve for my ribs, his teeth nipping at my earlobe.

I hate being tickled and try to clamber away, but he has

me, and he's much stronger. We are both laughing and kissing and breathing every moment of perfection that this is.

Then I look at him and catch my breath. "We've got twenty-four hours left, stop messing around and fuck me, Fairclough."

His eyes widen, the dark recesses flicker with deep emotion and then he pounces, and soon my cries of laughter have morphed into something else and I scream his name like it's the only thing left in my soul.

"So, food?"

My stomach is almost joining in our conversation as it gurgles and grumbles with hunger. I don't want to move though. My arms are wrapped around his chest tight. My cheek wedged against the firm and hot skin. I trail my fingers through the smattering of hair across his pecs, and breathe in the heady scent of him mixed with sex.

"I'm not hungry," I reply and tighten my clutch on him.

With a rumble of a chuckle which makes my stomach pinch with excitement, he manages to extricate himself from my hold. He grins as he slides me up to meet his gaze. His hands slide through my hair and hold it back from my face as though his gaze is seeking an answer to an endless riddle.

"What?" I ask and lean onto my elbows. His fingers continue to comb through my blonde strands. At the end of the lengths, his hands rub along the ink of my skin.

"You are incredibly beautiful." His lips curve into a sensuous and wide smile.

"Really?" I wiggle my eyebrows. "Many people would disagree."

"They'd have to be blind."

I shrug. "People don't like girls with tattoos, especially when they have as many as me."

The tip of his right index finger trails across my roses. "These blew me away when I first saw them."

My eyes skim the pink walls of my Bowsley bedroom, which after tomorrow will no longer be mine. "They'll remind me of you and this room." My throat tightens as I speak. "It's ironic really that I had them done because I wanted something pretty, and you who loves them so much are the only person who sees me as beautiful."

He watches me, his lips crimped together, for a long pause. I stare at him back and will him to understand the words I can't yet say.

"Come." He shakes his head. "Enough of this sadness, let's go."

Eli rolls from the bed and holds his hand out for mine. "Dinner."

My stomach growls again. It probably is time to eat something.

I follow him to the kitchen where we find a basket on the table with a note tied with brown string to the handle. *Enjoy!*

"She's a trouper, old Elaine."

"Are we going to the conservatory?" A tingle of excitement flares. I haven't spent enough time in that phenomenal place and now it's too late.

"Maybe." He smirks and holds out his arm for me to take. I link us together and anchor our elbows tight.

We don't go to the conservatory which is a disappointment, for a whole three minutes, until I see he's leading me down the kitchen gardens. "Where are we going?"

"Patience, Faith."

I chuckle a little. "I don't have any."

When he turns to me in the dark he steals my breath away. He's even more beautiful lit by shadows of cloud and moon.

He glances at the sky and I watch as the smile spreads across his face. "Why are you smiling at cloud cover?" I ask.

"Wait and see."

Finally, when we've been walking down the neat pathways and borders for a fair while he turns into a walled garden. The most delicious pungent scent fills the air, cloying and sweet, and I breathe in deeply.

"What is that? It's delicious."

He tugs on my hand and pulls me around for a kiss, the basket forgotten on the floor as his hands weave their way into my hair and his thumbs skim my jaw.

"You kiss like nothing else I've known." The words slip into the night air, but I can't really care or want to call them back. It's a statement of truth and I'll stand by it until my dying day. His kiss and the pungent air make my head swirl.

"This is the orchard." He pecks a kiss on the tip of my nose. "It's better at night."

I'll say.

"And you kiss rather well too," he adds with a cheeky grin. I just laugh. He makes me want to laugh; he makes me want to forget I'm the girl with tattoos, the girl with a past.

He lets go of me and busies himself setting out the blanket. I watch him enthralled. What the hell will my eyes look at when tomorrow is over?

The lightning bolt hits me smack in the grey matter with resounding clarity.

I can't walk away.

I'm going to fight.

While he sets out glasses and a bottle of champagne

with a gold foil top, I close my eyes and think of those Māori tattoos I have bound onto my skin.

Maybe those tattoos weren't meant to be for fighting Aiden and my father. Maybe they were for this. Maybe this is what I need, more than I need acknowledgement or apologies.

"Eli," I say his name. The tension in my stomach pulls and aches.

"Faith." He grins up at me and motions for me to come forward. He holds my hands and we sit on the blanket, two people fluid and free with one another.

"I'm just going to say this." The words are a fast train and they won't stop now for anything.

He nods, simple and precise.

"I don't want this to end tomorrow." My cheeks flare under the silver haze of the cloud covered moon. "I can't walk away from you. I thought I could, but now…" I shake my head as I think of the words I want to say but can't articulate. "I want to fight. I want to live rule free."

His hands slip around my face, his palms cupping my cheeks. His mouth catches mine and lingers with possessive attachment. "It's funny you should say that."

My heart hammers, loud and fast. "Why?"

He shakes his head. "I want you, Faith. Everything you are. The freedom you live with, the strength. I want that every day. And so we are starting backwards. We haven't even had a date yet, but." He grins and then pecks another kiss on my lips. "It's a start."

"What about your family? Grandbaronessy isn't going to take this well."

His eyes hold mine, fierce and determined. "I can live without money and the Fairclough name."

I almost crumple at his confession.

I kiss him, breathe him. Feel him.

Solid and firm, he holds me in his arms, his embrace gripping me to his chest as though he doesn't want to let go.

"We don't even know each other." I laugh, and it's on the verge of being water filled.

"We can start now." He grins and pulls away. Declarations are done, simple, easy almost. "Champagne?" He holds a glass for me.

"I prefer beer."

He shakes his head but then smiles with a warmth that makes my blood rush with heat. "Bottle of beer?" He slips his hand into the basket and pulls out two bottles of Budweiser, popping the lids off.

"Much better." I take it and we clink the necks of the bottles "Thank you."

"I hate bananas." he says out of the blue, and I snort a laugh.

"I hate oranges."

We both begin to chuckle and a bubble wells in my chest.

"I really like Take That," I say, but then wag my finger under his nose. "Don't tell anyone though."

"I quite fancy Gary Barlow myself."

And that's it. It can't stop laughing and tears begin to fall down my cheeks. This is it. Nothing more, nothing less. Him and I.

Every square inch of the blanket has been rolled on, my lips are bruised and I'm breathless. "I'm pretty sure you mentioned food."

His hands anchor into my hips, pushing me into his pelvis where he grinds his erection against the ache between my legs. I want him so bad it physically hurts.

"It's always about the food with you."

I bat him with my hand. "Hardly, I've nearly starved to death in this place." I kiss him again. Screw the food. "In fact..." I break contact to continue. "When your grandmother said on my first day they used to have starving artists stay here, I didn't realise she meant they were actually starved while they were here."

He chuckles into my neck and warm shivers of excitement wash along my skin. I let out a little groan of disappointment when he actually moves away from me in the search for food.

He passes me the basket. "Here, dig around and I'll set out the rest of the stuff."

"Jeez, I'll do all the work, shall I?" I snigger. Truth is when this two-week fairy tale ends tomorrow, I'm going to have to pull my socks up. Otherwise, he's quickly going to realise I live like a total pig—in fact pigs are cleaner I'm sure.

"How do you feel about reality television?" He's unscrewing two more bottles of beer while I'm looking in the basket.

"What do you mean?" I'm distracted by a wheel of brie.

"Reality TV, what do you think about it?"

"Do I look like the type of woman who sits about watching Love Island?"

He smirks, "Hey, I think that's perfectly reputable."

"And you sit there watching it in that swanky London Mews house you call home, do you?"

"Faith, I do all kinds of things in that swanky London Mews house you don't even know about yet."

I flush a bit pink. I can all too well remember what he did to me on that kitchen island. I get hot between the legs just thinking about it.

I raise an eyebrow. "Why are you asking anyway?" I

pull a pat of butter out of the basket. I don't know how big this thing is, but it seems to be full of endless food supplies.

"I've been in talk with Sky Arts. The team coming tomorrow wants to discuss the possibility of making a show based on our little summer experiment."

"Uh, no. I can't do that in front of other people."

He catches my hand and squeezes my fingers. "When are you going to see how talented you are? This place is a goldmine of unique art now, because of you."

"It wasn't all me." I don't add that really the art of the ball has nothing to do with me at all.

"Look at it this way." He hands me my new bottle of beer. "If we get funding then we don't need to worry about the Fairclough name or even Bowsley. Hell, the producer even said there are plenty of stately homes who would take up the opportunity. So when I get cut off tomorrow." He winks, although honestly there is nothing amusing about the palpitations fluctuating my heart rate. "It won't matter. The project is still ours."

"What about your job?"

He shrugs. "I don't know yet."

"What about Tabitha? You didn't want to leave her, like your..." I hesitate, "like your dad did."

He nods slowly. "I know. But she's a big girl and I need to do my own thing. I can't let this family dictate my life anymore."

I roll my eyes. "Shit, your mother is going to hate me even more." I turn my attention back to the basket. "How much food is in here, Eli?" My hand lands on a small black box. "What's this?"

I pull it free of the dark recesses of the basket. It's a little heart-shaped antique ring box. I should know, I grew up in

Brighton where the antique shops of the Lanes peddled these things to tourists.

His eyes are on me. My heart... it's near on collapsing. "Don't panic, I'm not proposing. Even I'm not that crazy." He grins, but it doesn't help the butterflies flapping their wings in my chest cavity.

"What is it?" I can hardly speak.

"Open it." He scoots closer across the blanket and crosses his legs as he watches me intently.

I flick the small brass latch and lift the lid. Holy shit.

The holiest of shits.

Nestled inside of the small box is a giant black tear-shaped solitaire, delicately balanced on a slender band of pave diamonds.

"That's beautiful." Tears sting my eyes. "I've never seen an onyx shaped like that before.

His lips quirk and he pulls the ring from the box, holding it in his fingers.

"It reminded me of your ink, and I hoped that one day maybe I'd be the one who stops your tears for good."

I'm breathless. There is no air left in the world for me to grab onto.

As I meet his eyes, my heart pounding, a droplet of rain splatters onto the blanket. Then another, and then another.

He smiles broad and wide and I know why we haven't gone to the greenhouse. "You remembered."

He nods, picks up my hand, and slips the exquisite ring onto my right-hand ring finger as rain begins to pour down.

"A kiss in the rain. It's the first that I get to keep." Then his mouth is on mine and the rain soaks our faces. Our lips slide as our tongue's tangle.

On my hand is a giant teardrop of ink. Tears he'll help me fight.

"I think I love you." I blurt the words. Crazy. Insane. Spontaneous.

He kisses me harder. His hands hold my jaw, his thumbs sweep my skin. "Nothing to think about."

We are lying in bed, my hands trailing across his chest. His fingers smooth my damp hair. "When did you know?"

"Know what?" A light pressure presses against my hair and I bloom from under his tender touch.

"That you loved me?"

His chest moves as he chuckles. "I can't tell you, it's too cheesy."

"Ah, but I love cheese."

Another kiss. "You love cheese, you hate oranges. I'm a quick learner."

"Stop stalling." I nudge him with my elbow.

"When you refused to sit down at The Ritz."

My face folds into a half-hearted scowl. "You were an arse that day."

"I told you, it's this family. It's what it does to me."

"I'm glad I saved you then." This time his lips find my mouth and I breathe in the hot scent of his breath. "And I'm glad I broke my rules for you."

My one rule seems so very far away now. I didn't know being with someone could be like this. I didn't know I could care so much my heart would ache and pull, and want to explode all at once.

He rolls me, his intent clear as he hardens against my body. "I've never been gladder of anything in my life."

Thirty-Seven

I stretch and point my toes when I wake. We didn't have much sleep. The first thing I see is the impressive onyx on my finger. I wiggle it a little in the morning sunlight and it sparkles and winks.

The second thing I notice is the empty pillow next to mine and the sheet of folded paper. *Gone to London to sort some things. I'll be back for the ball, Sunshine. xo*

My heart rate escalates just reading a handwritten note from him. I'm doomed to erratic behaviour forever it seems.

This enormous swell of emotion threatens to engulf me when I think that tonight isn't the end. It's the beginning. And for the first time in my life I'm not scared, not running.

My phone beeps, I reach for the bedside table and peer at the screen. *Dan.*

A stab of deep guilt burns when I think how bloody happy I am when he's going through shit.

Dan: Dad's not doing good, Faith. Sorry to break bad news over message but he's not going to make it past the weekend.

Struggling up from under the duvet, I hit dial.

"Hey," he sounds exhausted as he answers on the second ring.

"Dan, I'm sorry."

"Don't be. He's been asking after you, wants to know what you created."

I smile, but it's watery and weak. "Tell him I made my heart whole."

There's a pause. "You and Eli then, hey, Faithy?"

I nod even though he can't see me and stare at my ring. "Yeah, I guess. Odd, right?"

"Not really."

I drag in a deep breath. "Listen, I've got the ball today, all the kids are going to be here, it's a big thing. I'll be back tomorrow, tell Al I'm expecting to see him."

I should go now, I know I should. But I don't want to let Elijah down when he's gambling everything he knows on me.

"Sure, Faith, I'll tell him." There's another panful pause. "Abi's been here, I think she's coming by again."

"I guess her and Adam aren't coming to the ball?"

Guilt washes over me until it's as though it's pouring into my mouth and drowning me as I sit on my bed. "Screw it, I'm coming now."

"No." Dan cuts me off. "Don't. Dad would be cross, this ball's important, right?"

"Yeah, but…"

"Come tomorrow. Then you won't get a bollocking from the old man."

I laugh, but it's pathetic and small.

"See you tomorrow, Dan."

"Good luck, Faith."

I hang up the phone and send Eli a quick message.

Faith Hitchin: Al's not doing good. I'll have to go tomorrow.

I wait a moment to see if I get a response. When one

doesn't instantly vibrate my phone, I leave it behind on the side and get up to slip on some clothes. I've got to finish my centrepiece and I have to move the rest of the exhibition. It's going to be a busy day.

Damien calls me at about three. "Where do you want this frame? It weighs a fucking ton."

"You need to grow some muscles. I'll meet you on the drive and we can carry it together. I'll bring the brawn." He swears at me as I hang up, which I'm sure isn't a professional way to talk to a client.

I wave as I crunch over the gravel and find him balancing the frame out of the back of a transit van. The frame is wrapped in a black velvet covering which can only be a good thing. "Thanks, Damien. I appreciate this so much."

"It's fine, you can give Whitlocks all the exclusive pieces you are going to make off the back of this venture."

"That reminds me, did you know it was Elijah Fairclough who bought all my pieces?"

He shrugs. "Who cares, so long as they sell?"

I can't argue with that logic.

We both turn as Lewis crunches across the gravel. "Do you guys need some muscle?" Damien's eyes light with glee as he takes in Lewis' strong build.

"Yes, absolutely."

"Where's Tabitha?" I ask Lewis.

"In the kitchen." He nods his head. "She's not feeling great."

"Okay, she better not leave me to walk into this ball by myself. Can you guys manage to get this to the painting studio?"

They both nod, and I leave them to seek out Tabitha.

She's got to help me get into that white dress without making a hash of it.

"Hey, what's up?" I ask as I step into the comforting familiarity of the kitchen. It's just Tabs, Elaine must be busy somewhere. Tabitha's eyes are red-rimmed. "What's going on, have you and Lewis had a row again?"

There are a lot of teenage hormones in charge of their blooming relationship. Makes me kind of glad the last thing I wanted at her age was a boyfriend.

"I'm tired." She sags a little. "And Mother is being a bitch."

"Why? And do you mean more of a bitch than usual?"

This makes Tabitha smile, but it doesn't last long. "She's sending me to finishing school. I mean seriously, of all the bloody things. Why can't I just get a normal job, like a normal girl? I don't know why everything to do with the Faircloughs has to always be so over the top."

"Finishing school? Is that still even a thing?" I perch on a chair and grab her hand. My stomach plummets. Are they saying they will send her to stop Elijah being with me? Has he told them already? Sweat slicks my palms and I wipe them on my tatty jeans.

"Eli will sort it, you know he will."

I say the words, but inside I'm tangled into knots. Will Eli sort it when he could be cut off at any point?

All this is because of me.

Is this what love costs?

I blow a breath of air from my mouth and push back my hair. "Do you want to help me get the ballroom ready?"

"Sure." She pushes back from the table, but she looks green.

"You're not well enough, don't worry about it." I place a soothing hand on her shoulder, but she shakes her head.

"It's okay. You still haven't told me what you are putting in there anyway."

"I'm putting all Elijah's paintings in there. He's going to be the main artist."

Tabitha holds her hand to her mouth. "But that's a secret. Mum's always said."

I shake my head and shrug. "Some secrets aren't meant to be kept."

Three hours later the ballroom is ready. By the time I'd put all Eli's paintings pride of place, and surrounded them by the others from the project, it was too late for Jennifer to say anything. Although the look on her face said it all.

There is no hiding the *Eli Fairclough* swirled as a signature at the bottom of every canvas.

The roses, dressed in an eye catching and dramatic gilt frame, are at pride of place under the curved double staircase.

My own centrepiece is in the middle. A heart made of yin and yang glass pieces, sandblasted until the ruby red is iridescent and then held together with smelted gold.

I've never created anything like it. Never would have tried without Elijah. At three feet tall, the freestanding glass heart is the biggest and most unique thing I've ever created.

Gerard nods at it. "You should have saved it for your third-year finals."

"Gerard, I'm not finishing remember?"

He shakes his head. "I think you will."

I wave my hand at him and turn away. I'm not getting into it now. I've got a ball to get ready for.

Back in my room I check my phone, but before I get a chance to log into my messages there's a tap on my door.

He's here. I leap for the latch only to be disappointed when it's Saskia standing at the other side. "Hey."

"Expecting someone else?" She smirks a little and I stick my tongue out.

"Nope."

She breezes into my pink room and looks about. "Come on, let's get you ready."

"Why are you here helping me? Haven't you got to get ready yourself?"

"I want to see you in that dress and make sure you knock them all off their feet." She looks at my hand. "Nice diamond by the way."

I grab the ring and swirl it around my finger. "It's onyx."

She laughs and looks closer. "I'm no jeweller, but I know my diamonds, and that, my friend is a massive one."

The ring winks at me and I stare at in horror. "A diamond? Are you sure?"

"Yep."

"Shit, it's massive."

It really is ridiculously massive.

"About four grand's worth I'd say, so don't lose it when you're drunk later."

I grab my phone and send another message.

Faith Hitchin: A diamond? I can't keep it.

I'm relieved when he answers. He's been quiet all day and really, I was expecting him back by now.

Eli Jones: Well, it's yours to keep.

I don't have time to answer anything else because Saskia takes charge and pushes me into the shower room. Apparently, I stink.

The white satin pools at my feet. Saskia bought me a gift of some white satin Manolo Blahnik's which I'm sure cost as much as my dress.

I wish I wasn't going into the ball by myself.

But fuck it. I'm a big girl.

The doors open, and I glide through. All eyes are on me, on my skin, but I don't care. I see Dylan and Maisie over by the bar and give them a wave. Maisie gives me a thumbs up, which I think is a compliment. I can't see Tabitha though, or Lewis for that matter, but then there are lots of people, the room is busy and it's hard to focus—maybe they are here somewhere. Then I sense the blues, bright and intense. He gives me a small smile as he talks to a group of men in tuxedos, although none of them rock the tux with the intensity Eli does. That man could look good in a paper bag, and right now the black tux fitted and cut to perfection along his tall broad form is far from a bag you'd put groceries in.

He looks busy, and nerves put me on edge, so I don't step forward and greet him.

Jennifer works the room and I take a moment to watch her do her thing. She's perfection as she glides in black, and touches people on the arm when she greets them and makes them all think they are special. When she sees me her face falters. I kind of thought we'd got to the point of being okay, but then I don't know what Eli has said to her since last night. The silver bob of Connie Grandbaronessy comes into view and she whispers in her daughter's ear. Jennifer's eyes glance at me, briefly, before they both turn away.

Fine. I could worry about it. But truth is, I can't be bothered, Eli has told me how he feels and that's all that matters to me. I smile a little to myself and step further into the room ready to mingle. This is my ball, my art, and I'm going to make sure everyone knows.

I double check the placement of my centrepiece. I don't think I've ever been prouder of a piece before. I glance at the handsome man in the tux, whose lips I want to kiss again. I would never have made that without him, the idea would never have come to me. I'm smug knowing that he has my ying and yang on his skin forever.

When I don't find anyone to talk to and I can't see Damien from Whitlocks, or sadly anyone from the Tate Modern to launch myself at, I find my way to Gerard who's talking to a woman in gold lace. He waves me forward and I turn away from the blues and step up with a smile.

"This is the woman you want," Gerard says with a small wave in my direction. "This is the enormously talented Faith Hitchin." He turns to me. "Faith, this is Angela Bartlett, Channel Four's Head of Arts."

"Channel Four?" I'm confused. I stop myself from saying I thought Sky were coming.

Angela smiles. She's smooth and serene. Her pale blonde hair is neatly tied in a chignon and matches the pale gold of her dress perfectly. Seamlessly, she drops her fingers into her pale gold clutch and hands me a card.

"I hope we can talk, Faith. I've got some big ideas."

"Big ideas? I'm sorry, I'm confused." I shake my head and stare in bewilderment between her and Gerard. Gerard is grinning—which is really bloody annoying.

"Oh, yes," Angela continues. "We have the Bake Off now, I'm thinking something along the lines of an Art Off."

"Fart off? I'm sorry?" I can't help myself.

Gerard laughs loudly, but then downs most of his glass of champagne.

Angela smiles, and I'm honestly surprised to find her smile genuine. "Well the title needs work, I'll admit."

My mouth opens in horror. "Oh, crap, was that actually an idea for a show?"

With a high laugh, she pats me on the arm. "If you want to open a discussion, I'd love to see you... next week, maybe?"

I go to say yes, before my doubts and fears can eat away at my future, but then I remember Al and the fact I should really be with him right now. "I'm going to be home for a while I think, but when I come to back to London that would be great."

Her gaze sweeps the building. "It's an impressive display."

I nod, and a deep pool of pride overwhelms me. "I just put it together; the paintings are Elijah Fairclough's." I raise my voice slightly so more people can hear. There's a murmur around the room and then people begin to move around the easels and canvases.

A brush against my elbow pulls my attention and I know it's him before I've even turned around.

"Hi." I blush as his eyes sweep along the skin skimming white satin.

"Hi."

Eyes are on us from all around the room.

I wave to the retreating shape of Angela. "That was Channel Four." I grin at him. "This is mad."

If I expect him to smile it doesn't come. "Thank you for using my paintings."

"Eli." A cold shiver crawls up my spine. I place my hand on his chest. His heart thumps below my palm. Be dammed who can see. This is nearly over. He loves me.

He nods. "I think this will open some doors for you, Faith."

"Us, Eli. Us."

"Faith, I need to—"

Our attention is pulled by the band striking up an up-tempo fanfare.

His face drops. "I would have liked to dance with you in that dress," he says. I meet his eyes to ask him what he means, but Jennifer is on the small stage at the end of the ballroom calling for everyone's attention with the clink of two champagne flutes.

"Thank you everyone for joining us."

There's a murmur of responses. She looks regal up there in floor-length black. Small gems glitter across the full skirt of her gown. I'm sure her gaze rests on me for a moment, on my hand on Eli's chest with my giant diamond sparking under the lights.

That reminds me, I need to discuss the ring with him again.

"What a glorious evening this has been. The brain child of my wonderful and talented son, Elijah." There's a cheer for Elijah and my pool of pride doubles in size. "To realise he's been hiding this talent all these years, keeping his gift a secret." She shakes out her honey hair. "That all changes tonight. I'm proud to announce the Fairclough Trust for Art and Design. The first recipient of which will be our own Faith Hitchin, the leader of *this* year's event." There is absolutely no mistaking her emphasis on *this*.

I glance up at Eli. His face is a mask. Closed and empty.

Jennifer continues as I give a small wave to all the people who have craned their necks to get a look at me. "Tonight, we are not just celebrating the end of a wonderful event, one of which I'm so proud to be involved with." *Is she kidding me?* I turn to roll my eyes at Eli, but his face is a little on the green side, strained. There's a pulse thudding along the golden skin of his throat. I lean a little closer to ask him if he feels ill. Maybe he's got what Tabitha has? Jennifer is still chiming her clear-cut tones into the microphone. "Elijah, my darling. Sienna, Sweetheart. Come up here so everyone can see you."

"Elijah, darling, shall we?" A vision in red steps between us. It's her. *I'll see you both at the ball...*

Why is she being called up onto stage? It should be me...unless...

Oh, God.

He's lied.

The world tilts.

My hands fall to my sides and I look into his face.

Those blues that have taken me apart and made me change everything stare back at me with fathomless depths.

"I'm sorry." The words fall from his lips, but I don't really register them. Two words. *I'm sorry.*

Jennifer is still trilling away. "We are so delighted to re-announce the engagement of Elijah and Sienna. What a stunning couple they make and we know the timing is perfect this time for the happy couple."

I stumble back. My heart splinters.

I can't stop looking at him though. The liar. The traitor.

He lied to me.

How long has this been fact? Him and her?

I smooth my dress, breathing in deep.

More fool me.

Sienna links her arm through his, just like I did last night out in the garden, and I watch as they take to the stage and Jennifer air-kisses them. Eli is smiling, waving at the crowd.

It's like I don't exist.

Like this has all been nothing.

I step away, my chest labouring as I try to breathe. My heart cracks and aches until I want to stop breathing.

I've let another man hurt me.

The red glimmer of my glass heart catches my eye.

Fuck, how foolish have I been? Did I think this was a fairy tale? Did I really believe in a prince on a white horse?

I know better.

In three steps, I'm next to the heart. My own is pounding and squeezing.

"Faith, don't." It's his voice that cuts through the chatter. How fucking dare he?

I push at the heart, so it topples off balance, and then I watch in slow motion as it shatters into a million tiny red shards. Gold and red destroyed across the floor.

"Faith." Gerard tries to grab my arm. "Don't throw everything away."

I don't listen though. I walk. I hold my head high and I walk away, and never, *ever*, will I allow any man to lie to me again.

"Faith." Elijah's fingers electrify my skin as he rushes behind me and tries to catch a hold of my hand.

He's too late.

I'm already gone.

The tear of ink on my finger glints as I steal back to my room and lock the door.

It only takes me moments to pack. A few clothes stuffed into a bag, the same as I arrived with.

Tears course down my face and I swipe at them as I try to see through the pools gathering along my lashes.

I slide off the dress and stuff that in too, not worried about creases. I'll burn the damn thing, I don't care how much it cost.

I slide on my familiar jeans and vest, then I pick up my phone. On the screen is a message. The one I've been dreading.

Dan: *He's gone.*

And then everything I know falls apart and I know I will never forgive Elijah Fairclough for being the man to finally bring me down.

To be continued ...

To follow Tears of Glass release please sign up here: Subscribe

You can join the exclusive Facebook group here
http://bit.ly/TearsofInk

THANK YOU

Thank you for reading

Please as always remember that authors love to hear from their readers, and reviews are as valuable as fairy dust. Your time and review are always gratefully received.

Acknowledgments

As always these are the hardest part of any book to write. There are so many people to thank in the process of what I do.

After a year filled with empty void of a lack of words to suddenly find myself inspired with characters again was a welcome relief.

That inspiration came in the form of Ally Sky, who's stories, life and love reignited my love of the written word and inspired me to create a book that not only am I in love with, but also immensely proud.

With love to Andrea, I always feel every manuscript of mine should appear with wine and chocolates to see you through the mess I create. Thank you for understanding my words even when I don't.

Nikki and Elena, thank you for your sharp eyes and nit picking!

My tribe of author friends who are with me every day and carry me in my darkest moment. My Indie girls and Lianne, and Nikki as always have a special place in everything I do.

Little Annie Hughes, having you as my cheerleader has

changed my life and given me laughter and love when I need it the most.

My beta readers I hope you know how much I value you. Everything you say makes me want to work harder for you to give you words you love and look forward too.

To my children who put up with mummy working more hours a day than any sane woman should, always know that I do this for you, so that one day you will dream and aim for the stars.

To Wes for understanding even when at times you don't want to understand at all.

For my parents for encouraging my love of books and my sister for keeping me in check and accountable every Sunday!

And lastly. For every woman who has ever experienced the fear of an unwanted touch. The past doesn't define, it doesn't create, it makes us stronger and harder until we are unbreakable. I wish you the strength and determination to speak and seek justice.

This series is for you.

Anna Bloom
Surrey, England. 2018

Printed in Great Britain
by Amazon